To: Claire

a
monster
like me

You are the magic that makes everything else shine!

All my love!

Pamela Bankston

a
monster
like me

PAMELA SPARKMAN

Edited by The Editing Sweetheart
Cover Design by RBA Designs
Photographer by Anna Pototskaya
Cover Model: Valery Kovtun
Interior design and formatting by

E.M.
TIPPETTS
BOOK DESIGNS

www.emtippettsbookdesigns.com

About
a
monster
like me

"I love the peculiar silence of shadows. They exist but leave no mark."

Zeph had been a child, thrust into a war that wasn't his. When he was older, he discovered he had landed on the wrong side of everything.

He'd been fighting for sweet revenge, because of lies he'd believed—and those lies proved to be his ruin. Falling into despair, Zeph decides living is too painful. So, he writes his final act with poison and chooses to end his story.

But Fate has other plans for Zeph and when he finds himself in the hands of his enemies, he has to decide: Does he want to live? Or does he want to die?

Or maybe that choice is no longer his to make.

Ruled by shadows and armed with secrets he never intended to share, Zeph will be put through his toughest battle yet: the war within himself.

"He isn't a lost cause. He's just—lost."

That's what Arwyn believes. She sees the monster he has become, but what she also sees is someone worth fighting for. Armed with secrets of her own, she's determined to help Zeph fight his demons, because there was more on the line than Zeph's soul. So much more.

Revenge may be sweet. But redemption is sweeter. The question is, can Zeph find the boy he used to be, or will he always believe that no one could ever love—a monster like him.

"You are everything good. And I am everything children are afraid of."

CAUTIONContains a brief descriptive scene of childhood rape.

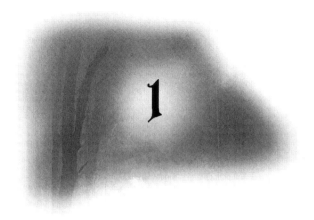

Zeph stood at the highest point in all of Faery, on the barren cliffs overlooking Death Sea. He looked out from a safe distance, listening to the ocean-song as the waves crawled benignly to shore, the palpitating pulse steady and peaceful.

The flint-gray skies above sagged with heavy rain clouds, but the winds were sweet-tempered, blowing through Zeph's long hair gently, like a warm summer's breath.

He closed his eyes and listened to the chorus around him. A symphony of gurgling and humming—of murmuring and lapping. But the chorus within his soul drowned out the music of the land with the *thump, thump, thumping* of a heart shattered, like a drum roll on a death march.

He squeezed his eyes tighter and threw his hands over his ears. A wounded cry eked out of him, causing him to double over from the pain of it. He begged—begged for this agony to stop.

"I'm sorry," he said around dry, cracked lips, his voice sounding sharp and jagged, like the edge of a knife scraping against stone. "I'm so sorry."

The air was salty, but it did little to alleviate the metallic tang of blood that stung his nostrils, his clothes soaked and stained in his sister's blood.

"*Elin*," he breathed.

He held his hands out in front of him. The sight of her blood on his skin made the memory of her dying in his arms slam to the fore. It wasn't supposed to be like this.

"It should have been me!" he shouted to the universe. "I'm the monster! You should have taken me!"

He swallowed the acid rising from his gut and wrenched his tabard and tunic over his head, casting them to the ground, offended by them. He took a few wobbly steps to the edge of those barren cliffs and heaved all that he had within him, hoping he could dislodge the rot he felt inside.

And through the heaving, he cried, "It should have been me."

Days came. Nights went. Zeph slowly lost his sanity. Deep into his depression, on the eighth day, consumed by grief and guilt, he poisoned himself with a concoction he'd made, one that would work quickly in his Fae blood. He could have Faded, the way Elin, his sister, had once tried to do, but Fading would allow his spirit, his essence, to be absorbed back into Faery, and he had no desire for that. He just wanted the pain to stop. Losing Elin was the final act that broke him, irreparably so. He didn't realize how much his life was tied to hers—until she was gone. Now, he wanted to be done, completely done with this life.

Weak and listless, Zeph rolled onto his back, shards of rock digging into his skin. "How long?" he said to no one, his voice too thin to be heard.

How long must he feel this desolate?

The song of the sea played on while Zeph's turbulent chorus raged within. He closed his eyes and a vision of a young boy crept slowly toward him. In his mind's eye, he could see him clearly: fair skin, hair the color of milk. But the downward curve of the boy's mouth told the story. He was sad. Zeph felt compelled to reach his hand out toward him.

"Find me," the boy said just as Zeph touched the boy's cheek. "Please."

Zeph's heart lurched. He pulled his hand back and curled onto his side.

"Go away," Zeph muttered in a quiet rasp. "You're not real."

The poison was working into his veins now. He was hallucinating. He would have laughed at himself had he not...

"Find me," the boy repeated. "I can't hold on forever. Please, you have to find me."

"You're not real," Zeph murmured, clamping his hands over his ears. "You're not real."

"I'm going to get you help," a feminine voice said.

Though his mind was foggy and unclear, he thought he felt himself being lifted from the ground and cradled in arms that felt too soft, too kind.

"Shh," she soothed. "Everything will be all right. I'm going to get help for you."

He didn't deserve it—her kindness—her compassion. He certainly didn't deserve her help. Even the imaginary kind. "I don't want help," he mumbled. "Leave me be."

"Shh," she soothed again.

She crooned a melody in his ear as he felt himself being lifted higher and higher, then sailing through the warm, salty air. He sobbed at the distant memory of when his mother used to sing to him, cradled in her arms. The mother he had killed...*murdered*, by his own hands.

He didn't deserve to live.

"Show me no mercy," Zeph pleaded. His eyes were too heavy to look up and see the face of the woman he imagined, but he imagined saying it to his mum. Sucking in his last breath, he made one final appeal before his world faded to black.

"A monster l-like me deserves n-no mercy."

2

ll was quiet, save the sigh of the wind outside the monastery, lazily ruffling the ivy that crept up the thick stone walls. But the air inside the monastery was eerie stillness, as if each room, each darkened corridor, was holding its breath.

Lanterns lit the halls, providing Searly a sallow path as he casually walked the east wing, his mind a restless thing, his heart a troubled well of confliction. Since leaving Faery, Searly had felt a perplexing thrum underneath his skin, a gnawing sensation that left him feeling raw and agitated. Adjusting back to normalcy after his internment in Shadowland, a realm within Faery, proved to be more difficult than he had anticipated. There, he had been beaten and tortured, and he nearly succumbed to the seduction of evil. Try as he might, he hadn't been able to forgive himself. He tried to immerse himself in prayer and monastic activities, anything to ground him in the present. Only his mind ceased to rest, and his worriment further vexed him beyond reason. He had become anxious and ill-tempered. He hated that about himself. Searly had always been calm and levelheaded, a voice of reason in the face of despair and uncertainty. How could he lead his fellow monks if his leadership abilities took leave and left him floundering and toiling about, questioning his own stability and honor?

He had thought coming back to Mirova, his childhood home, would have eased his night terrors. He had told no one he suffered them. But Searly no longer wanted to sleep at night. Thus, he found himself walking the halls when everyone else was snug in their beds. And in so doing, his mind was never at rest.

He often thought of Zeph, the one responsible for killing Thaddeus, his brother monk—the one responsible for his and Elin's interment in Shadowland—the one who shattered Elin's world when he killed their parents—all because he was seeking revenge. Revenge, as it turns out, for lies Zeph had been told and had believed. A long story, but the short of it was Zeph had been taken from his family as a child, abused, and led to believe his family never cared for him or sought to save him. The truth was that his family believed Zeph had been murdered and fled Faery to save Elin, his sister, lest the same fate befall her.

It was during their interment that Searly had learned those parts of Zeph's past and why he had turned out to be so diabolical, so unfeeling. And while a part of Searly felt compassion for what had happened to Zeph as a child, he also couldn't excuse the murder of one's own parents, for which Zeph was guilty. Or the cold-blooded murder of Thaddeus, who had been entirely innocent and simply in the wrong place at the wrong time.

Searly had also witnessed another side to Zeph—troubling glimpses of a soul fighting the evil that lived within. It was those glimpses that kept Searly awake at night, aside from the night terrors. He didn't know why, because Searly loathed Zeph for what he had done…and yet…

He shook his head, trying to dislodge the thoughts that plagued his mind on a continuous loop. Reconciling the two sides of Zeph only served to vex his already frayed nerves. It wasn't his place to figure Zeph out. He was gone, and hopefully he would stay gone. They hadn't seen him since the day they all thought Elin had been killed. Well, she *had* been killed, but Lochlan brought her back with his ability, his gift, to bring back the dead, but that was a whole other story.

Searly's place was here, serving, so he needed to recommit himself back to the holy order of business and get on with his life. He had people who needed him, relied on him. Like Arwyn, an elf, who had lived with Zeph inside Shadowland. This was a girl who needed care. Her family had been slaughtered by Unseelie, and surprisingly enough, Zeph had saved her from that slaughter and hid her, keeping her safe inside his keep. For years.

When he, Elin, and Lochlan left Faery, they'd convinced Arwyn to follow. He had told her he could offer her comfort, a place to mend her brokenness, a place to regain a sense of equilibrium. But he couldn't even offer himself these things. A fool he'd been to think he could offer them to another.

The frustration of it all rose up, and Searly clenched his fists and bit the inside of his cheek to keep from swearing. He stopped his pace and leaned against the stone wall, the coldness of it seeping past his robes and into his skin. He breathed out, his breath uneven and shallow, so he tried for another. In time, he could do this again. He could breathe without feeling like he was losing a piece of himself with every exhalation.

"One day," he murmured, and pushed himself off the wall.

One, two, three, four…

He had resorted to counting his steps. Fantastic. He had once considered himself a prince of wise men. Now he was babbling like a loon and counting his steps like a sophomoric imbecile.

"Fantastic!" he shouted, his voice echoing off the walls, his fists clenching again at his sides.

He paused mid-stride and closed his eyes, trying to regain his composure. He needed to get a handle on himself before his inner turmoil affected more than just his own well-being. He had others to consider, others who depended on him to be solid and sure. Resilient in all things.

A door closed somewhere in the distance with a heavy *bang* and Searly startled, his eyes opening in fright. *Dark dungeon. Chained and bound, the sound of a whip tearing his bare skin.* Panic blackened the edges of his sight. He bent over at the waist, placed his hands on his knees, and breathed through the memories, his wooden cross dangling in front of him. He gripped it with one hand and repeated a prayer he had said many times.

"Lord, stay with me and feed me Your strength."

His heart was a drum, pounding with urgency to flee, to run. He gripped the cross tighter. "Lord, stay with me and feed me Your strength."

He repeated the prayer over a dozen times, and after, he stood, doing his best to ignore the hammering inside his chest. If the other monks could see him now, what would they think?

He scrubbed his hands over his tired face and laughed sardonically. "They'd think me mad."

Maybe he was mad. Maybe his sanity had finally snapped. Could anyone blame him?

"No," he murmured to himself. "I haven't the luxury of going mad." He had responsibilities and that was that. He pushed himself forward, no destination in mind; he just needed to keep moving. Maybe he would tire and fall into a deep, restful sleep.

If only.

He passed by the communal room where his brothers often gathered to converse. He considered perhaps a fire to warm his soul would help ease his troubles, so he turned back, and only then did he catch something out of the corner of his eye.

The silver disk of the moon hung low, peeking past the corner window, casting a watery haze across the sparsely decorated room. Arwyn sat stiffly on a chair, her spine a straight line, her shoulders square, staring off absently. Her lilac hair fell down her back in thick spirals and her pixie face glowed from the moonlight. She appeared neither young nor old; rather, Searly thought of her as a living relic, preserved for all of time, like the saints he often prayed to for guidance, for she had been a saint to him not so long ago.

He shouldered the doorway, his ruminations carrying him back to when he'd first met her. She had been shy at first, hovering just outside the room where Searly sat vigil at Elin's bedside, back when Elin had tried to Fade, when she had willed herself to die. Compassion suffused Arwyn's face, and she had taken one tentative step towards them, catching Zeph's eye briefly, as if to say *I'm coming in whether you like it or not.*

Searly's mouth twitched at the memory.

He had watched Zeph with a sharp eye, waiting to see what, if anything, he would do. Zeph had only stared at her as she crossed the threshold. When she made her way to the foot of Elin's bed, Searly had held his breath. He knew nothing of her and was prepared to protect Elin against all manner of things. Even from a delicate woman with pointed ears. But she had simply closed her eyes and whispered a prayer for Elin. The lilt of her voice and the kindness in her eyes was enough for Searly to release his breath. When he realized there was nothing to fear from her, he was grateful to her in that moment. Grateful, because he had thought he was alone in his hell—and then she showed up—like an angel sent from God.

It had been an awful time, and Arwyn had helped Elin and him through it.

When he heard a tiny whimper, he pushed off the doorway and walked tentatively toward her. She hadn't been the same since leaving Faery. She wasn't the same elf girl he'd grown to care for. She was removed, distant. Sad.

As was he, he'd come to realize.

Softly, he asked, "Arwyn, are you all right, luv?"

When she didn't answer or acknowledge his presence, he frowned. "Arwyn?" he said, moving closer. "Did you hear me?"

No movement. No response.

He knelt beside her and touched her hand. "Arwyn?"

She blinked when she felt his touch and recoiled slightly, though her eyes were focused on nothing.

Searly placed his hand on her forehead. "Are you feeling well?"

She turned her eyes to him then, a tear slipping down her cheek. "I can't feel him."

"What do you mean? Can't feel who?"

"Zeph," she said, turning to face the window. "I can't feel him." She lifted her hand and placed her palm over her heart. "In here." Her chin quivered. "I can't f-feel him."

"What are you saying?"

"He was so lost," she whimpered.

Searly sat back on his haunches, not knowing how to respond. Eight days. It had only been eight days since leaving Shadowland behind and the hell they had gone through. If he felt himself unraveling at the seams after only spending a short amount of time there, he could only imagine how Arwyn must be coping, considering she had spent *years* there.

He sighed an exasperated breath, realizing how selfish he'd been, wrapped up in his own inner struggles. He had promised Arwyn he would look after her, care for her, and he hadn't. Clearly, her sanity was slipping.

He was about to reach for her hand…convince her rest was in order, when a sharp and sudden pain hit him hard in the chest. It felt as though he'd been pierced with a blade.

Confusion lit his face as he stared up at Arwyn.

She leaned forward and pressed her hand to his head. "I need you to see."

Visions of Zeph standing along a jagged cliff swam in Searly's head. Despair and agony overwhelmed him. He watched as Zeph staggered in his bereavement, like a drunkard, succumbing to vomiting, ripping the clothes off his back while drowning in sorrow and desolation.

Searly felt it like it was his own pain. He fell onto his backside and fought the nausea that overtook him.

"Stop," Searly muttered. "Stop. Please."

Searly clutched his head, pulling his hair, feeling open wounds along his skin where Zeph had exposed himself to the elements for far too long. He felt blisters that oozed, felt rocks dig and cut into his skin. He felt the rot that consumed him, and he felt his heart breaking—all in the span of a minute.

Searly rolled over and vomited on the floor. "Make it stop," he begged. "I can't—I can't take anymore."

In an instant, the pain, the heartbreak, and the nausea faded, though the dullest of sensations still lingered. Weak and brittle, Searly lifted his head.

"Why?" he said, his voice sounding thick and desperate. "Why would you do that to me?"

"I'm sorry," Arwyn said, moving off the chair to cup Searly's hand, her pixie face tracked with tears. "But I needed you to know."

"Why?"

"I had a vision. Never has it happened to me before, but I—"

In the distance, another door opened and closed, followed by pounding of footsteps on the stone floor. Two sets. One set heavier than the other. Voices carried and echoed down the corridor.

"Searly!" Lochlan shouted.

Searly did not answer. His eyes stayed on Arwyn.

Arwyn looked toward the sounds coming down the corridor and then her gaze slid back to Searly's and held on, as though she were begging him to *hear, feel, see.*

"Searly!" Lochlan shouted again. "Elin said something was wrong. She said we had to come here! Searly, where are you?"

Another wave of pain came over him. This time it was Arwyn's. It started out small—like a tiny pinprick at the apex of his heart. Then it became more than a pinprick. It grew into something sharper, something wider, until it consumed the whole of his heart. His breaths drew shorter, more labored. He jerked away from Arwyn, needing to stand...move...catch his breath. Anything to make this...this...*ache* go away.

Then Lochlan's voice was at his back, directly behind him, calling his name. Searly couldn't answer. He could barely breathe, for he felt like he'd lost something. Something precious.

Searly surveyed the room. Everything appeared to be in its place. He spun to the left, and to the right. Something was missing. He could feel it.

"Searly," Lochlan cautiously said.

"Do you—do you see anything missing, milord? I feel like I've lost something."

A crease formed between Lochlan's brows. "What?"

Searly leg's wobbled beneath him and Lochlan was at his side, holding him steady.

A flash of silver bedimmed past him and Elin was there, pulling Arwyn into a hug. Searly could only watch them, because, presently, he couldn't do anything else.

The sound of wood shattering made everyone in the room bristle.

"She's here," Arwyn said faintly.

There was a cacophony of shouts and heavy footsteps as Searly's fellow monks came out of their cells at the sound of invasion.

"Ease. I am not here to hurt anyone," a feminine voice declared, a soft echo that drifted to Searly's ears, as though it was meant to soothe him.

The footsteps persisted, and after a moment, a woman carrying a limp body stood in the doorway, flanked by monks on all sides of her, wide-eyed and frightened, yet they each held a weapon in hand, ready to defend if need be.

When Searly recognized the person in her arms, it wasn't the woman the monks feared, Searly realized. It was whom she carried that drew their harried responses. But Searly's response was different from theirs. He instantly felt— loss.

"It's you," Elin said. She moved toward Lochlan and clutched his arm, confusion imprinted on her face. "From—from the bath—after my parents died. Francesca."

"Yes," the woman said. There was a flicker of light behind Francesca's eyes before she smiled sadly. She looked down at the lifeless body in her arms. "I need to put him down."

Elin rushed to a long, slender table. "Here," Elin said. "Put him down here."

Searly's breath caught when Francesca raised her head and looked directly at him. She was a woman, yes, but also a thing of otherworldly beauty, not of flesh and blood, clothed in gold gossamer with long, flowing hair as fine as gold threads and eyes that sparkled like crystals. It almost hurt to look upon her, but look upon her he did. Then, suddenly, she appeared wan and fatigued, ordinary, as she had when she first entered the room.

Searly looked around at his friends and wondered if anyone else had seen the seraphic beauty he had, but it appeared not.

The woman, *Francesca*, carefully placed Zeph on the wooden surface. The moment she stepped away, Elin was there, picking up Zeph's hand, tracing the lines on his skin with a careful, delicate touch.

"Elin," said Lochlan.

"He's my brother."

"He killed your parents."

Elin's eyebrows knitted tightly together, as if she were holding back tears and memories. "He also saved Arwyn. And healed Searly. I can hate him and love him at the same time. Don't tell me how to feel, Lochlan. I don't know what I feel, but don't tell me what I mustn't feel—what I shouldn't feel. Don't tell me—"

"I'm sorry," Lochlan said, sounding contrite. "You're right. I'm sorry."

Elin and Lochlan's gazes met and locked, the moment pulling into an uncomfortable stalemate, until Elin blinked and nodded ever so subtly. She let her eyes fall back to Zeph, who lay lifeless before them. She brushed the hair back from his face with a gentle hand. "Where did you find him?"

"On a mountain," Francesca said. "He poisoned himself, Elin."

Elin's eyes snapped to Francesca's. "Why?"

"How do you know this?" Lochlan asked. "Who are you?"

"It does not matter how I know. It only matters that I *do* know."

"It matters to me," Lochlan said, stepping closer to her.

"Lochlan," Arwyn said.

Holding his hand up to Arwyn, he asked Francesca, "Why did you bring him here?"

Francesca stood up straight and walked to where Lochlan stood, meeting him in the eye. "I need you to bring him back."

Lochlan let out a huff of a laugh. "Bring him back? From the dead?"

"That is your power, is it not?"

He narrowed his eyes at the woman who didn't cower under his glare. "My power was to bring *Elin* back. Not Zeph."

"You have the Kiss of Life. It was bestowed on you for a reason. And you do not get to decide what that reason is."

Lochlan stepped closer. They were nearly nose to nose. "And you do?"

"Stop," said Arwyn. "Lochlan, please…" She moved to stand before him, her skirts rustling in her haste. "I beg you…if you can bring him back, and I know you can, please, you must. You have to."

"No," he said. "I don't."

"Don't do it for me," she countered. "Do it for Elin."

Lochlan bristled at that. "I'd do anything for Elin, but asking me to bring back—"

"Is asking too much?" Arwyn bit out. "Then don't say you would do *anything* when clearly that is not the case."

"Both of you stop," said Elin.

"Acushla," Lochlan said, sidestepping the women and briskly walking toward her. "Do you want me to bring him back—the person responsible for your mother and father's deaths? Are you asking me to do that?"

Elin lifted her chin in a regal gesture. "Yes. I-I believe you are supposed to. I don't know why. I just feel like you're supposed to save him. My mother…"

Elin swallowed and let her eyes fall to her brother. "She told me to save him." Her eyes drifted back to Lochlan, who now stood before her, holding her hands like they were precious things. "I have to believe there's a reason he's supposed to live."

"Elin, I don't know if I can—"

"Do it." Searly's voice sounded unusual and Lochlan instantly went still. "Bring Zeph back, milord." Searly glanced at Arwyn, still feeling all the things she had made him feel: the loss, the pain, the heart-bruising ache that continued to throb. He watched a tear slip down Arwyn's cheek. Then he looked at Zeph. It felt like someone had punched him in the gut to see him lying there. Something feral rose up within him, and he could no longer separate his feelings from Arwyn's, and that was the damnable thing of it. Gritting his teeth, he looked Lochlan dead in the eye. "Bring him back. And do it now. Do it now, milord, or so help me God, I will—"

"All right," Lochlan said, the tip of his mouth curling upward. Everyone knew Searly could not physically take on Lochlan, but at least Lochlan was polite enough not to contradict him. "I'll do it." His eyes roamed to Francesca. "What do I need to do?"

Arwyn breathed a sigh, relief washing over her delicate features. She mouthed...*thank you...* and it was then Searly understood. It was at Searly's behest that Lochlan conceded. Arwyn had known it would come to that. Still, Searly felt violated.

"Same as you did before with Elin. You need to kiss him."

Disgust lit Lochlan's face. "There's not another way?"

"I would not have brought him here if there was. Truthfully, you are the only one who has this gift. Now please, hurry. There simply is no more time. It has to be now."

The room went unnaturally still, everyone eyeing Lochlan with expectancy. In the quiet of the room, a clicking sound could be heard, as if Lochlan had snapped his teeth together, a grim expression on his face.

He shifted his position away from Elin to stare down into the face of Lochlan's greatest enemy. "Ye gods," he muttered. "I feel ill."

Elin gingerly placed her hand on Lochlan's back in an attempt to soothe him. "Please, Lochlan. Please hurry."

His lip curled like he'd tasted something bitter. "Bloody hell."

Slowly, Lochlan bent at the waist, hovered over Zeph, and whispered something in his ear. Then, quickly, he placed his lips over Zeph's and gave him the Kiss of Life.

3

eph opened his eyes wide with an audible gasp, his breath sharp with fear. He sat up quickly, his heart tattooing a frenetic rhythm against his ribs, then cursed inwardly when tiny pricks of light dotted his vision and dizziness took hold. He dropped back to his prone position and groaned an indecipherable slur of words, his tongue too thick to form them properly.

His head lulled to one side. Soft ribbons of moonlight filtered in through a window. Zeph watched the dust motes float and dance in the silvery beams. Pain ebbed and flowed throughout his limbs, then crested over him in waves. He swallowed. It was too much.

Too much.

A log popped and hissed. His attention slid to the fire inside the hearth, and for a long moment, he watched the flames dance too, craving its warmth. Cold had seeped into his bones, freezing his joints until he thought they might shatter. A whimper broke from his dry-cracked lips.

"I know you're in pain." A woman's voice slid over him like honey, thick and sweet, and eyes like diamonds glanced down at him, shadowed by golden-winged brows. "Where does it hurt?"

Everywhere.

As though she could read his thoughts, she nodded. Her eyes slid from his and said to someone he could not see, "You may heal him."

No, don't touch me.

Feminine hands appeared above him from behind his head. He followed them until they came to rest on his bare chest. Warmth suffused him instantly, thawing his bones and melting his pain. Another whimper escaped. He fought to keep silent.

He'd never had anyone touch him with such tenderness before. He'd never known care like this. Not since he was a child.

Heat feathered over him like summer, his limbs loosened, his pain subsided. Lethargy weighed on him until fatigue pulled at his eyelids and he was forced to close them.

"It's all right," the honeyed voice said. "It will be all right."

That was a lie. Zeph would never be all right, though he was too tired to put words to his thoughts. He succumbed to sleep and sometime later he awoke— his mind a muddled mess—lying prone on a hard surface. He stared up at the polygon-shaped ceiling, tracing the lines of the Gothic architecture until they ended in a sharp point.

Confusion stabbed his mind.

"Zeph," said a male voice, deeply quiet, liked wrapped thunder.

With a jolt, he sat up. Cool, narrowed eyes—eyes that he had always found to be striking for a churlish being—stared back at him. Zeph plopped down again and cursed. "I'm in hell," he said with a bitter laugh. "Sard it all."

Of course he was in hell. This would be his punishment, an illusion of Lochlan to taunt him in death. Inside, he thrashed, yet remained perfectly still for anyone viewing him from the outside. He closed his eyes and mumbled, "I am buggered."

"Most likely."

Zeph's eyes snapped open, finding the lout staring down at him. The firelight made Lochlan's features appear sharper, more angular, like his face was chiseled from stone.

"I do believe I hate you," Zeph muttered. He couldn't help his lips from quirking upward when Lochlan snarled. "Don't take it personally, half-breed. I hate everyone."

Lochlan answered by continuing to hover over him like a giant insect.

"By God's bones," Zeph hissed. "Would you kindly get out of my face?"

Lochlan inched back, but only slightly. Zeph rolled to his side, wincing as he rose to an upright position. He swung his legs over the side of the table and dizziness made him grasp the edges. His head pounded like someone had driven a spike through his skull.

Sard it all.

A heavy scent of incense punctuated the air. His stomach rolled and contracted with a tang of acid on his tongue. He hated the smell of incense. It reminded him of the...

Hesitantly, he raised his eyes. Religious artifacts were thoughtfully placed around the room. The muscles in his jaw tightened. "I'm in the monastery?"

Zeph peered to the right when he saw movement. Searly moved toward him, silent as a cat, wearing an expression that bewildered him, although to be fair, he was bewildered by everything at the moment. Zeph breathed through his nose, trying to steady himself, for the dizziness refused to leave him.

"Yes," Searly answered. "You are."

"How did I get here?" Zeph snapped.

"Someone brought you here. A woman with—"

When a figure moved to his left, Zeph's head swung in that direction, and suddenly he couldn't hear the rest of Searly's explanation over the thudding pulse in his ears. His lungs nearly collapsed at the sight before him: silver eyes, silver hair. His ears buzzed as memories of her limp in his arms pushed to the fore. He blinked and shook his head, believing she was an illusion. She wasn't here. None of this was real. *None of this was real.*

"Zeph," Elin hedged.

"No," he said, jumping off the table, ignoring the splintering pain in his side. He backed away from her. "You're not real." He squeezed his eyes shut, placed both hands on his head as he rocked and chanted, "You're not real, you're not real, you're not real."

Elin knelt before him, taking his hands off his head. "Zeph, I am real. I am alive. And so are you."

"No," he said. "It's not possible. I was there! You died!" He held up his hands to show her he still had the stain of her blood on him. "You died!"

"I'm not dead," she said quietly.

He detached himself from her and stood. "Look at me!" he shouted, with his hands out. "I still have your blood on me! Look at me! You *died*!" The room spun around him, a pain shot behind his right eye and he very nearly fell back to his knees. He turned his back to her, unable to look at her. *Too much.* "I'm hallucinating," he murmured on wobbly knees, reaching for the table to hold himself up.

"Quiet," Lochlan hissed. "Elin? Are you all right?"

Zeph turned in time to see Elin's head snap up, eyebrows drawn tightly together. "I…" Her eyes fell back to her hand. She dropped it to her side. "I'm fine," she said. Then she moved toward Zeph, her expression now a blank mask. His eyes widened as she neared. When she placed a smooth palm on his chest, they both gasped a startled breath.

Zeph reared back like she'd burned him, stumbling in retreat a few paces, shocked by his sister's actions. "What are you doing?"

Lochlan dashed toward Elin, and when Zeph saw him reach for her, Zeph roared, "NO! You'll kill her!"

Zeph lunged for him, but Lochlan saw him coming and shoved him, hard. All the air whooshed out of his lungs when his back slammed into the wall on the far side of the room.

"Don't," Lochlan seethed.

"He didn't know," Elin said. She twined her fingers through Lochlan's and pulled him toward the door.

Searly knelt beside Zeph, put a hand on his shoulder. "Lochlan's curse was broken. He wouldn't have hurt her."

Zeph pushed himself up, keeping his back against the wall for balance as the room tilted around him. He stared at their joined hands, unsure what he was seeing. Then he looked down at his body, touching his chest where Lochlan's hands had shoved him. He shouldn't be alive. When was the curse broken? And *how*?

"You think I would ever harm her?" Lochlan seethed. He jabbed his finger in the air at him. "That's something *you* would do. Not me."

For a moment, he let Lochlan's words drift in the air between them and settle on his skin, the truth as fragile as frost on a spider's web. Lochlan was right. He *had* hurt her.

"I—I *had* died," Elin entreated, trying to explain. "But Lochlan brought me back. I'm not dead," she said again. "You're not hallucinating."

"How?" Zeph asked, feeling like he might swoon. "*How* did he bring you back?"

"By the Kiss of Life. He can bring back the dead—with a kiss. He brought you back, just as he did for me."

God's teeth, Zeph's head felt brittle. None of this made sense. He'd never heard of anyone bringing someone back from the dead.

"*How?*" he questioned again, moving away from everyone, sliding his body along the wall, needing the distance. His head was full of cobwebs, and thinking rationally was proving to be difficult. "Explain it to me."

When she did not answer, he forced himself to look at her, though she was not looking at him. She was still staring at her hands with blank dispassion, rubbing the tips of her fingers together.

Zeph's eyes darted toward Lochlan. "Explain!"

"She's already explained it to you," Lochlan said. "I have the power to bring back the dead."

Zeph's nostrils flared, his fists curled at his sides. The longer he pondered the hows and whys, the more tumultuous he felt.

"Calm," Searly said. "Lochlan was granted the Kiss of Life. We know only what we were told—that saving Elin was his destiny. It is a gift and a long story. Now, perhaps once you've had a chance to recover, we shall talk further. I can imagine it is a lot to take in," Searly said, sounding so very reasonable.

Zeph opened his mouth to push, to demand to be told more. It didn't make sense. This was just too...

He remembered what Elin had said. *He brought you back, just as he did for me.*

"Was I dead?" Zeph asked, his voice a shadow, thin and dark. "Was I dead when someone brought me here?"

Searly nodded.

Zeph's eyes shot to Lochlan's. "Did you use your *gift* to bring me back?"

"Yes."

Zeph scrubbed his hands over his face. "Bloody hell. Why would you do that?"

"They asked me to. If it was up to me, you'd still be dead."

Beside him, Zeph's shadow unfurled, hushed as the night, and danced between the flickering light until it stilled, surveying him, waiting to mimic his motions; an immaculate outline of his shape, an echo of his movements. His shadow was a lifetime companion, a silhouette of darkness, and a friend. His *only* friend.

Zeph kept his back against the wall for balance as the room tilted around him. He forced his eyes to hold Lochlan's scathing glare. He had only ever brought pain to those he cared about. He didn't deserve to be here. He would end this now. He dug deep, finding the fight that still lay within him. They should have let him stay dead.

He grinned as he straightened, standing to his full height. "Tell me something, half-breed…this *Kiss of Life*…you had to kiss me to bring me back? On the lips?" Lochlan's anger vibrated and hummed like a colony of bees, and Zeph's grin widened. "Did you like it, darling? Truthfully, I don't remember it, so for me, it was quite forgettable." Zeph shrugged. "However, I imagine it will forever haunt your dreams."

A low, animalistic growl rumbled in Lochlan's throat.

Zeph smiled brightly, like a blade catching the light of the sun. "Excellent. A boon for me, then. At least something good came from it."

Lochlan made a move toward him, but Elin pulled on his arm. "He's trying to anger you. Don't give him what he wants. Come with me," she said. "Don't do this."

Lochlan's eyes narrowed into thin slits. Zeph put on a good show of being unaffected, something he was quite good at, even though his own rage coiled within him, readying to strike. He wanted a fight. He wanted Lochlan to take his life. *I want to not be here. I don't deserve a second chance.*

Zeph was disappointed when Lochlan turned away and allowed Elin to lead him out into the corridor. Disappointed and *angry*. He made a final attempt to provoke his nemesis. He was not long for this world, and he would make sure of it one way or another.

"You're weak," Zeph hissed. "Fight me!"

Lochlan's steps faltered, his shoulders lifting, his muscles tightening underneath his cloak. "No," Lochlan said with surprising calm. "It wouldn't be a fair fight."

It wouldn't. Zeph could barely stand. Even more of a reason to provoke. It would be over quickly. "Fight me!" he bellowed.

"No."

Zeph could hear the scrape of Lochlan's teeth as he gritted them together, and Zeph pulled at his hair, furious with the situation. "Why, then? Why *did* you bring me back?!" When Lochlan did not answer, Zeph picked up the nearest object he could find and slung it across the room, pleased with the crash it made against the stone. "Was it to torture me? Make me stay in a world that only brought me pain?! I DON'T WANT TO BE HERE!"

Lochlan simply shrugged, still keeping his back to him.

Zeph went for a wooden chair, something he could throw. When he managed to get to it, he needed it to steady his balance.

Sard it all!

Leaning against the wooden frame, the guilt of his sins pressed upon him, like waves swelling and crashing over him. He could barely catch his breath. The fight he had wanted drained out of him and he crumbled to the floor. He knew his sister was watching him, analyzing his every word, trying to make sense of him. He couldn't look at her. He knew what he would find: hate, sadness, sorrow. He'd had a lifetime of it and he just wanted to be done.

He rubbed the place where Lochlan had shoved him, feeling bruised, and asked the question before he could think better of it.

"How did you break the curse, half-breed?" His voice was a rasp, his head a throbbing, aching thing, and his heart was a useless organ that beat a steady rhythm, robbing him of the one thing he wanted. Death.

Lochlan held Elin's hand, squeezed it once, and started for the corridor once more.

"I didn't," Lochlan said. "You did."

Arwyn flinched when she heard something crash against the wall. She had taken leave before Zeph had fully come to and stepped into the hallway, where she listened on shaky legs to every harsh and bitter word Zeph spoke.

She knew his reaction would be this way when he realized what had taken place. She could not bear to see it, though she could not bear to venture away too far either, so she dithered outside the communal room, pacing about, afraid to face him. Not because she feared him. She never feared him. But because…

"I suppose that went as well as expected."

Lochlan's voice wasn't loud, though it roared like the inside of a shell. The stale and stagnant air turned frosty with his presence. Arwyn tried not to shudder from the sudden chill.

Arwyn halted her pacing and absently tugged on a cuff sleeve. "I heard. I—"

"Where did Francesca go?" Lochlan questioned, cutting her off. He glowered at her like she was a well of secrets, as if *she* were someone not to be trusted. She bristled under his accusing glare before she straightened and answered with a proprietary tone.

"I don't know. I did not see her go."

The woman, Francesca, had disappeared shortly after Lochlan had brought Zeph back to life, though not before she had asked Arwyn to ease his pain so he could rest. No one had seen her leave. She had simply been there one minute and gone the next.

"This was a mistake," Lochlan groused, rubbing his hands over his face. "I should never have—"

"No, it wasn't," Arwyn said, keeping her voice low. "It *wasn't*," she said again with more insistence, more bite. Her eyes fell to Elin, desperately needing her to agree, but Elin was staring off behind her, toward the room she'd just exited, obviously not part of their conversation. Arwyn's eyes drifted back to Lochlan's and asked, "Are you angry with me?"

"Yes!" He scrubbed his hands over his face and leaned against the wall. "No." Leaning forward, he pressed his palms to his knees. "I'm sorry, Arwyn. I don't know why I'm taking my frustrations out on you."

Lochlan's tone was no longer icy. It was a warm blanket, and the frost in the air dissipated like morning mist.

Arwyn moved toward him with the intent to comfort. She extended her hand, about to lay it gently on his back before she caught herself, suspending her hand in midair, forgetting that until recently, Lochlan had not been allowed to touch or be touched. His curse forbade it, lest dire consequences ensued. For five hundred years it had been so. And though he was now free from his curse, he had not yet had time to get used to the idea of it—touching. Elin was the only person he was comfortable with touching him. Arwyn felt his unease the moment she started his way, felt his pulse thrum faster, felt his panic. "It's all right," she said, snatching her hand out of the air, pretending to be none the wiser to his emotions. "I'm sorry for snapping at you earlier. I was just..." She sighed. "Desperate."

Lochlan relaxed and rose from his bent position and a faint, humorless laugh escaped. "I'm trying hard to understand you and Elin. I really am."

Arwyn's smile was small, though she managed it nonetheless. "Well, when you have us figured out, mind sharing? Because, presently, I'm having a difficult time of it myself." She glanced behind her, at Elin, and asked, "Is she well? She seems—"

"Out of sorts?" Lochlan finished.

Arwyn nodded.

Lochlan let out an exasperated breath and shoved off the wall. Taking Elin by the hand, he asked, "What's wrong? You don't seem yourself. Ever since—"

"I'm fine." She swallowed and blinked, as if coming out of a trance. "I just feel rather...odd."

Arwyn's brows knitted. "Odd?"

Lochlan tucked Elin underneath the pit of his arm and kissed the top of her head. "I'm worried for you, acushla."

"I just need some air, I think." She touched her clammy forehead with trembling fingers. "It's been a long night."

"Are you sure that is all?" Arwyn asked, concerned. "You seem more than a little shaken." Arwyn felt the oddity Elin felt, and like Elin, she couldn't explain the feeling either. It truly was *odd*.

"Lochlan just brought my brother back from the dead. Of course I'm shaken. Who wouldn't be? And I don't know how to even talk to him. *If* I should even try. I hate him. I hate him so much." Her eyes drifted back to the room where she'd left Zeph and said, "Just now, when I looked at him, I remember the boy he used to be." Her lip trembled. "The vulnerability, I remember how different he was then…before he was taken, and I want so badly to hug him. And then I want to slap him."

Arwyn understood the sentiment.

"Did I fail him?" Elin asked, her voice wobbling. "Did I?"

Lochlan squeezed her shoulders. "No," he said softly. "You didn't fail him. You didn't know—"

"I know," Elin said. "Logically, I know. My heart is objecting, however."

He kissed her head once more and held her tighter. "You're right; it's been a long night. Let us try to get some rest. We'll stay close in case there's any trouble. There's nothing you can say to him tonight that will help."

She lifted her head off his shoulder. "You're not worried to leave him alone with Searly?"

"No. He can barely stand on his own." To Arwyn, Lochlan said, "You'll be here, though, right?"

She waved him off. "Go. I'll not leave. You have my word."

He hesitated briefly and then nodded. "Thank you."

She made a feeble attempt to smile. "Of course."

Together, he and Elin walked away, leaving Arwyn to her troubled thoughts. She pressed her back against the wall and blew out a nervous breath. She would have to see Zeph now. She had hoped she could put if off a bit longer. Tomorrow, perhaps. But now…

"*Bugger me.*"

She let her head fall against the wall as she shut her eyes, listening to what was being said on the other side. She heard nothing but quiet. She tried to imagine Zeph when they were last alone together. White hair that fell past his shoulders, swept back and neat; dark, striking brows that shadowed eyes clear as rain; and a jaw sharp as a blade. There was an elegance about Zeph, the way he moved. He didn't walk across a room. He prowled…like he was always searching for prey. Something she most certainly should not admire, yet she did. She always had.

"We don't want him here," a voice said, coming up beside her.

Arwyn's heart squeezed. Xavier.

Opening her eyes, she said carefully, "I know."

"Do you? He *killed* our brother, Thaddeus." Xavier's voice was low yet stern. "And now he is in our midst and we are supposed to—what? Forget?"

He gesticulated wildly as he voiced his displeasure—his anger—about Zeph being inside the monastery. She listened with a quietness, a stillness that never wavered, taking in Xavier's hurt and heartache, anger, and bitterness. In the absence of Thaddeus, he needed to be the voice of his brother monks, most of whom had taken a vow of silence. They had been present the day Zeph had walked into the monastery, killed Thaddeus upon entering the library, and gave a wicked blow to Searly's head before carting him off, taking him to Shadowland against Searly's will. And the monks could do nothing about it except watch it happen.

Arwyn knew this. Their sufferings were as much a part of the monastery as stone and mortar was. And knowing Zeph had done this to them fragmented her heart into tiny pieces.

She wiped a tear. She could *feel* all of Xavier's emotions. Her father had called it a gift. To her though, it never truly felt like a gift. Most days, it was all she could do to hold herself together. She didn't just have to deal with her own pain. She had to deal with the pain of the whole world.

"I'm so sorry," she said. "I—I don't know what to say."

"Tell me he won't stay here. Tell me you didn't demand Lord Lochlan bring him back from the dead to torture us more."

She reared back as though she'd been struck. "No," she said. "Never would I do that."

"Then why?" Xavier implored. *"Why?"*

How could she make him understand?

"We deserve an explanation. This is our home and we have no say?"

"Of course you do."

"Then tell me—"

"My family was slain," Arwyn said softly, so softly in fact that Xavier had to lean in close to hear. His mouth snapped shut when her eyes lifted to his. "Unseelie came into our home and slashed my family's throats. I listened to the sounds of their wet gurgles while I hid. I understand what it is to watch someone you love be murdered in front of you while you do nothing, afraid to make the tiniest sound for fear they'll come after you too. I know what it is to listen to someone take their last breath. I know…"

Another tear slipped down her cheek and she angrily wiped it away.

Xavier's expression softened, and his tone became softer as well. "I am sorry you had to endure that." He moved closer, put his hands on her shoulders. "But how would you feel if those who killed your family were underneath the same roof as you now? How would you feel knowing that they were steps away from you, standing in your *home*?"

Arwyn couldn't stop her heart from racing at the thought, though she also knew she wouldn't be standing here now, telling Xavier her story, had it gone a different way.

"He saved me," she murmured.

"Who saved you?"

"Zeph."

Xavier drew in a sharp breath. "What?"

Arwyn needed room to breathe. She detached herself from Xavier's hold and folded her arms across her middle. "Zeph found me, hiding underneath the bed. He gestured for me to keep quiet." She bit down on her lower lip to stay its quivering. "I didn't know what he would do. I obviously thought the worst. I listened as he stood and left the room. I heard him tell the other Unseelie no one else was in the house. They all left. Sometime later, Zeph came back. He took me to Shadowland and promised to keep me safe." Her eyes held Xavier's when she said, "He kept that promise."

"Arwyn, you were his prisoner."

"I could have left. I wasn't imprisoned there."

"Then why did you stay?"

"And go where? Where would I have gone?"

"Arwyn—"

"No. I know who he is to you—a monster, and rightly so. That is not who he is to *me*." Xavier started to speak but she held up her palm, cutting him off. "I was alone with Zeph in his keep for years. He had every opportunity to harm me if he had wanted. I won't get into the particulars of what I came to know of Zeph while in his company. However, know this…there is good in him. I've seen it. Small flickers of light. There is good in him. He is—"

"He is a lost cause," Xavier said between gritted teeth. "You were lucky he never harmed you. You'd do well to stay away from him."

"I can't," she said.

"Why not?"

"Because he isn't a lost cause, Xavier. He's just—lost."

An audible scoff escaped Xavier's lips, and the veins in his temple began to bulge. He lowered his hands to his hips and shifted his weight from one foot to the other, shaking his head like she was a dimwitted child.

All right, she thought. If she was going to make him understand, she would need to speak his language. "Wasn't Saint Paul once a murderer?" Arwyn asked.

Xavier's head snapped up. "What?"

Arwyn tilted her head. She had read and studied a plethora of things while at the monastery, sacred texts included. Saint Paul's story had given her hope. "Paul was a murderer, was he not? Before his redemption?"

Xavier's head nodded a fraction, as if he hated to admit it.

Her eyes dropped to the cross that hung around Xavier's neck. "Why do you suppose your Lord allowed Paul to become so wicked before saving him?"

Xavier rubbed the back of his neck uncomfortably and she waited for him to answer.

"Well?" she prompted.

"To encourage those who think they are too sinful to have hope," a voice behind her said, but Arwyn wasn't surprised by the interruption. She had felt Searly's presence in the doorway. And behind him—she'd felt Zeph's.

Searly went on, his eyes on Xavier, "To put our Lord's perfect patience on display. To show that anyone can triumph over wickedness. To prove that *no one* is a lost cause."

She counted the seconds before anyone spoke. Fifteen had passed.

"I believe that is the answer you were seeking, Arwyn," Searly said, tilting his head toward her, a smile on his lips. "It was also a lesson I needed to be reminded of. Thank you."

Something passed between them then. Something warm and tender. And her spirits were raised. She had felt so badly for what she had done to him before. She had been desperate, and though she wasn't proud of the way she had manipulated her friend, she couldn't be entirely sorry, either. She did what she had to do.

"Yes," she said. "You are welcome."

A quiet fell over the four of them, weighted and full of discomfort. No one knew quite what to say. She stared at the floor, the walls, the ceiling. When Arwyn gathered the nerve to glance at Zeph, she found him watching her. She quickly looked away, thankful for the shadowed corridor, for a blush stole over the crest of her cheeks. It was never her intention for him to hear her defend him like some love-struck fool, but the timing was what it was, and nothing could be done for it now.

"I will be along in a while to speak to you and the others, Xavier," Searly said, breaking the silence. "Get some rest. We will talk it all out when we've all managed a bit of sleep. Yes?"

"Of course, brother."

Xavier did not look Zeph's way, nor did he spare Arwyn a glance. Arwyn tried not to think of the conflicting emotions that warred in Xavier's soul. Like the rest of them, it would be a struggle to sort them out and know which ones to act on.

"I'll take you to the infirmary, Zeph. You can clean up and rest there if you like. I'll have some soup brought to you as well."

But Zeph did not move. He simply stared—at Arwyn. Arwyn pretended to be otherwise distracted, brushing off invisible lint from her sleeves.

"Zeph?" Searly prompted. "This way."

When Zeph failed to move or even speak, Arwyn forced herself to look at him again, allowing herself to truly take in his condition. For a moment, she struggled for breath. He appeared so frail, like one strong wind could blow him away. Her heart lurched.

When Francesca had first brought him in and placed him on the table, Arwyn had seen how he was. But he was alive now. She expected him to be the same as before.

He was not the same. Not at all.

Francesca had not allowed her to heal him fully. She had said, "Let him feel the consequences of his actions, child. We only need to *ease* his suffering, not end it. When he wakes, let him feel pain so he will know that he is alive."

Arwyn did as Francesca bid, though she had wanted to argue. Truthfully, it was one of the reasons she had removed herself from the room when Zeph woke. She would have wanted to heal him completely. Even now, her hands trembled with the desire to do so. She was a healer, after all. It wasn't like her ability to feel others' emotions—or transfer emotions to others, as she had done to Searly. This was something she actually loved about herself.

She fought the sting of tears as she looked at him, holding her tongue, afraid to utter a sound. His hair was a bedraggled mess. He swayed on his feet, wobbled with each intake of breath and shuddered with each release.

But his eyes never wavered from hers.

Where does it hurt?

"Zeph?" Searly prompted once more. "If you will follow me, please?"

"You look well," Zeph said, surprising her. His eyes lowered, traveled the length of her torso and back up. "Different."

She fought the urge to fidget, her spine stiffening. "You look terrible," she said, frowning.

The corner of his mouth lifted. "You always know just what to say."

"Yes, well, I believe in honesty. Something you've always struggled with."

He did not flinch, nor did he look away. "I've struggled with many things, darling," he said, his voice trembling defiantly. His expression closed off then, giving away nothing of what he was feeling. Even the pain she had seen in his eyes was now hidden from her. "Do me a favor, luv. Stop trying to save me. I am not a saint, nor will I ever be one."

"I'm not asking you to be a saint, Zeph."

"You're asking for me to be *something*. Aren't you? Something I can never be."

"Go with Searly," Arwyn said. She focused on the wall behind Zeph's head, no longer able to look at him. She was breaking inside and desperate to be alone, so she could shatter quietly. "Please go." When Zeph refused to move, she picked up her skirts and said, "Fine. I'll go. Searly, please see he gets to the infirmary. Wouldn't want Zeph passing out in the halls."

She was a few steps away when Zeph called, "Your worry for my well-being is touching."

She stopped, turned, and bustled over to him. He grinned when she got in his face, but his eyes gave away his insecurities.

"You were given a second chance, you stubborn ox! I'm not trying to save you! No one can do that. You must save yourself. I will not coddle you. I will not make excuses for you. But I will fight for you when you're too tired to fight. I will be there for you. I will challenge you. Because I know there is good in there somewhere. And you know it too! You're just too damn scared to try! I never thought I'd say this to you, Zeph, but you're a coward!"

Zeph's features turned to stone and her blood began to boil.

She laughed, but there was no joy. "Why do I do this to myself?" She picked up her skirts once more and made to leave.

"Why?" Zeph asked quietly.

She paused. "Why what?"

"Why would you fight for me?"

She closed her eyes, grateful her back was to him, for she couldn't stop the quiver of her chin. She had to swallow several times before she could speak. This. This was why she kept trying. He was vulnerable as an orphan, deposited in a world full of hate.

"Because," she whispered, "you won't fight for yourself."

"There is simply nothing to fight *for*, Arwyn." His tone was no longer confrontational. "You value truth, honesty," he said. "I'm giving it to you now." She turned to face him. He extended his arms out to the side, as though he was offering a glimpse of himself to her. "Don't you see? I am everything Xavier said I was. And I agree with him. You'd do well to stay away from me."

She took a step forward, and then another, and another, until she had closed the gap between them. She startled him when she pressed her palm to his chest. He fought the flutter of his eyes as he refused to close them.

"Where does it hurt?"

A strangled sound escaped his dry lips. She knew the effect she was having on him. She felt it. Warmth absconded over him like drops of sunshine, heating his muscles, clearing his mind, easing his pain.

"Where does it hurt?" she asked again, wanting him, *needing* him to say it.

He covered her hand with his and repositioned it over his heart. "Here," he said. "Is this something you can heal? Can you mend broken hearts, Arwyn? Because if you can, I'll let you have a go at it."

She wanted to sob. "I'll try. If you'll let me, I'll certainly try."

He closed his eyes, and a single tear slid down his cheek. A moment later, Zeph pulled away.

To Searly, he said, "Please lead the way if the offer for a bath and rest is still on the table."

Searly simply nodded, and on legs that barely seemed solid enough to hold his weight, Zeph followed. They traveled down long, darkened corridors, past statues of those who came before him, men and women better than he could ever hope to be, and all the while, a shadow, a long, thin echo of Zeph, trailed closely behind.

4

lagued by dreams of a lost boy, crying, begging for someone to save him, Zeph sat up and rubbed his eyes. The first time he'd seen the boy had been on the mountain. Now, every time he slept, he saw him.

He heaved a sigh. All was quiet. Even Zeph's shadow, which was usually a restless thing, was still and unmoving.

Days had passed since Zeph arrived at the monastery. In those days, he had not left the infirmary once. He'd convinced himself it was so he could heal, and he had, to be sure. He felt stronger than ever. He sat on the edge of the bed and looked down at his hands, palms up, then he turned them over before squeezing them into fists. He should leave now that he was healed. But where would he go? He had no place to be, nowhere to retreat, and no one waiting for him to return.

He stood and moved toward the window. Darkness had not yet surrendered to the light, though the sky was more of a metallic gray than an abyss of black, glistening with the occasional spear of light through the clouds. A subdued quiet filled Zeph's soul. He didn't want to be here. Then again, he didn't want to be anywhere. Least of all in a place surrounded by people who hated him. He had been surrounded by hate most of his life. He should have felt at home. But he hadn't felt home anywhere in such a long time.

He closed his eyes. A vision of Elin framed his mind, as though she was an answer to a question he hadn't asked. And then he felt her—in his room, the air shifting around him, growing heavy, finding it harder to breathe in her presence. He ignored the organ inside his chest that thumped once, then twice. Same as it always had whenever she was near.

"You look better," she said without preamble. "Although you should really do something about your hair."

He nearly smiled. He had not seen her since his arrival three days past, but she was always on his mind. How could he not think of her? She had consumed his thoughts for as many days as he cared to recall.

"You don't like my hair, sister? I am hurt." He didn't turn around. Instead, he stared at the sun cresting over the horizon, slowly covering the pearl morning haze bit by bit. He couldn't fight the sun. He could only watch as it dragged him into a new day against his will.

"It is not your best look," she said with no inflection in her voice, nothing that would indicate her mood.

He combed his long fingers through his white locks, doing his best to tame it. He realized then how unsettling he must appear. After Searly had deposited him in the infirmary, he had washed away the gore but had done little else since. He looked unkempt, and for some reason, he wished to appear more pleasing to his sister. Less monstrous.

With a snap of his fingers, he changed into his usual attire: white breeches, white tunic, and a white robe that reached the floor. His hair now tied away from his face, flowing down his back in one long sweep.

"Better?" he asked.

He heard her take a sharp breath. He turned in her direction, surprised to find the startled look on her face. One dark brow lifted as he clasped his hands behind his back. "What?" he asked.

Her eyes fell to the floor. She shifted her feet and cleared her throat. "I wasn't expecting the sudden transformation is all."

He observed her. The way she'd enter the room without a sound—how she stood there now—like the floor might give way underneath her if she but moved in the wrong direction. Every step was careful, precise, and so light she made no sound at all. Most people would likely see her fear. Zeph saw her bravery. Afraid of him, and if not afraid, then she most assuredly was wary of him. Yet she came.

At length neither she nor he spoke. He returned his focus to the window while she stayed by the door. An easy escape, he surmised. She didn't trust being alone with him. Then, because he had to ask, he turned to her again, the question falling from his lips. "Why are you here?" Her silver eyes found his and the organ inside his chest thumped once more.

Tilting her head as though she was considering a thoughtful response, she said, "I don't rightly know. I just felt..." She rubbed her hands and smoothed them out over her dress.

"Go on," he said. "You just felt..."

"Don't rush me," she said, her voice bristling like a cat's fur.

Zeph held up his hands, flashing a grin, like a blade gleaming from concealment, before disappearing under his cloak of indifference. "Take your time." He faced the window. The forest beyond now seemed to glow, haloed by soft shades of gold. "I've got nothing but time," he mumbled to himself.

"Why did you do it?" she asked, her question bubbling up like a pot of boiling water.

He cut his eyes toward her. "I'm afraid you'll have to be more specific. I have done many things."

He didn't want to have this conversation, feeling sure she was asking about their parents and why he had killed them. His reasons now seemed so unjustified. He had not thought so at the time, of course, not caring about consequences. But he knew the moment he had slain them, calling forth the smoke monsters to do his bidding, that he would live to regret it. And regret it he did. But what did it matter? He couldn't bring them back.

"Why did you change your name?"

"Pardon?" he asked, caught off guard. Certainly not the question he'd expected.

She casually walked to the table beside the bed and pointed to the bread wrapped in a cloth. "May I? My stomach is a bit unsettled."

Searly had brought the bread to him the night before along with a bowl of thick soup. The night before that had been fish and beans. Searly had not overstayed his visits on either night, seemingly sure Zeph wanted no company, which was true, but Searly had also been the only visitor he'd had, and some part of Zeph appreciated his visits all the same.

He nodded once and watched her pinch off a piece before placing it in her mouth. She chewed slowly, as though she was using food to keep from using words.

"Why are you asking about my name?" Looking at her proved to be painful because he longed to hug her, to apologize for every wrong he had ever done, yet he could not muster the courage to try. He'd rather assume her rejection than know it outright, so he turned away from her and let his eyes roam the view outside. The sun was becoming increasingly ambitious, illuminating the land one crevice at a time.

"Because I want to know. Why did you change it?"

He chuffed. "I was told to."

"By whom? Lolith?"

"No. By the Unseelie King."

"The one you killed?"

When they were in Shadowland, he had killed the Unseelie King. And he had done so in front of Elin, Searly, and Arwyn. However, had Arwyn not interfered and stabbed the king in the neck with her blade, Zeph would have been the one to perish that day. He had merely finished the job by lobbing off the king's head with his sword.

"Yes, the very one," he said.

"Do you…" she paused. "Do you ever wish to be called Zuriel again?"

"No," he answered without hesitation. "I do not."

"Why?"

He closed his eyes. "Eliniana, I am not that boy anymore."

Again, silence fell between them, thick and weighty. He cleared his throat after a time, but he couldn't think of anything to say. She needed to leave. No good could come of this.

"Zuriel. Eliniana. Pyric. Hiamoli." She said the names in a whisper. That worthless organ taking up space underneath his breast thumped again. "You named yourself after all of us. You, me, Mother, and Father." She came around the bed to stand beside him, realization dawning on her, her mouth curving into the shape of a crescent moon. "That's what Zeph stands for."

He neither confirmed nor denied. He simply let her words stand as truth as he willed his heart to stop beating like an anvil while he forced himself to stare at the world outside the window. Birds began chirping as the sky now burned a pale orange. How much simpler life would be if he were just a bird.

"Were you really going to kill me?" she asked, whisper soft, perhaps hoping he would say no.

"Yes," he said, looking directing at her, needing her to believe him. "Yes," he said again.

"Liar."

He scoffed and shook his head and began to pace the width of the room. "Why are you here?" he asked again. "Do you want to reminisce? Is that it? All right. Remember the time I killed our parents? Or how about the time I stole you right underneath your half-breed's nose and dumped you in a tomb? What about the time I took you and Searly and hid you inside Shadowland, refusing to let you leave? Quite the memories, right?" He stalked toward her, but she held her ground and refused to be backed into a corner. "What about the time I killed a monk? Oh, right…you weren't there for that. Searly was, though…and the rest of them," he said, waving his hands toward the door, his voice growing louder, harder.

It wasn't until the words died in the air that Zeph realized they were nose to nose, his chest rising and falling in quick succession.

"Do you remember the time you saved me from the Unseelie King?" she asked, her tone matching his in volume.

"You wouldn't have been in danger had I not brought you there."

"Please. I have always been in danger. I had just forgotten."

"What are you doing?" Zeph asked, lowering his voice. "You can't erase what I've done with one decent move on my part."

"Oh, believe me, I know that."

"Then what is this, Eliniana?"

"Don't call me that."

"Why?"

"I am not that girl anymore."

Wasn't she, though? For a moment, he could only stare at her. She still had that beautiful innocence about her. The kind of innocence he'd once had. But when he looked deeper into her eyes, he saw the pain that existed there. Then he laughed, all joyless and bitter because he'd robbed her of that innocence and in the cruelest way imaginable. He bit the inside of his cheek, hard enough to taste blood because the alternative was to smash his fists into the stone wall. "No, I suppose you're not."

"So, if you're not that boy anymore, and I am not that girl, who are we?"

"Enemies," Zeph answered, swallowing. "We are enemies."

Elin repeated the word *enemies* like she was trying it on to see if it fit. She walked to one side of the room and then the other. Zeph watched but kept his distance. He had to. He was feeling too much. Her being alive and him being alive—it was all too damn much. He wanted to hug her so badly that he ached all over.

"You know what I think?" she asked, completely unaware how quickly he was unraveling.

"No," he said, his voice tender as a wound.

"I think if we changed once, we can change again. Be different people."

"I'm surprised the half-breed has left you alone with me this long," Zeph said, changing the subject.

Elin's mouth twitched. "He's on the other side of the door, to be sure," she said. Glancing at the door, she smiled. It clung to the edge of her lips like a sunrise—slowly creeping until it was warm and glowing.

"Is he good to you?" Zeph asked, the words rushing out before he could stop them.

"I do not believe that is something an enemy would ask," she said, her smile guileless. "Do you truly care?"

He ignored her taunting and redirected his attention out the window once more. The morning dew glistened as the sun climbed higher, eating away the morning fog. Movement from the corner of his eye caught his attention. A white-tail deer crept along the outer edge of the tree-lined forest. Zeph couldn't help thinking the animal was much too delicate for this world. He thought of his sister in much the same way. When he had first found her, she'd had that same gracefulness, that same demure quality, and had been completely unsuspecting of the creatures that lurked in the dark to devour her.

"Zeph?"

He blinked and glanced over his shoulder.

"Did you hear me?"

"No." He pressed the heel of his hands into his eyes. "Did you say something?"

"What is it?" She walked to the window and peered out. "What are you looking at?"

Zeph stepped away, the swell of emotion inside of him threatening to bubble over. "Nothing." He went to the side table, the one by his bed, and picked up the bread, tearing off a piece. He chewed it as slowly as she had. To him, it tasted like nothing. "The food in Faery is much better," he said without thought. "How have you eaten this every day for so long?"

"Mother's cooking was quite good…" Her voice trailed off, but not before Zeph heard the catch in her throat, the bread now tasting like a lump of clay.

Zeph tossed the rest of the bread back onto the table. He squeezed his eyes closed, let the guilt consume him. "You should go," he said. When she didn't move, he shouted, "Leave!"

Elin moved toward the door in a swish of skirts, her face contorted in anger and grief. She opened the door and stood there, staring out into the hallway.

Lochlan, who had been leaning against the wall, stood up straight, his eyes roaming hers.

Zeph watched his sister, wondering what she was waiting for. Then she closed the door again and pressed her forehead to it. "I hate you," she said. "It burns like fire in my chest." Her hands began to glow, the flame inside a lantern against the far wall arched higher, and the room began to heat.

That stupid organ thumped, thumped, thumped in his chest. "This is not news, luv," he said, with all the callousness meant to drive the wedge further between them. He did not want her forgiveness. He didn't deserve it, yet, on some level, deep in his soul, he yearned for it, hoped one day, maybe, she could forgive him. He shook his head and put those thoughts out of his mind. He wanted her free of him. "I'll be gone by the day's end," he said. "Don't come looking for me this time."

A sob escaped Elin's throat. She clasped her hands over her mouth, and her shoulders shook and trembled.

Zeph had seen many horrible things in his life. Things no creature should ever see, but seeing his sister's pain was the hardest thing he'd ever witnessed.

"Go!" he yelled. "Leave!"

She flinched, then opened the door, allowed herself a moment to gather her wits, squared her shoulders and walked out, moving with utter control, despite her fury and her sorrow.

For the longest time, Zeph didn't move. He waited for the numbness to take hold. It did not. Not this time. He sat down on the edge of the bed, and with his elbows on his knees he placed his head in his hands. He fought off the tears for as long as he could. He deserved this. He deserved her hate.

In the resounding silence, he couldn't ignore the cadence of his heart, whispering regret for his words—for his deeds. Losing the battle, he let the tears flow. He lost himself in his misery and wept like the lost boy he so often dreamt about.

"We were kids," Elin said tenderly.

Startled, Zeph stood and whipped around. He had not heard her come in. She moved toward him on silent feet, cautiously. Once again, he saw her bravery. Afraid, but still she came.

"The Unseelie were planning to steal me. You hid me…with your…your shadows…like you did in Shadowland."

He blinked. Then blinked again.

"I remembered," she said. "How it happened. It was you they stole instead of me because you cloaked me in your shadows and they couldn't find me. So they took you instead." She stalked toward him now. He took a step back. "Do you remember that, Zeph?

"Stop," he said.

"You protected me."

Lochlan stood in the doorway, watching. Zeph's eyes bounced between the half-breed and his sister. Zeph's head began to swim. He clutched his head. "Leave me, Elin. Just go."

"No."

Zeph felt her hand on his shoulder. He looked up. Her quicksilver eyes glowed. Little by little her skin illuminated. As radiant as a sunrise. And so beautiful, he couldn't look away.

Shadows danced by the light she created. Zeph felt his own shadow rise up and become that restless thing he knew so well.

"*I love the peculiar silence of shadows,*" his mother once told him. "*They exist, but leave no mark.*"

Zeph blinked, fighting the sting of tears at the remembrance of his mother's words. He turned away from his sister.

"I have a question for you, Zeph, and I need you to tell me the truth." He swallowed. "If I am the Faery of Light. What are you?"

"*Do not fear what you are, my sweets. For we all sleep in the earth's shadow, more commonly known as night.*"

"Your brother," he answered, his voice a mere rasp.

"No," she said. "What *are* you? Why did they keep you? What did they want from you?"

His mind raced with the possible answers he could give. But his thoughts scattered when she was near. "Stop," he said, hand clasped tightly over his ears. "Please stop."

"No," she said. "What are you?"

"Nothing!" he yelled. "A black hole! You were always light, Elin. I was always the darkness. All right? The best thing for you is to stay away from me."

"*You give dimension to your sister, Zeph.*" His mother's words again, only this time it sounded like she had whispered them in his ear. "*You ground her to this world.*"

He spun around, casting his eyes around the room, halfway expecting to see his mother standing beside him.

"No, you're not," Elin said, coming to stand directly in front of him. "Tell me the truth."

Teetering on the edge of insanity, Zeph gripped her by the shoulders, wanting to shake her, make her see. "It is the truth!" he shouted.

A spark passed between them then and she gasped, her eyes widening. They broke apart and stumbled back.

"What was that?" Elin asked.

Zeph was still wide-eyed and blinking.

"What was that?!" she repeated, louder this time.

"Nothing," he answered. "You need to go."

"What are you, Zeph? Why do I feel this way whenever I'm near you? When we touch, why do I feel…why do I feel like I'm…" She closed her mouth and yanked him by the arm, forcing him to face her. She held on to him with a firm grip. "Why do I feel invincible when I touch you?"

"Do you?" he said, a strangled sob lodging in his throat. "Unhand me."

"Tell her the truth," his mother would say.

"No," he whispered, shaking his head. "No." She didn't need to know. It would only hurt her more. She'd forgotten so much. So much. Zeph thought the less she remembered about him, the better.

Concerned, Elin held his face between her palms. "Zeph, what are you not telling me?"

"Nothing," he said, looking down, away from her.

"Zeph," Elin said, dipping her face, forcing herself into his line of sight. "Tell me."

His eyes found hers. "It'll only hurt you. Let me walk away from you. Let me go, Elin. I've hurt you enough."

"Care about her enough to tell her the truth," Lochlan said.

Zeph's eyes cut to his. "Stay out of this."

"Tell me," Elin said. "Here. Now. Tell me."

Zeph's jaw tightened. "Fine." He straightened to his full height. "I am not just your brother," he said, strangling on his words. "I am your twin. Are you happy to know now?" he asked, stepping away from her and marching toward the door, his shadow trailing behind as always.

She had not moved or made a sound, although he had glimpsed disbelief behind her eyes before he'd forced himself to move away.

But before he could reach the door, Elin dashed across the room, a blur of light, and then she was blocking him, preventing his escape.

"Twins?" she asked.

He sighed. "You're older by one minute."

Her eyes fell to her feet. "How did I…how did I not remember that?"

"I shouldn't have told you."

Her head snapped up. "So that's it, then. You're a Faery of Light, too. That's why they kept you."

"No," he said. "I am not a Faery of Light." He would have laughed at the notion if he'd had it in him to do so. "Not even close."

"Then what are you, Zeph?"

"By God's bones, Elin," he hissed. "You control the elements and I control the space in between," he said, stepping back and flailing his hands in the air.

"The space in between. What does that mean?"

He breathed in a long pull of air and let it out in slow measures. "I am darkness. You are light. That's what we are. Night and day. You are everything good. And I am everything children are afraid of. That's why they kept me! Because they could use me! Send me out to do their bidding. I am a black hole! But you didn't believe that, did you? Well, believe it, luv."

Zeph clamped his mouth shut then. He'd said more than enough. He took one last look at his sister, his dark brows knitting tightly together, and wished from the depths of him that he was different—that he'd been born with her goodness—her light. But wishing was for romantics and little girls and he was neither, so he turned away from her and did the only thing he could do well, even if it wasn't right.

He disappeared—into a whirl of shadows. And in the air, his words lingered…

"I believe that makes us *enemies*."

5

The young lad stared at the large stone structure in front of him. It lay like an old man on a hill, moss clinging to the base like a straggly beard with vines of ivy twisting up the pitted and scarred walls. A forest of trees surrounded it like a great army defending its citadel.

A smile inched across his face. Weeks of traveling by ship and he had finally arrived. His smile only grew the longer he took in the view. Even the gloomy drizzle could not lower his spirits. Years he had waited, setting sail the moment he was able to do so, though his mamá did not want to let him go. *"The world is so big, hijo. Stay with me. Do not make me worry so."* But he had to make the journey. It was something he had longed to do for as far back as he could remember. He could not be swayed to stay. He'd promised her he would send word by courier the moment he'd landed at port, and so he had. *I am well, Mamá. Do not worry. I have made my destination and I am safe.*

He adjusted his bag over his shoulder, shifting the weight to his other side, inhaled a deep breath, and took a step forward. Soon his steps quickened, each one feeling monumental. By the time he passed through the entryway, he was full of excitement. His first time away from home on his own, a dream come true, a promise to himself fulfilled—it was all he could do to keep it contained within.

"May I be of assistance?" a monk asked, approaching from an expansive corridor on the right.

Sliding his hands over the straps of his bag nervously, he spoke in a thick Castilian accent, "*Sí*. I am here to see the abbot, Searly."

"I shall let him know he has a visitor," the monk said, bowing gently at the waist. "May I have your name, sir?"

This time when the young man smiled, it was with his whole face, and as brilliant as a flower bursting out of winter earth. "Favián," he said. "Tell him his nephew is here."

Searly leaned forward, staring into the cup he held in his hands. A slight drizzle of rain had descended upon the land, forcing the light of the sun to stretch and yawn its way through the clouds. The library appeared gray and colorless until Lochlan lit a lantern, an arc of gold against the dreariness. "What do you mean—twins?" Searly asked.

Lochlan reclined back into his chair, tracing the arm of it with his fingertips. "I have no more information than that. Zeph left immediately after."

"Where did he go?"

"I don't know." Lochlan stood and walked over to a shelf, plucking a book from it, flipping it open. "I've contemplated finding him. I want to know where he is for my own peace of mind."

"Why have you not?"

Lochlan closed the book and placed it back on the shelf. "Elin asked me not to." His words were laced with worriment and underscored with a hint of resentment.

Searly sighed and put the cup to his lips, tasting the bitter wine on his tongue. "How is she?" he asked.

"Confused. Conflicted."

Searly nodded. "Understandable. And how are *you*?"

Lochlan ran a finger over the spines of the books in a casual caress. "I suppose I feel the same as she." Lochlan rarely looked Searly in the eye in moments such as these, afraid to show vulnerability. Foolish man for thinking it a weakness.

"Does Arwyn know?" Searly asked, still watching his friend peruse books that he wasn't truly seeing.

"Do I know what?"

"Saints in Heaven, child." Searly clasped a hand over his heart, feeling the rapid beat against his palm. "How long have you been standing there?"

"I was on my way back to my room when I heard my name." Stepping further into the library, Arwyn asked, "Do I know what?"

"Why are you carrying a bow?" Lochlan asked.

Searly took notice then. Arwyn was dressed in all leather: boots, breeches, and a jerkin with a white linen tunic underneath. In one gloved hand she carried a bow, a leather guard on her forearm. And on her hip, a quiver.

"I was practicing my…" she paused and said primly, "never mind that. What were you discussing?"

Lochlan let out a sigh. "Arwyn, perhaps you would like to sit."

She leaned her bow and quiver against the wall. "No. I'd rather stand. What is it?" She looked to Lochlan, then to Searly. "Tell me."

"Zeph left early this morning," Lochlan stated.

"What? Why? Where did he go?"

Lochlan filled Arwyn in on the details of what had taken place, and Arwyn seemed to be handling it well. That is, until she sat, stood, and sat again as if she was at war with her own mind.

"He must be…" Her words trailed off.

Searly set his wine aside, moved toward her, and kneeled. It was a natural instinct for him to offer a comforting hand, and was about to do so when he promptly remembered the last time he'd been in this position. He kept his hands in his lap. "Finish your thought, child."

"Upset," she said. "He must be upset." She stood in a flourish, the heel of her boots slapping hard against the floor.

"Where are you going?" Lochlan called.

"To find him," she called back.

Neither one tried to stop her. Pointless it would be. Arwyn was on a mission where Zeph was concerned, and if Searly had learned anything about the lovely elf girl, it was that she had her own mind and it was mostly led by her heart.

A long silence befell the library. Searly and Lochlan were both trapped in their own thoughts before Xavier knocked to alert them to his presence.

"My apologies, brother. Someone is here to see you."

"Do you know who it is?"

"Favián, he said his name was. Your nephew?"

"Favián? He's here?"

"Aye."

Xavier stepped back, gesturing for someone to come forward. Favián crossed the threshold. Searly stared unabashedly, trying to rectify the last image he'd had of his brother's son, a chubby-cheeked babe, to the image before him now. He was brown of hair and skin and eyes, his face broad and high-boned, like his father's. Searly gaped at him…taking in the sight of him.

"Saints in Heaven," Searly said softly.

Favián's feet carried him forward, his eyes shining with a misty haze as he set his bag on the floor. "*Tío*," he said in a choked whisper.

Searly met the young lad halfway and embraced him firmly. "I wasn't expecting you," he said, his voice quivering like wheat in a light summer wind. "Did I miss one of your missives?"

"No. I wanted to surprise you."

"You succeeded." Searly pulled back just enough to see his nephew's face. "Gracious, you are a grown man now."

"*Sí, Tío* Searly."

Searly loved his nephew deeply. He was family and they shared a bond. As soon as Favián had been old enough, Searly had arranged for him to attend a monastery school, where he was taught to read and write in multiple languages. They had fostered a relationship through letters, both sharing an affinity for poetry, though Favián's affinity surpassed even Searly's. This, of course, was something Favián kept private, only confiding in Searly his love of them. Favián's father, Joran, was a warrior, a man-at-arms, who had served his king when called upon. Growing up with Joran meant learning to fight, and from the letters, he was quite good, though Searly suspected he was better than he let on.

"An introduction, Searly?"

Searly turned his head toward his friend, his expression ever so inquisitive. "Oh, yes, Favián, allow me to introduce you to Lord Lochlan, my friend and my family, the one I've written to you about. Lochlan, meet Favián, my nephew from Ontiverós."

Lochlan bowed his head slightly. "Pleased to meet you, Favián. So, you're the nephew Searly wrote to."

"*Sí*," Favián said, casting his eyes to the floor. "*Tío* Searly and I have been writing letters since—"

"Since you were a wee lad," Searly finished, clapping his hands over Favián's cheeks. "I cannot shake the surprise of seeing you. Come, sit." Searly moved swiftly, leading Favián by the elbow to a chair. "Tell me, how are your parents? Your mother is well, yes? And your father?"

"*Mis padres* are well. They send their love."

Xavier, still lingering in the doorway, asked, "Shall I prepare a room for you? Will you be staying?"

"Yes, he will be staying," Searly answered quickly, in case Favián had other ideas. He would put that little matter to rest at once. "Prepare the room across from Arwyn's. Thank you, Xavier."

"Certainly," Xavier said, leaving the three of them alone.

To Favián, Searly asked, "Are you tired, my boy? Were the seas rough? Have you eaten? I shall have a bath drawn as soon as possible so you may freshen up."

Favián laughed. "I fear you have replaced *mamá* with all the fussing. I am perfectly well. A bit tired, I admit. But, mostly, I am happy to see you."

"Searly is a bit of a mother hen, I'm afraid. You will get used to it." With a grin, Lochlan added, "He is an acquired taste."

"Never mind him," Searly said, the light still twinkling behind his eyes. "It is a rule of mine that anyone under my care is well fed and well rested. My only rules, but I daresay I strictly enforce them."

"Your only rules?" Lochlan quipped.

Searly cut his eyes to the hulking brute, dressed in black from head to toe. "You are in rare form, milord. It's nice to see you in a chipper mood. Even if it is at my expense."

"Am I?" Lochlan seemed to ponder that a moment. Then, looking to Favián, he asked, "Do you intend to stay long? I know your uncle would like that very much."

"I intend to stay for a while, *sí*. If that is all right with you, *tío*."

Searly waved away his concern. "Try to leave and I'll have Lochlan hold you down."

Favián lifted a brow, amusement in his features; however, Favián was a polite lad and chose to answer as a proper gentleman. "It is settled, then. If you show me to my room, I would like that bath you mentioned earlier."

The air was damp, trees veiled in the lightest of mists, smothering the greens of the leaves and the brush underneath until all that was left was the same stony gray as the nebulous vault above.

Arwyn's worried eyes scanned the edge of the woodland, searching for Zeph. She wasn't a hunter like her brothers had been. She couldn't kill a wild animal and bring home supper. But she could close her eyes and sense the world around her. She could listen to nature and understand its sounds. She could press the palm of her hand to a tree and feel its energy, absorb it into herself. "One with nature," her father had told her. She could even feel energy and emotions at a distance, though she had to make a conscious effort to do so if the distance was great. When she was little, her father often worried about her. As an empath, Arwyn was hypersensitive to everything, and when she was much younger she would cry every day and then she cried never, withdrawing from everyone around her, trying to distance herself from all that plagued her until her father taught her how to gain control over her ability. He, too, had been an empath, and so, he trained her in how to deal with all the emotions that threatened to drown her by teaching her the art of archery.

Nyokou, her father called it, *the pursuit of truth, goodness, and beauty. "It is where attitude, movement, and technique unite in a state of harmony. A true shot in Nyokou is not just the arrow meeting its intended target. It is the belief the arrow existed in the target before its release."* Courtesy, compassion, and non-aggression, these things her father also taught her, for a proper archer retained her composure and grace even in times of great stress. Goodness was shown by displaying proper behavior and respect at all times. And then there was beauty which enhanced life and stimulated the spirit. The elegance of the bow, the artistry of the arrow, were both beautiful, though her father considered truth and goodness to be the beauty of the art.

Before Arwyn's fifteenth summer, she could shoot an arrow as sure and true as the master who'd trained her—her father. Archery, for her, had not been about mastering a weapon. It was about physical, moral, and spiritual development.

"Through repetition," her father would say, *"one's true self-perfection emerges."*

He taught her how to position herself: the bow in her left hand at the grip, placed on her hip, the string facing outward, and the arrow in her right, a standing meditation if you will, with her back straight, shoulders flat, and elbows flared out to the sides. She had to shed all strife, and when she moved, she had to be pure of heart and mind. Each step she took had to be graceful and deliberate. No unnecessary movement, and each action taken served a specific purpose.

"A river is calm on the surface, quiet, unassuming, but underneath a tremendous power is hidden deep within its depths."

Even though Arwyn had left her bow behind at the monastery, she moved as though she held it, in the midst of silence and practiced control. If one was to spy her, one may think she was performing a meditative dance. Or perhaps, they would simply presume she was mad. Most, she imagined, would not understand her methods.

"Streams may appear powerful because they are loud and rebellious, but underneath they are shallow and wield no real powers."

Her father had had three sons—and her, teaching them all the skill of Nyokou from the tender age of seven, although he had spent particular care with her. *"The control of the breath and mind generates power, Arwyn, a cessation of thought. It is the final emptying of the mind as the arrow is released."*

Two hours every day, he taught her how to shoot an arrow and meet its mark. Then two hours became three—three became four. *"Practicing technique improves the shooting, but improving the spirit improves the man."*

"Or woman," she would say.

"Yes, or woman," he would answer.

The slightest smile touched the corner of her mouth as she mentally prepared her bow and concentrated on her target, emptying her mind of all things except him. This was how she would find him. Nyokou taught her how to ignore the noise of the world, allowing her to focus on just the things she needed to, and what she needed was to find Zeph.

She released her mental arrow, finding her mark. She may not be a hunter, not in the usual sense, but her aim was always true. She sensed him, some distance away. His pain was an itch underneath Arwyn's skin, like a burn trying to heal. Sometimes, if she was deeply connected to another, it was impossible to tell where her feelings began and theirs ended. They crowded out her own until all she felt were theirs. Like now. She leaned against a tree, needing to take a moment to meditate, *control* her ability before it took control of her.

"Breathe," she murmured. "Just breathe."

"Sometimes you will hit the target but miss the self. Find yourself in the target, Arwyn. Posture, balance, and stillness. Clear the mind, release the energy."

She inhaled deeply and let it out slowly. Each time she exhaled, she regained her balance. She did this until she felt sure she had her abilities under control, and then she continued making her way toward him.

The scent of rain still hung in the air, but the sun's amber glow managed to punch its way through, golden fingers slanted through the trees. Its warmth was an elixir after an age of grayness. Birds sang out, softening the air with their chorus, gently waking the woodlands from its nap. Then shards of light descended, highlighting a path before her. She followed its winding curves, careful to dodge the sharp points of branches that protruded her path. It led her straight to a clearing where a river cut through the forest. That was when she saw him, sitting alone, near the water's edge. She couldn't help her heart from quickening. A few long, white strands of hair had fallen from his neat queue at the base of his neck, softening the sharp line of his jaw. He sat, staring at the water, dominated by a profound sadness, fatigue engraved on his face. No longer could Arwyn see that spark of fire in his eyes. All that remained was a hollow soul.

Hand to her heart, she rubbed the spot where it ached, blinking several times to keep her composure. She waited the time she needed, then she spoke when she was sure her voice wouldn't betray her. "May I sit?"

Without even turning his head, Zeph answered, "If you must."

"Did you know I was—"

"I always know when you are near, Arwyn."

Oh. She didn't know quite what to say to that, so she said nothing. She took her seat beside him and turned her gaze to the river before them, a ribbon of turquoise winding its way through a land she knew very little about. It flowed like time, always onward, toward its destiny, and as she watched eddies swirl and disappear, she wondered what her destiny was. She didn't know. She hadn't known anything with any certainty since the day she was robbed of her family. She was adrift, alone, and afraid of losing something she never truly had. Her mouth pulled into a frown, scolding herself for such thoughts.

Zeph shuffled something in his hand. Five small round pieces were tossed in the air. Flipping his hand over, he caught two on the back of his hand. He put one aside and kept the other. He tossed it again, picked up two of the three objects that had hit the ground and caught the other still in the air. Putting two aside, he threw another into the air, picked up the remaining object on the ground, and caught the one he'd tossed again. Then he repeated the process.

"What are you doing?"

"Baking a pie."

"Ha. Ha. Perhaps when you get bored here, you could try for the position as court jester."

"I don't think they would be fond of my particular brand of jokes."

Arwyn's mouth twitched. "I'm sure you're right."

"If I had a quill, I would write down the date."

"What for?"

"I don't believe you have ever said I was right about anything."

"That's not true. Whenever you call yourself a fool, I always agree."

A sliver of a smile etched across his mouth, and Arwyn basked in it until it disappeared from view. "So, what *are* you doing?"

He shrugged. "Playing a game."

"And what are those?" she asked, pointing to the objects in his hand.

He flattened his palm, lining them up in a neat row; all five pieces were shiny and varied in size and color. "Polished stones."

"They're beautiful. Where did you get them?"

He stared at the stones like they were jewels. "I've had them since I was a boy. Elin and I used to play with them," he said, a trembling edge to his voice.

"Oh." The sadness of his words made her heart tender, but she refused to look away from him. Too many others had looked away from him already.

Clearing his throat, he said, "Hold out your hand." She did. He placed the smooth stones in her hand, not missing the way his fingers gently grazed the tender part of her palm. She had to bite the inside of her cheek, not letting on she could feel his pain burn through her like hot embers. "I'll teach you the rules," he said.

"All right."

"You can use only one hand. Toss the stones up. You want to catch as many as you can on the back of your hand. It's easier to catch them if you spread your fingers a little. Toss them up again from the back of your hand, turn your hand over quickly and catch them in your palm. Choose one of the stones to be your taw—the one you throw in the air. Put aside the others you caught. Repeat the steps until you've caught them all."

"All right." Arwyn cleared her throat. She followed his instructions. She managed to catch two on the back of her hand. Putting one aside, she tossed the taw and managed to pick up the other three pieces and catch the one she'd tossed before it hit the ground. "I won!" she declared rather excitedly.

She saw it, the way the corner of his mouth curled up the tiniest bit, but he said nothing. No compliments. No encouraging words.

For the next few minutes she played with the stones, and for the next few minutes, Zeph watched. She tried not to let that fluster her, concentrating entirely on her task. Surprisingly, she found she rather liked this game. She managed to forget the world for a brief time. Perhaps that was what he had been doing too—forgetting the world.

After the fifth round, she scooped up the stones and handed them back. He took them, cleaning off the dirt and dust before placing them inside a small drawstring pouch, then tucking it inside his pocket. Silence stretched and lengthened into something that seemed impossible to pull away from. It was an entity unto its own. Cruel in the way it bared down on her already bruised heart, threatening to dismantle all her well-crafted aloofness. She wanted to pop the bubble that found its way into her throat, suffocating her, and shout at him—shout at the whole damned world for this…this…

And then she remembered why she'd never left Shadowland all those years ago.

"Stay," she murmured.

"Arwyn," he hissed, "don't."

"No," she said. "That was what *you* said to me a long time ago. I tried to leave Shadowland once. Do you remember? You found me before I could. And you said, '*Stay.*'"

She had wanted to leave, needing to go back to her home and give her family a proper burial. After that, she hadn't known what she would do; she only knew staying and hiding felt wrong, so she had attempted to leave, uncertain about telling Zeph. She was going to slip away unseen, but he'd slipped out of the shadows, as though he'd been waiting for her. She remembered his words clearly, so she repeated them.

"You wanted me to stay. I asked you to give me a reason why I should, and you said, '*Because I'm asking. Because out there I can't keep you safe.*' I stayed, Zeph. I stayed. Because for some reason you needed me to and I needed to be needed. I never got to bury my family, Zeph. It has always troubled me." Arwyn stood abruptly and walked closer to the water's edge. Her father's words whispered in her ear. "*If the spirit is strong, one will appear like a deep flowing river.*"

"I am a river," she whispered to herself. "I am a river."

"Can you give me a reason to stay?" he asked quietly. "I have many reasons why I should go." She felt his presence at her back, then he faced her, his eyes settling on hers, those unfathomable colorless eyes that she always got lost in whenever she stared too long. "Can you give me one reason why I should stay?"

Me, her heart whispered, but she knew that was not the answer he sought. "Your sister loves you. She is angry with you, yes, but she loves you." Thinking of her brothers, her father, her mother, the hurt she kept deep inside bubbled to the surface. She shook her head. "You have an opportunity I will never have. If you walk away from her, you will regret it. It will eat you alive. Do not let your past ruin your future, Zeph. Do not let it."

He chuffed. "Future."

"Yes, *future*. Lochlan brought you back to life. You have a—"

"This isn't a life, Arwyn! This is *existing*!"

"This is a second chance! And you're wasting it!" She stepped into his space, jamming her finger into his chest. "I told you…I *told* you—" She cut off her words, her emotions or *his* emotions clogging her throat. *I told you I would try to heal you.*

She had to walk away for a moment. It was too much. She would drown in everything if she didn't let some of it go, so she leaned against a tree and cried the tears he refused to cry. And damn him for making her cry.

Forever went by before either of them spoke. Finally, she broke the stalemate. "Don't leave," she pleaded, finding her voice again.

"You don't understand," he said, gripping his hair by the roots. "Nobody does."

"Then make me understand."

He laughed. It was cold and callous. "Look at me!" he yelled, thumping himself hard on the chest. "Look at me! What do you see?"

"I see more than you could possibly imagine."

He scoffed, shaking his head like she was daft. Opening his arms wide, he asked, "What then…do you see?"

"Currently, an impertinent fool."

His lips curled upward a fraction. "You wound me, darling."

She marched toward him, her boots pounding hard against the earth. His eyes were like glaciers as they locked on hers. Slowly, the ice in them began to melt as they drifted lower, to her mouth.

"What is it you think I do not see?" she asked. "Your shadows? The darkness within you? I may not understand how they manifest, but I know they exist. I know they are a part of you. And I am not afraid of you."

"You should be," he croaked.

"It is only at night that we can see the stars, Zeph. Darkness doesn't have to be scary. It can be beautiful. You have just forgotten."

He shook his head. "No."

"Would I..." Her words died on her tongue as something sharp pierced her, causing her to lurch forward. A burning sensation rent through her right shoulder. Blood spilled down her arm. Her eyes were wide and frightened when Zeph caught her in his arms. "Zeph? What's happening?"

The look in his eyes was fear and anger. Together, those two emotions collided in an epic maelstrom when he peered over Arwyn's head and saw who or what had shot her with an arrow. Zeph let out a roar so loud that the ground rumbled beneath them. Holding Arwyn firm with one arm, he launched one, two, three giant fireballs with the other.

All Arwyn could hear was the wailing cry of a creature before Zeph turned it into ashes. She was losing consciousness. The world was fading fast.

"Arwyn, stay with me. Stay with me, Arwyn." Zeph broke off the shaft of the arrow, keeping the tip inside, lest she bleed out before he could heal her. "I have to get you back to the monastery. I can't heal you here. Others may be coming. Stay with me." He scooped up her legs and cradled her to his chest, his perfectly white attire now stained red with her blood.

"T-Turn into sh-shadows," Arwyn murmured, teeth chattering. "H-Hurry."

The next sounds Arwyn heard were the crashing of a door and Zeph yelling, "She's hurt! Arwyn's hurt! A poisoned arrow!"

Arwyn surrendered to the darkness soon after.

Z eph had entered through the east range of the monastery, until he reached the infirmary, and carried Arwyn to the bed. He laid her down gently. Shouts of directive orders were given. "She needs healing! She's been wounded! Fetch Searly! Fetch Elin!"

Those were his shouts, his orders, although no one was around to hear them. His own echoed voice was his only greeting.

The room was mostly bare, lit by a few low-burning lanterns. A stash of clean linens lay neatly by a bowl of water on a table on the far wall, and the bedside table had been cleaned off, housing nothing at all.

Arwyn moaned and his eyes came back to her. Sweat beaded on her forehead like glistening pearls. His hands shook, his heart trembled. "I'm going to pull the tip of the arrow out, luv. No, don't close your eyes. Stay alert. Stay with me." He gently turned her on her side. "You're going to be fine."

Arwyn cried out when Zeph removed the broken arrow. His hand covered her wound as he knelt beside the bed. Blood coated his palm, warm and sticky. He had to shut his eyes against the sight of it, the scene reminding him of when

Elin had been stabbed by Lolith, how the blood coated his skin exactly the same way. It frightened him that he might fail at saving Arwyn the way he had failed at saving his sister.

He swallowed thickly. "Heal," he murmured. "*Heal.*"

Heat and light emanated from his palm. He pressed harder, easing onto the edge of the bed, the cloying scent of blood permeating the air. "Heal," he chanted. "Heal, heal, heal."

Voices carried from somewhere outside the infirmary doors, footsteps of a dozen men or more coming closer. Zeph was past hearing them, his sole focus on Arwyn. "Stay with me," Zeph pleaded. "Do not die. I forbid it." He swallowed again, unable to quiet the tremor that swept throughout his limbs. "Do you understand? I forbid it."

"Zeph," Arwyn mumbled.

The heat from his hand became hotter, brighter, but her wound would not mend. She burned with fever, her teeth clacking together.

"Shh." He was now on the bed with her, tucking her against him in order to warm her as she drifted in and out of consciousness. "Tell me how to heal you, luv," Zeph begged. "I am not at all good at it."

Why would he be? He hadn't used his healing abilities for most of his life. Healing wasn't something valued by the Unseelie. Or by Lolith. His mother and father were the only ones to ever nurture that side of him, and that had been too many years ago—he had forgotten too much. Perhaps that was why he couldn't save his sister. Or heal himself when he'd been injured by the Unseelie King.

But he *had* healed Searly when he'd been whipped and beaten. He could do it again. He could heal Arwyn. He *could*. He had to.

"I'm so c-c-cold."

"Shh," Zeph said again.

He hated the way her brows pinched in an expression of pain, and the way she shivered so violently. He repeated the chant, *"Heal, heal, heal."* His voice grew angry with each passing minute she lay in his arms with no improvement. She was a delicate thing, all muscle and fine bones. Though looking at her now she was just—frail.

Venenum a te release. Whispered words spoken in his ear, a voice as familiar as yesterday, and Zeph's stomach fluttered. An odd flush of something tingled through his body.

"Mother?" he asked in a tremulous voice, and then immediately swore underneath his breath. His mother was dead, and he was losing his mind. Pinching his eyes shut, he held Arwyn tighter.

Venenum a te release.

His eyes snapped open, darting around the room.

Venenum a te release. Venenum a te release. Venenum a te release.

The room echoed in the whispered phrase, and Zeph didn't know if he had finally succumbed to insanity or if the spirit of his mother was truly present.

Zuriel carried his sister through the door of their home. "Mother! Eliniana's been bitten! Help!"

Their mother rushed into the parlor. Upon seeing her daughter's face, which had gone ashen, she dropped whatever she'd held in her hands and rushed toward them.

"What happened? What bit her?" She took her from her son's arms and carried her to the kitchen and laid her upon a long wooden table. "Tell me what happened."

"A snake," he said, trying hard to hold back his tears. "Is she going to be all right? I tried...I tried to pull her away, Mother, but the snake...it was so fast..."

"She will be all right. I need your help. Can you do that? Can you help me?"

He nodded, tears wetting his cheeks.

"Place your hand over the snake bite and repeat these words with me... Venenum a te release."

"Zeph."

Zeph blinked at his sister, who hovered over him. A window of his childhood had been flung open. Surprise flashed behind his wounded eyes. Then they drifted to the robed monk standing just behind her. "Searly," he heard himself say. A blur of others behind him. He'd never heard them enter. "When did you all come in?" he rasped, confused.

"A while ago," Searly answered, his tone queerly pitched.

Elin eased forward like she was unsure if she should. He looked down at himself, covered in blood and sweat. He couldn't blame her. He looked wild and untamed.

Ignoring his own appearance, he brushed the hair out of Arwyn's face, still pale and wan, but no longer shivering.

"You were—chanting." Tears welled in Elin's eyes and her voice sounded jagged. "You were in some sort of trance, I think."

He moved cautiously, careful not to jostle Arwyn. He needed to see where the poisoned arrow had entered her shoulder. He had managed to knit her wound and stop the bleeding. And her fever was no more. Zeph felt oddly emotional, like a man reprieved from the gallows.

He had healed her.

He shook his head repeatedly, desperate to reconcile what had taken place. The presence of his mother...that had been real. *Hadn't it?*

"Zeph," Elin asked, "are you all right? You look unwell."

"I think...I need...to wash the blood off me," he said, easing himself out from under Arwyn and covering her up with the wool coverlet. His heart was filling up with something strange and uncertain and the room was too crowded for all of them.

"You're not going to tell us what happened to Arwyn?" Elin asked.

He pressed the heel of his hands into his eyes. "We were talking in the forest...by the river, and then she was..." The image of Arwyn slumped against him, frightened and confused, swam in his mind. He struggled to remain calm.

"She was shot with an arrow. I knew it was poisoned by the way she reacted to it. I think the arrow was meant for me. It was one of Lolith's hounds. I killed it. And if I could, I would bring it back to life so I could kill it again."

He removed his hands from his face and was struck by how everyone stared, unmoving, but not unmoved, particularly how the half-breed stood in the back of the room, watching, like a raven on a tree branch.

Elin stepped closer, her hand reaching for him, to console no doubt. "And what happened to you?"

He stepped to the side, away from the reach of his sister. "I need to wash the blood off," Zeph said, his voice sounding both jarring and vulnerable, like a cracked bell.

He quit the room then. Not one of them attempted to stop him.

Later, when Zeph returned to the infirmary, he stood, looking out the window into the starless night. Arwyn lay asleep, resting peacefully. Zeph closed his eyes and thanked whatever benevolent god spared Arwyn's life. Everyone, save Elin, had left, but when he had returned from donning crisp, white attire, even she slinked out the door on those oh-so-quiet feet. He thanked the benevolent god for that as well, for he was not in the mood for council.

The fear of almost losing Arwyn still swirled around him, like dust in an old cellar. Even now, he couldn't take in a full breath of air; his lungs were heavy as cold mud. When was the last time Zeph had had the luxury of staring into a starless sky with peace of mind—to have common thoughts about common things? If only he could...

"Zeph."

Oh, buggering hell. Could he have a moment to his thoughts? Was that too much to ask?

Turning, he gave his intruder a withering glare. A lesser man would have cowered and begged off. Unfortunately for Zeph, he wasn't dealing with a lesser man. "What do you want, half-breed?" he asked, his voice clenched like a fist. "I'm rather busy."

"Doing what?"

"Controlling my temper."

"Ah. Good luck with that. Perhaps a walk with me might do the trick."

"Pardon?"

"A walk, Zeph. I would like to talk to you. And I wish not to disturb Arwyn."

"A midnight stroll? Alone? Do you think that's proper? What would the monks think?"

The edges of Lochlan's mouth twitched ever so slightly. "I promise to be the perfect gentleman."

Zeph returned his gaze to the window, careful not to let the half-breed see the edges of his mouth lift a fraction. Lightning winked across the flat black sky, and distant thunder rumbled. "I'd rather not leave her. Not just yet," he finally answered.

"Zeph—"

"She almost died today."

"She's completely healed. Thanks to you. We won't be gone long. And I have someone outside the door. Searly's nephew. He'll stay until our return in case she's in need of something. She'll be safe here. You know that."

Zeph did know that. Still. The residual fear still lingered, and he could not shake it. He walked to the side of the bed and watched Arwyn's chest rise and fall. Her lavender hair spilled around her pillow in fine, smooth loops. He twined a piece of it through his fingers, feeling the silkiness of it. Someone had cleaned her up, changed the bed linens, and changed her clothes.

"Elin," Lochlan said, as if he could read Zeph's mind.

Zeph nodded, making a mental note to thank his sister later. He let his eyes roam over Arwyn's delicate features. He smiled at the veil of freckles across her nose and cheeks, like a sprinkle of gold. Had he ever told her she was beautiful?

"Zeph?"

Zeph blinked and released the lock of hair. Clearing his throat, he put on his cloak of indifference and proceeded to the door. If it had been any other night, Zeph would have told the half-breed to go take a walk by himself, preferably off a plank. As it was, he was too tired to put forth the effort. "After you," Zeph intoned.

Once they were in the hallway, a young man, who had been leaning against the opposite wall, stood to his full height.

"This is Favián, Searly's nephew," Lochlan introduced, leading Zeph toward him.

Zeph distractedly nodded in Favián's general direction.

Favián answered with a nod of his own.

"This is Zeph," Lochlan explained. "Elin's…" He paused to glance at Zeph. "Her brother," he finished.

Favián said something, but Zeph wasn't paying attention. He felt odd, like he was wearing his skin inside out. He glanced over his shoulder, to the door he'd just stepped through. He didn't want to go for a walk. He wanted to stay right where he was.

Every time he shut his eyes, he saw the panic in Arwyn's, and something inside him would swell until he thought he would burst. And every time he had to temper that feeling like a bed of banked coals before he ignited like a flame.

"Zeph."

At the sound of his name, Zeph realized he had retreated whence he'd came, his hand on the latch to the room that housed Arwyn.

"This way," Lochlan said with a sly grin.

Zeph released a steadying breath, counted to ten, and counted ten more. It was a pure force of will that he moved away from the infirmary door. One day, he thought to himself, he would wrap his hands around the half-breed's throat with delight and he would…*squeeze.*

The two of them ambled forth down one hallway, then another, both with their hands tucked neatly behind their backs. They walked sedately, side by side, slow and purposeful, but separately…like they were accustomed to being alone, even in the presence of others.

Lochlan waved his hand at the lanterns on the walls, making their flames burn taller, brighter. The brighter flames meant more heat. The heat wasn't an entirely unwelcomed feeling. The expansive corridors were rather drafty places, though they were exposed to the outside elements once they crossed from the east range to the west. Zeph felt his throat constrict the further away they ventured from the infirmary, and was of a mind to end this *midnight stroll* when Lochlan stopped outside a doorway that lacked a door and uttered a quiet, "After you."

Zeph lifted one dark brow. "And what room is this?"

"A dwelling room," the half-breed explained dryly. "Searly and I are the only ones to ever use it anymore."

The doorway was low and Zeph was rather tall, so he had to bend at the waist to pass through, as did Lochlan. Once inside, they could stand to their full height. It was a large space, longer than it was wide. The walls and ceiling were made of rock and mortar. To the left, two openings were cut out for windows in different sizes; one small, the other nearly the entire length from floor to ceiling. If the moon had shown this night, the moonbeams would have been all the light one would need. As it was, it was hidden behind ribbons of black clouds, so lanterns had been lit, casting a pleasing honeyed hue. A large bench seat extended from the doorway to the corner wall to the right, upholstered in red with stripes of blue, and Zeph couldn't help noticing how the same fabric had also been used as a rug to cover the floor. Three low standing tables were strategically placed between the bench and wall, and seven gold embroidered cushions were, Zeph assumed, extra seating, tossed about on the floor.

This space was meant for entertaining, though, perhaps a more apt word for monks would be—*gathering*. But Lochlan had said he and Searly were the only ones to ever use the room and…

Zeph's throat bobbed, a realization dawning. He had killed one of their fellow monks some time ago. Regret clawed at a heart that had long since stopped feeling, or so he had thought, and Zeph no longer wished to be in this room, a room, that if he hazard a guess, the murdered monk had been in many times before, laughing and enjoying his fellow brethren, and Zeph had taken that away from him.

He started for the door.

"Sit down," Lochlan said, blocking his path.

"I want to leave."

"Sit. Down."

"I need to get back to Arwyn."

"Yes, let's talk about that."

"Let's not."

"I can make you sit down," Lochlan said.

"And I can make you *move*," Zeph hissed.

A fit of anger was as lethal as poison, Zeph knew, but so be it. He had lived in a fit of anger for most of his pathetic life. He would not be forced to stay where he did not wish to be. Especially by this churl!

Zeph's shadow rose like an unwelcomed tide, covering everything around them, like a sea erasing footprints, leaving only stillness and breaths. Lochlan, to his credit, did not cower, nor did he flinch. He stood tall, undeterred, and at length, neither hedged a withdrawal from their stance.

That is until Lochlan let out an audible sigh. "I do not wish to fight you." He removed himself from Zeph's path and walked to the other side of the room, where he fetched a wine sack and a goblet, pouring himself a healthy dose. He dipped his head back to swig rather than sip.

Zeph's shadow retreated, his ire abating now that his path was no longer hindered. The honeyed hue of the flickering light returned, as well as the warmth. "Bloody hell," Zeph murmured, scrubbing his hands over his face, then crossing the room in a huff. "Is there enough in there for me?"

Lochlan glanced over his shoulder and made a fine show of holding the wine sack to his ear, shaking it. "There might be some left for you." He fetched another goblet, pouring the remaining contents into it, and extended his arm out to Zeph.

Zeph accepted the wine without words. However, he had no intention to sit, so he examined the sights of the night by leaning against the wall and gazing out the window, which was something, Zeph realized, he liked to do. There was always something to see if only one looked closely enough. Or perhaps, what he was truly doing was looking for ways to ignore what was on the inside.

"Arwyn means a great deal to you," Lochlan said. It was a simple statement, a declaration. So why did it feel so infinitely *personal* to Zeph's ears?

Gritting his teeth, Zeph chose to remain silent. What he felt or didn't feel for Arwyn was no business of Lochlan's.

"You mean a great deal to her as well, you know."

"Don't," Zeph said.

"Does she know?"

Zeph forced himself to sip his wine, feigning ignorance. "Does she know what?"

"How deeply you care for her?"

"She was injured. She was…" Zeph swallowed. "I couldn't live with myself if anything happened to her. She's an innocent. That is all."

"I saw the way you looked at her."

"Leave it be," Zeph said.

"Why?"

"Because it does not matter."

"I see," Lochlan said.

Zeph made no qualms of scoffing rather loudly. "You see nothing."

"I have been watching you closely. Earlier this morning with your sister, and then later this eve with Arwyn, and with both encounters I saw a great deal.

It pains me to say it, but I finally understand where the confliction lies within Elin and Arwyn regarding you."

"Well," Zeph said. "If you remember, I was leaving when Arwyn—"

"If you leave, you will destroy them both," Lochlan admitted. "And I think you have destroyed them enough."

Zeph breathed deeply through his nose, still staring out into the inky night. "What am I supposed to do? I cannot stay. I cannot. And yet…"

"And yet?"

Zeph looked over his shoulder. Lochlan was staring…intently. Zeph said in defeat, "I cannot leave either."

"I know."

Zeph, again, returned his focus to the outside. "They could be in danger if I stay. But if I *don't* stay and something happened to one them…"

"I know."

"What am I to do?"

Lochlan let out a puff of air and took a seat. "I think it is mad that we are having a conversation at all, so if you are asking what I think, which is doubly mad…"

"Can something be doubly mad?" Zeph stole a glance over his shoulder.

Lochlan grinned. "As I was saying, you should stay. You need to mend your relationship with your sister if that is a possibility. Your *twin* sister. I imagine there is a bond I cannot possibly understand. I do not know what happened to you as a child, Zeph, or how it changed you. Speaking from experience, however, I do know what it is to do something so egregious…" Lochlan's voice grew to a sharp raspy sound, like a door hanging on a rusty hinge. Clearing his throat, he continued, "So egregious that nothing we do could ever absolve us."

Zeph raised a curious, albeit hesitant, brow.

"I killed my father."

Zeph stared at the man sitting down, staring into his cup, clutched in both hands, looking forlorn and every bit as lost as Zeph felt.

"Beg your pardon?" Zeph queried, for surely, he had misheard.

"I said…" Lochlan looked up. "I killed my father." Each word was akin to a physical blow, though nothing as brutal as Lochlan's eyes, for in that moment, they resembled twin pools of still water from which Zeph saw himself.

He could only blink, disbelieving. Shaking his head, he asked—no, he demanded—Lochlan to explain himself. "What do you mean, you killed your father? Was he cruel? Did he put hands upon you?"

"No," Lochlan said. "He would never." Zeph didn't miss the quiver in the half-breed's chin.

"Then *why*?"

Lochlan dropped his head into hands and for a long moment, he was still as a grave, motionless. An intense silence came between them, as if there was a third presence in the room.

Zeph took a seat after all and fixed his eyes on the wall, the truth falling across him like a velvet curtain. "It was an accident," Zeph theorized.

"How do you—"

Zeph looked him in the eye. "You live in a monastery because your best friend is a monk and you would rather be here than anywhere else. My sister…I have to believe she cares for you because of the man you are, even though you are a…" Zeph snarled. "Half-breed. Also…" Zeph cleared his throat, "Arwyn holds you in high regard. You are not a murderer. You may have killed your father, but it was an accident. I am certain of it."

Lochlan shook his head. "He wouldn't have died had I never been cursed, had I never been born. I touched him on my thirteenth year. I didn't know what would happen." Lochlan stared at his hands. "Five hundred years I have lived with a curse. My father's death marked the day it began. It doesn't matter that it was an accident. He died because of me."

"He died because of Lolith. She is the one who cursed you. And you killed her."

Lochlan nodded. "I know."

"Good. Stop with the guilt. It is unbecoming. You have so much more unlikeable qualities to overcome." He finished his wine and stood. "May I get back to the infirmary now? Or are we not done strolling?"

Lochlan waited a moment before standing, grinding his teeth into dust if the sound was any indication. Eventually, Lochlan got to his feet, and stepped around him. On his way out the door, Zeph wasn't sure, but he thought he heard Lochlan mutter, "I do so hate you."

I have known what it feels to conquer a man in battle
To lift a weapon and turn it on another
I have been trained by my father, a warrior
I fear no man
However,
A fear hides deep within me
It has nothing to do with bows and arrows
Swords or daggers
It pierces my heart all the same
For I feel it every time I breathe
Slicing deeper until I am sure I will die
Bleeding me dry
Who can save me from this fear?
This fear I cannot identify

~Favián's journal

Favián sat outside the room where Arwyn slept while he wrote in his journal, trying to quell the unfamiliar feeling that had been gnawing at him since he'd arrived. His uncle had spoken a great deal of Lochlan through letters over the years, so Favián felt he knew him somewhat, though Favián learned he and Lochlan were not the only guests within the monastery. After a very detailed account of who everyone was and why they were here, Favián was amazed that he had remained upright. It was not every day that one was surrounded by mystical creatures. Had he not already known about Lochlan, he may have believed his *tío* was having him on.

So far, aside from meeting Lochlan, he had only met Elin. He wasn't going to count the brief introduction to Zeph in the hallway. He would reserve judgment on that one until he got to know him. But Elin, he had liked her instantly. Her kindness and goodness quite literally glowed around her. She had put him at ease, conversing with him as if she had known him all her life. Since he considered Lochlan part of the family already, having read about him since he was a child, he'd never felt more at home when they had dined earlier together that day. That's when all the commotion had happened, and he'd learned that Arwyn, the elf, had been shot with a poisoned arrow. Later, when Lochlan had asked him to wait outside her door until he and Zeph returned, he hadn't hesitated to oblige. Of course he would wait.

Favián paused and listened, sure he had heard something. A soft moan. She was waking up. He made quick work of putting away his quill, placing it inside a small pouch and tucking it and his journal underneath his belt. Then he made sure the inkwell was securely capped, that small secret compartment inside his necklace, and rose to his feet.

Tapping gingerly on the door, he waited for a sound, a voice, *something*, before he entered a lady's sick chamber unannounced. He could hear his *mamá's* voice now, scolding him for even thinking of entering, but as he looked down both ends of the hallway, there was no one else about to see to her needs.

He tapped again, this time a bit louder than the first. He put his ear to the door.

"Yes?" a small, raspy voice said.

Favián cleared his throat. He hadn't really thought beyond knocking. What was he supposed to say? He cleared his throat again. "Erm…do you need anything, *señorita*?"

He heard her say something; unfortunately, he was unable to make out quite what. "I'm sorry?" he said. "I didn't hear you."

"Do come in," she said, louder and much more authoritatively.

Favián turned the latched and pushed open the door. Slowly. He had never been alone with a woman in her bedchamber before. He had no idea how he was supposed to behave or what he was supposed to say.

"You are new here," she said.

Favián could not find it in him to look at her as he nodded. For propriety's sake, he should at least keep his eyes averted.

"What is your name?" she asked.

"F-Favián. Searly's nephew." His eyes were cast low, taking a sudden interest in the style of his boots…and the rather dull coloring of the floor: stone gray, smooth from wear.

"Oh, how nice to meet you. I am Arwyn."

Favián's heart ratcheted inside his chest. Her voice was a melody, a beautiful melody.

"Favián?"

He blinked at the sound of his name. He had yet taken his eyes off the floor. "Y-Yes?"

"Are you all right?"

"*Sí*," he said, and because he felt he needed to explain why he was there, he added, "Lochlan asked me to wait with you until they returned."

"Until who returned?"

"He and Zeph."

"Lochlan and Zeph are together?"

"*Sí*."

"Alone?"

"*Sí*. They went for a walk."

"How long was I asleep?" she muttered.

Favián didn't answer. He was more than a little uncomfortable being alone with her. When he had agreed to wait outside her door, he'd rather assumed it would have been for a short time and he would simply be on one side of the door and she would be on the other.

"Favián."

"Hmm?"

"You can look at me. It's all right."

"If *mamá* knew I was in here with you, she would—"

"Favián," Arwyn said, making an ardent attempt not to laugh. "It's all right. Really."

He smoothed his sweaty palms over his breeches, took one fortifying breath, lifted his eyes, finding hers, and finding a faint, slow smile clinging to the edge of her mouth like an age-old secret.

"Tell me," she said. "Will you be staying…" She winced as she tried to sit up. "…long?"

"*Sí*. Allow me to assist," Favián said, stumbling over his feet before reaching her. He managed to break his fall by grabbing hold of the edge of the bed. "Sorry," he murmured, his cheeks burning with embarrassment.

She watched him curiously while he awkwardly righted himself then awkwardly fluffed her pillows. He cleared his throat for the third time and stepped away from the bed. He placed his hands on his hips and let his eyes roam around the room while she adjusted herself in a more comfortable position. Helping her to sit up wasn't an option. Where would he even place his hands? Under her arms? What if he accidentally brushed against her…

Did it suddenly become hot in here? Favián pulled at his cravat, desperate to loosen the strain around his neck.

"Are you all right?" Arwyn asked once she found a new position.

"*Sí*." It was a garbled sound even to his own ears, and Favián had to shut his

eyes and pray that God would have mercy and would take him now, full body...
just lift him right out of this room and put him out of his misery.

"Perhaps you would like a drink of water?" she suggested.

Water! Excellent idea. He marched toward a table across the room where a
ceramic pitcher and cup were stationed. After pouring himself a cup, he gulped
it down and poured himself another.

"May I have a cup as well?" she asked, a hint of a smile in her voice.

Favián froze, realizing his behavior was not that of a gentleman. *She* was
the one in the sick bed. "I beg your forgiveness, *señorita*."

He kept his back to her while he poured a fresh cup. His hands shook so
badly that water splashed over the edges. He used a linen cloth to clean it up
then he made his way toward her. His eyes floated up briefly and darted away.
She was too beautiful. It hurt to stare.

She took the cup. "Thank you. Do I make you nervous?" Her tone was not
mocking, simply...curious.

Favián, for all the skill he had as a fighter, he had zero skill with a woman,
especially a woman who was like *her*. How to admit that? He thought about
lying, saying he had a fever, which could explain why he was breaking into a
cold sweat, but his eyes drifted up and found hers again. They were watching
him ever so closely. Inexplicably, he knew that if he lied, she would know.
Somehow, she would know. So he nodded his head and murmured, "*Sí*."

Still, she studied him, like she was listening to what he said between his
words and beneath them, tilting her head and leaning in. Then she smiled. It
was the most breathtaking and devastating smile Favián had ever seen.

"You and I," she declared, "are going to be good friends."

"We-we are?"

"Yes!" She beamed. "We are."

Favián swallowed. Because now it was clear. The fear he could not identify
before, the one he had written about, the one that would pierce his heart, it had
a name.

Arwyn.

7

Favián's eyes were innocent, like those of a newborn babe, wide and full of wonder whenever he allowed himself a moment to look at her. Arwyn had never felt such reverence before, so she forgave herself the thrill whenever his large brown eyes slid over her face like he was paying her a compliment, one slow blink at a time.

"We are going to be great friends," she stated.

"We-we are?" Favián asked.

"Yes, we are."

His eyes lit up like wind-whipped embers. It made her smile. It couldn't be helped. *He* made her smile. He had gaped at her at length after her little announcement of friendship, and she felt something stir and shift in the air. She smiled demurely, now feeling the stirrings of shyness herself as he looked at her like she was something remarkable. Truth be told, she rather thought there was something remarkable about Favián as well.

But then he settled, and the air settled and soon they were talking. She sipped her water and asked him questions about himself, where he came from, what his home was like. He found an uncomfortable-looking wooden chair in the corner, pulling it beside her bed, and obliged her by answering softly, a sweet-sounding lisp replacing his nervous stuttering, and as he grew more comfortable conversing, he became more excitable, his words dancing with a flourish, and sometimes whole words exploded on his tongue.

"You talk too fast," she joked.

"You listen too slowly," he countered.

A ripple of laughter escaped her, like a scattering of loose coins. Favián's whole face lit up at that and wrinkles of laughter leaped into sight the more they talked.

And so it was, the two falling into a friendship, just as she had predicted. And then…

Zeph was standing in the doorway, filling the space like a snow-capped mountain, his countenance blank, void, like a still, breezeless day.

Anxiety flowed through her body like a current. There was something in the way Zeph didn't move, a frightening stillness. The air was knotted in silence before he withdrew from the doorway and crossed to the other side with nary a word, the heel of his boots striking against the floor. Arwyn and Favián's laughter hung in the air like a foul smell. When he reached the window, he simply stared out, unseeing.

A dark form came up beside her. Her heart leaped; she was startled until she realized it was only Lochlan. With a hand clutched to her breast, she murmured, "You scared me."

"My apologies. But dare I say you scared us all."

With chagrin, Arwyn looked at Zeph, his white hair hanging long and loose down his back. "I'm fine. Really. I'm sorry to have scared everyone."

Zeph slowly turned around, though he spared her not a glance. No, he looked directly at Favián, crossed his arms over his chest, and said, "Get out." Zeph's eyes were as hard as the polished stones he kept inside his sash and every bit as indestructible.

"Zeph!" Arwyn hissed.

Arwyn slid her gaze to Favián as he rose from his seat.

"Get out," Zeph ordered again.

Favián mimicked Zeph's mien. "If Arwyn wishes me to go, I go. If she wishes me to stay, I stay." His remarks were thrown like daggers as he held Zeph's cool glare.

"Favián, it is quite all right," Arwyn said, touching his arm. "Why don't you and Lochlan go on to bed? It's late, and I know you must be tired."

Favián slid his eyes from Zeph's to hers, softening immediately. "Sí. Are you certain you want to be alone with him?"

Zeph took one step forward. "Get. Out."

"I'll be fine," Arwyn rushed to say, though her words might as well have been weightless leaves for how quickly they were whisked away.

"I think I should stay," Favián said, his eyes veering back to Zeph, sharp as wet blades.

She turned to Lochlan. "Please, you have to do something."

"Are you sure? You're not at all curious—"

"Lochlan!" she scolded.

"Right. Favián, come with me. Arwyn will be well without us here, I assure you." Then he turned to Zeph and said his name.

"What?" he barked.

"He only did as we asked."

Zeph said nothing. He and Favián stared at one another, each taking the measure of the other. The air was rife with contention, a viscous silence, and unformulated words. When Favián finally gave in and followed Lochlan out, Arwyn felt she needed to say something.

"Thank you, Favián, for seeing to my well-being. I hope to see you in the morning. Perhaps at breakfast, and if not, then perhaps lunch?"

Favián paused, though he did not turn around. "Sí. Sleep well." A tired disappointment underscored his words. He closed the door behind him and

Arwyn felt the pang of disappointment as well.

She waited several minutes before speaking again. Zeph had turned his back after they had left, and she contemplated throwing something at him. She considered the empty cup in her hand, weighing it. Instead, she set it aside and counted off in her head. When she thought she could speak to Zeph without temper, she asked, "Why did you do that?"

Zeph's shoulders stiffened, though no words passed his lips. His gaze remained fixed on some far-off place he always seemed to retreat.

Arwyn's lips pursed at his haughty demeanor. She folded her arms in a huff, her eyes narrowing at the back of his head. She opened and closed her mouth three times, longing to lash out at him. The way he came into the room like a silent storm, demanding Favián to leave. Thinking of it now made her nostrils flare. And the longer he stood there not speaking, the more she realized she was rather angry with him. Quite, actually.

Then he dropped his head, and suddenly he looked disconsolate, miserable, like a man who had watched too long from a window to glean an answer to a question he had posed, or for a sign from a god he had prayed to and finding none.

Her anger crept away like fog.

The night had been particularly dark, a mild storm had passed through, but at that moment, that exact moment, the moon had lifted the darkness, cutting a swath through the black, and for a whole minute, Zeph was bathed in a silver beam of light. And wasn't it just like Nature to know how to paint the greatest effects with just moonlight and shadows. She didn't know why she remembered it then, but she recalled his whispered, desperate plea…*"Tell me how to heal you, luv. I am not at all good at it."* But he had healed her, hadn't he? He alone. She marveled at how he had taken care of her. There was goodness in this man, for she had seen it, more than once.

"How do you do that?"

Arwyn blinked, surprised he'd spoken. "Pardon?"

"How do you do that?" he repeated.

"I don't know what you mean."

"Just now…you were smiling."

"Was I?"

He nodded.

"Well, it's quite simple, really," she explained dryly. "You lift the corners of your mouth like so." She used her index fingers to demonstrate. "Perhaps you should try it sometime."

She wished she understood better what he was feeling. His emotions were a confusing, tangled mess, and so were hers.

"That's not what I meant," he whispered.

"Then what did you mean?"

He sank into the wooden chair beside her bed, his eyelids drooping as though they weighed considerably. "I don't know," he murmured.

Time passed like centuries between them, the silence rolling and breaking against her ear. Arwyn opened her mouth several times to speak. Each time, she chose not to. She had accused Zeph of being a coward, and maybe she was a coward too, afraid of saying the wrong thing at the wrong time. With Zeph, she never knew.

"You almost died," he said. His voice was splinters and broken glass and oh, how she wanted to reach for him—to hold him.

"I remember certain things," she answered, her brows wrinkling.

"What things?"

He sat with his eyes closed. She leaned against her pillow, staring up at the ceiling. "Well," she said, the corner of her mouth tugging upward, opting for a bit of levity, "You were very high-handed. Something about forbidding me to die."

There was a brief pause before Zeph spoke. "You scared me, did you know?"

Arwyn's heart expanded, filling up with so much tenderness that she couldn't possibly have room for it all. It leaked out the corners of her eyes. "I'm sorry," she said. "Thank you for…for saving me."

Another pause, and then… "Thank you for not dying."

A hush prevailed once again. This time it hummed rather than roared. She liked the melody of it.

"I buried them," he said, so quietly she barely heard him.

"What?"

"Your family. I buried them for you, right after I brought you to my keep. There was an old elm tree behind your home. You can find their graves there if ever…if ever you want to visit them."

Arwyn closed her eyes, pinching them tightly together, tears falling like rain, a sob escaping her throat.

"I just thought you should know."

She heard the creaking of the wooden chair as he moved to stand. She felt his eyes watching her. And then…she felt his breath on her cheek and the barest brush of his thumb as he wiped her tears.

The only thing she'd ever wished for, a proper burial for her family. He had given that to her.

"Thank you," she whispered when she was able to say the words.

He didn't hear her. He had already left the room.

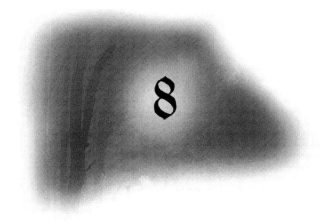

8

Zeph sagged against the door. An unnatural thrum beat unsteadily inside his hallowed chest. An ache coursed through his veins that left his limbs weak and his mind conflicted. He hadn't meant to disclose to Arwyn that he had buried her family. He never wanted her to know. He didn't want her to think he was a kind sort, because he wasn't. He didn't want her to think he had a soft heart, because he didn't. He had wanted to spare her the disappointment. It had always been enough that he knew what he'd done for her. At least, it had been until now.

Now, it seemed imperative that he give her a bit of peace.

The corner of Zeph's mouth tipped up in a bewildered smile. What an odd sensation that Zeph could bring someone a sliver of peace. But he had, hadn't he? Even though she had cried, he felt certain they had been tears of relief. In return, Zeph had felt something wholly unfamiliar; a fragile emotion swept through his body like a clumsy visitor, leaving him dizzy, off-balance. It was why he had left, and it was why he was now leaning against the closed door. He needed to regain his senses.

He let his head fall back against the century-old wood and he breathed in the redolence of incense. The day had started so long ago, it seemed. What he wouldn't give to crawl into bed and not be disturbed for days and days.

He laughed to himself bitterly. His bed had been the one Arwyn was currently occupying. He had nowhere to go. Again. Resigning himself to sleeping in the hallway, he slid against the door until he reached the cold stone floor. Reaching into his pocket, he pulled out his drawstring pouch where he kept the polished stones. He didn't take them out; rather he just felt the weight of them in his hand, remembering how animated Arwyn had become when he'd taught her how to play his childhood game. His throat tightened, and that useless organ inside his chest was expanding, contracting, and at times, it felt like it had been set aflame.

He didn't like feeling this way. He didn't like feeling robbed of breath and vulnerable, and this was as vulnerable as he'd felt in quite some time. He realized he was squeezing the pouch in his hand when he heard footsteps approaching. Releasing his grip, he slipped the stones back into his pocket and waited for whomever was roaming the night to appear.

A silhouette of a man ambled toward him, and as he neared, Zeph recognized him with a bit of surprise and asked, "Why aren't you abed?"

"Demons," Searly answered. "We all have them, and mine keep me awake."

One curious brow lifted. "Why would demons bother with a holy man?"

"You don't think you're so special to assume you're the only one who dances with the devil, do you?"

Zeph huffed in disbelief. "You? Dance with the devil? How absurd."

"Why is that absurd?"

Rubbing his temples, Zeph was too tired to venture into this particular conversation. "Because I suspect you're a terrible dancer."

Searly let out a soft chuckle. "Get up. No need to sleep in a drafty old hallway."

"I'm used to drafty hallways."

"Get up," Searly said again. "The infirmary was never meant to be permanent. Come, I have a room for you."

Getting to his feet, Zeph smoothed out his clothes. He rather liked the idea of a warm bed; however, he only managed to take two steps to follow Searly when he gave pause. Searly was well ahead before he realized Zeph was no longer following.

"This way, Zeph," he said, looking over his shoulder.

Zeph realized he wanted to stay right where he was—close to Arwyn.

There must have been something in Zeph's expression, because Searly said, "She's safe now."

Zeph only repeated, "I'm used to drafty hallways."

Searly walked the steps back to Zeph. His eyes flickered between him and the closed door. "She's safe," he said again.

Zeph jutted his chin forward. "I like drafty hallways."

"She would want you sleeping in a proper bed."

"I doubt she would give where I sleep much thought."

"Then you are a bigger idiot than I gave you credit for."

"The fact that you spend time thinking about me makes me all aflutter."

"You are as infuriating as Lord Lochlan, you know that?"

Zeph's jaw flexed. "Devil take me."

"It's true. You two are more alike than you are different."

A frown pleated the ivory skin of Zeph's forehead. "Now you're just being mean."

A suspicious tension outlined Searly's mouth, as though he were fighting a grin. "Let me take you to your room, Zeph. If it pleases you, I'll come back and stay with Arwyn. I can't sleep anyway, and it is obvious you are in desperate need of it."

Zeph *was* in desperate need of it. No use denying it. Reluctantly, he agreed with a magnanimous nod, but only because it was Searly and only because he knew Searly would never let anything happen to her. He had seen his loyalties on display enough to know that Searly watched over his charges with a fierce protectiveness.

When they reached the room, Searly pushed open the door and directed Zeph to walk through. None of the rooms inside the monastery were special. All were modestly designed with simple furnishings, but the bed big enough for one seemed like Heaven to Zeph in that moment. He couldn't help the stirrings of appreciation flit through him.

"Thank you," Zeph said.

Searly nodded. "Of course."

He meandered over to the bed and sat; his bones and muscles feeling the reprieve instantly. Searly watched him from the doorway and Zeph wondered what he saw—if he could see the shift that was taking place underneath his skin, the rearranging of thoughts and feelings that were currently wreaking havoc in his soul. He hoped he couldn't, though he couldn't help feeling a small part of Searly had an uncanny ability to see far too much.

"You can leave now," Zeph said as he draped across the bed, turned away from him, and closed his tired eyes. "I don't need a nursemaid."

"Of course," Searly repeated. "I'll see my way back to Arwyn. Rest well, Zeph."

The door closed with a snick and Zeph was alone in the dark, alone with his confusion, alone with his troubles, and alone with everything he hated about himself.

But Arwyn was alive, and Elin was alive. His lips twitched into a weak smile. He would deal with his confusion, his troubles, and his self-hatred tomorrow, for tonight he would sleep.

And he had…for a short time. But like Searly's demons, his demons would not allow him to rest. They came quietly, like whispered secrets in the dark, nudging him awake. Zeph covered his ears. "Go away. Leave me be. Leave me alone."

His demons nudged harder, whispered louder, until the whispers turned into shouts and the nudges turned into punches. Zeph's pleas morphed into cries as he curled into himself on a bed big enough for one but which no longer felt like Heaven.

Favián did not see Arwyn the following morning. In fact, he had made it his mission not to see anyone for as long as he could get by with it.

He had lost his head with Arwyn, forgotten for a time she wasn't like him, forgot that she was a magical being. She had made it so easy. He had gotten swept up in her beauty, in her laughter, in the way she had made him relax after his bout of nervousness.

He plunked his head against his pillow and groaned. Pressing the heels of his palms into his eyes, he sighed. He had gotten swept up in everything that was *her*.

"*El cielo me ayude*," he murmured. *Heaven help me.*

Frustrated with himself, he sat up, swinging his long, muscular legs over the edge of the bed, and rested his forearms on his knees. For hours he had tried to forget the way she had made his heart thrash widely when she smiled. Mostly, though, he wanted to forget the look in her eyes when Zeph had entered the infirmary. His heart had gone from thrashing to crashing. Just like that. Funny how a look…a singular look…could tell a story. Hurt. Sadness. Anger. Longing. Favián shut his eyes, shook his head, essentially closing the book on this particular tale.

He stood from his bed and moved toward the window. He didn't have much of a view from his room. Well, perhaps that wasn't a fair assessment. His view was the cloister, a square open space, divided into four paths, with a fountain in the center of the garden. He had spent an inordinate amount of time sitting in the cloister back home, writing, thinking, dreaming. Whenever he wasn't training with his father, that was.

He watched from his window as monks milled about, some sitting quietly as others cared for the garden, pulling weeds and watering plants. After a while, he decided to dress and join them, tired of being alone. However, by the time he'd made his way down, the monks had dispersed to the chapel for prayer and Favián was alone once more.

He walked to the center of the garden, not knowing if he wanted to stay or go, so he stood there, imitating the statues of the saints: still, quiet, unmoving. A million thoughts wrestled through his mind, all of them leading back to a lavender-haired beauty with pointed ears and a—

"What are you doing?"

A voice like quiet music. Turning slowly, he found the woman that ensnared and enchanted him against his will. He looked away, his brows knitting tightly together.

"What's the matter?" Arwyn asked.

He touched his finger to his lips and shook his head. She tilted her head in confusion. He gestured to a gate leading out and pulled gently at her elbow for her to follow. She nodded once, giving tacit permission. His fingers trailed down her arm until his palm curled around her palm, then his feet set into motion as he led her outside the gate.

Once outside, Favián explained, "The cloister is not a place for conversation." He cast Arwyn a side glance before returning his attention straight ahead. "It is for reflection and contemplation. One must never speak inside."

"I didn't know. I'm sorry," she said as they continued to walk.

Her voice was silk and lace. It wrapped around Favián like a soft caress. He didn't trust himself to speak just then, so he tried for a smile and a shrug, but his smile was wan, and his shrug was stiff.

Her fingers flexed against his and he realized they were still holding hands. His fingers flexed back, refusing to let go. She grinned up at him. He grinned back, her grins being contagious beasts.

"I missed you during this morning's meal," she said.

He looked away and out into the scythe-mown grass with flowering meads of primroses and periwinkle. "I was tired," he said, his voice queerly pitched. He cleared his throat, making a show of it. "Sorry," he said, tapping his chest. "Swallowed a bug."

Arwyn regarded him with amused suspicion. "Are you all right?"

"*Sí.*" He cleared his throat with finality. "I hate it when that happens."

"Mm," she said with an arched brow. "I, as well."

"What? Why are you looking at me like that?"

"Why were you avoiding me this morning?"

"I wasn't."

"You were."

This time Favián was the one to arch his brow. "I was tired, Arwyn. I have traveled far and have had little rest."

"Don't do this," she said.

"Do what?"

"Avoid me. Please don't."

His breath hitched when he saw the sadness in her face. She hugged herself as she stared off into a sea of yellow and purple blooms. His fingers twitched, wondering when they had stopped holding hands.

"I'm sorry," he said. "I didn't know my absence would upset you."

"It shouldn't," she replied.

"But it does," he said softly.

"It does," she answered.

"Why?"

She shook her head, still not meeting his eyes. "I had brothers once. Last night...for a minute, I remembered what it felt like. I remembered..." Her lip trembled, and Favián moved to hug her.

"Shh," he soothed, stroking her hair, holding her to his chest, her head tucked neatly underneath his chin. Her arms came around his middle. He pretended this embrace was something more than what it was. *I had brothers once.* She thought of him as a brother. He frowned. And then he got over himself. "What happened to your brothers?"

"Killed."

"And your parents?"

"Killed."

"I'm sorry," he said.

"Me too," she replied.

He held her for another minute before letting her go. "I can't replace your brothers." He tucked a ribbon of hair behind her pointed ear, tracing the curve of it, then took a step back. "But I can be your family." He smiled even as his heart curled in on itself. He knew she would never look at him the way a woman would look at a man—or the way she looked at Zeph.

"Thank you," she said.

He nodded and stared off, knowing that this changed everything…and nothing. "You're welcome."

They spent the afternoon together. She asked more questions about the proper etiquette of monastery living, which he explained in detail. Then he explained the daily tasks.

"Washing and cooking. Reaping and sowing. Binding and thatching. Providing education to boys and novices. In between the chores are the calls to prayers and reflection. A monk's life is hard and exacting, but if one is called to it, it is a satisfying life. At least, that is what *Tío* Searly always says."

Arwyn's mouth twisted into a wry smile. "Searly," she said with great care, like his name was made of something fragile. Then she looked at Favián, taking in the planes of his face, documenting his features. "You have his eyes."

Favián had thought his uncle had the kindest eyes of anyone he'd ever known when he'd met him in the library the previous day. He tucked his hands into his pockets, feeling rather honored. "Thank you," he murmured.

"Tell me more about—"

"I'd rather hear about Faery," Favián interrupted. "What is it like? I imagine it is most beautiful."

"Well," she started, "it is…" Her voice trailed off, her eyes wandering off to some distant place.

"Arwyn?"

"It is hard to explain," she said. "Faery is…a wild beauty, untamed, like a lion. It's probably best to admire it from afar." She cut her eyes to Favián and gave him a devilish smirk. His skin prickled with unease. "Magic, you see, is unpredictable."

"Right, of course."

She shrugged with nonchalance.

He stole a few quick glances at her as they walked. Arwyn was all graceful lines and soft angles, although he got a distinct impression that Arwyn held herself too tightly, keeping her emotions buried too deeply. It wasn't in her words and deeds that made him think and feel thus. It was in the way she moved, like a river maneuvering across the land, an artery of blessed strength, with her smooth, seductive curves. But underneath her calm, mellow harmony, Favián felt the pull of an undertow, and any moment he feared she would lose her balance and get swept away. His fingers itched to reach out and hold on to her.

He shook his head. "You want to see something other than the monastery?"

"Like what?"

"We could walk to the village."

"Village?"

"It's not far. I passed through it on my way here." He pointed to her lavender hair and her pointed ears and grinned. "You may want to cover your head. Humans, you see, are unpredictable."

"Right, of course," she said with a laugh, tucking her hair into the hood of her cloak.

"Shall we?" he asked, offering her his arm.

"Lead the way."

Walking down the worn cobblestone road of the village square, Favián noticed that Arwyn kept her head down, not looking anyone in the eye. He knew why. The Human realm and the Faery realm were strictly divided. Each was supposed to stay on their side of the seam and had been so for centuries. In the Aeon of Isis, Faeries and humans co-existed peacefully, but with peaceful existence, an unwritten rule had been established between both races: humans and Faeries were never to forge romantic relationships. In the eye of man, it was deemed ungodly. And the Fae wanted to remain pure and untainted. But the King of Kaelmor had fallen in love with a princess of the Seelie Royal Court, and together they created a child. That child was Lochlan.

That was the story his *tío* had told him in his youth. It was written a war broke out between Fae and Man, each blaming the other for the abomination that was created between them. Eventually, a treaty was drawn and signed into power and a wall was built between the Faery and Human realms. Permissions had to be granted to cross. As long as the treaty held, the war would cease. It was his *tío* who had told him about the curse…how the Seelie Queen had cursed the king and his child, ensuring that the child would never be accepted by either Fae or human and how the Fae Princess was also stripped of her immortality and died during childbirth.

The curse had finally been broken, and it was only the previous day, during his meal with his *tío*, Lochlan, and Elin that Favián had learned the rest of it. They had told him about the Seelie Queen and how she had *not* been the one to issue the curse against Lochlan. It had been Lolith, who had killed the queen, deceived both sides into believing she was the true queen, and history became quite muddled after that. She was also the one behind Zeph being taken as a child. But she was dead now, and they were still trying to put the pieces together.

"What are you doing?" Favián asked as he walked casually beside her, doing his best to smile at everyone they passed.

"Trying not be noticed."

Favián's mouth twitched. "You could never go unnoticed, *mi corazoncito*."

"It seemed like a good idea when you suggested it. Exciting, even."

"What? Coming to the village?"

"Yes."

"And now?"

"And now I'm afraid we made a mistake."

The villagers knew about Lochlan and had accepted him. He had lived among them for generations; however, it had only been recently that the villagers truly considered him as one of their own. They did not know about Arwyn or Zeph's presence yet. Lochlan, his *tío*, and the other monks had made the decision to not make any of this known for many reasons, which meant Arwyn was shackled to the monastery and its property indefinitely with nowhere else to go. Much like she had been in Shadowland. Even though he understood their reasoning, the idea of it did not sit well with Favián.

Arwyn tugged at the hood of her cloak again.

"You needed to get outside the confines of the monastery, Arwyn. You were suffocating."

"Yes, I was."

"You are safe with me."

"I know."

"Do you?"

"I don't need a protector, Favián. I can protect myself."

His mouth was in a perpetual state of grinning when he was with her. It should have been embarrassing; however, he couldn't be bothered to care. "Is that so?"

"Yes."

"Then maybe you should be protecting me."

She cut him a sideways glance, tossing him a smile like a child with flowers. "Maybe."

Two women walked by, one whispering to the other.

"Do you think they know what I am?" she murmured.

"No. Most likely they assume we are foreigners. Nothing more."

"This was a mistake. We shouldn't have come here."

"Let us ease their minds. I will stop up ahead at the next vendor and allow a conversation. I will explain I am from *Ontiverós* here visiting my *tío*."

"What about me?"

They were walking with arms linked, his hand covering hers. He looked down at her, a secretive smile playing on his lips. "I know you think of me as a brother, but we look nothing alike. Perhaps I should tell them we are betrothed, yes?"

"You are enjoying this."

"A little."

"Very well," she said, straightening her spine. "I can't believe I let you talk me into this."

"A positive influence already. My *tío* will be so proud."

It would turn out that Arwyn and Favián would have an enjoyable time in the village. Curious gazes were only that…curious. This particular village was not largely populated, yet the province of Mirova, because of its seaports and trade, attracted its fair share of travelers, thus the tiny villages throughout Mirova often saw foreigners, so they didn't stand out any more or less than any other. However, Favián did notice a peculiarity.

"People here seem a bit odd," he commented.

"In what way?" Arwyn asked.

His eyes discreetly scanned the crowd. Merchants sold their wares; women wore faint smiles with tired eyes as they pulled their children along while husbands and fathers paid the merchants and then loaded their supplies into wagons. There was nothing unordinary about any of it. But there was a hum in the air, a patient expectation in their weary gazes, like they were waiting for something to happen.

Or perhaps he was just a tired fool, having not slept well the night before.

"It's nothing. I spoke out of turn. Come, maybe we should go."

"No, wait," Arwyn said, tugging on his arm and coming to a halt. She glanced to her right, then to her left, her forehead wrinkling. "I think I understand what you mean." She looked at him with a gimlet eye. His skin tingled underneath her scrutiny. "How perceptive of you."

"So, it isn't just me?"

"No," she said with a tilt of her head.

Favián noticed a woman watching them, her face obscured by the hood of a thick wool cloak; her knobby hands were wrapped around the top of a walking stick. Unthreatening she was, though there was something unnerving about the way she observed them.

He offered Arwyn his arm, which she accepted. "Shall we return to the monastery now, *señorita*?"

A wary smile surfaced on her lips. "All right."

Upon returning, Arwyn knew something was wrong. Zeph prowled and paced near the front of the monastery, with his sister by his side. From a distance, it was uncanny how alike they appeared: long pale hair. Hers silver. His white. Slender frames, and although Zeph was taller, they both held an air of something *other* that could not be defined. At least not now, as Arwyn's mind wrestled with whatever could be the matter. Zeph looked panicked.

"Zeph?" Arwyn said, calling out to him.

Zeph's head turned at the sound of her voice. He was within three paces of them within a matter of seconds, his colorless eyes raking Arwyn from head to toe. "Are you injured?" Zeph asked, his voice wavering like a thread of smoke.

"What? No," Arwyn answered, blinking owlishly. Noticing how red-rimmed his eyes were, she asked her own question, "What happened to you?"

Elin had come up beside them and spoke softly. "Zeph only recently became aware you were gone. After yesterday," she said, "he became quite worried for your safety."

Regret speared Arwyn's heart. She hadn't considered he might worry. Had he ever worried before? Before she could explain, however, Favián spoke.

"We ventured to the village. I thought Arwyn needed to get awa—"

Zeph's hands were around Favián's throat in an instant. "I could kill you right here."

"Zeph! Release him!"

Zeph smiled nefariously, white, sharp fangs descended against his lips. "No."

"Please let him go," Elin entreated. "You don't want to do this."

Zeph's only reply was to squeeze harder.

Then something happened. Favián's elbow met Zeph's nose, breaking the chokehold around Favián's neck, then Zeph's nose met Favián's knee. Blood coated Zeph's face and fangs, his white clothes splattered with red.

The rhythm of time sputtered, rocked back on its heels, and was stunned into stillness, save for a twitch, like the tail of a great cat.

Arwyn and Elin stood poised in surprise. A sudden shock struck somewhere inside Arwyn's chest as Favián breathed heavily, angling his body into a fighting position, ready to defend, standing his ground. Not running as would be expected, but waiting.

Zeph wiped his nose with his sleeve, his eyes burning with hatred.

"Zeph," Arwyn said, touching his chest, pushing him away from Favián. "Let's go inside. Please. I'm fine. Please."

Zeph's gaze dipped to hers. What she saw in them nearly knocked the breath out of her. She had to slam her eyes shut against the tumult of emotional anguish and remember her father's words. *Sometimes you will hit the target but miss the self. Clear the mind, release the energy.*

He removed her hands from his chest and backed away. "Leave me alone," he said. "Don't come near me right now."

"Zeph," she protested.

"No," he said, turning from her and heading back inside. "Stay away."

Arwyn and Favián parted ways after that and Elin walked with her for a bit.

"I hadn't seen Zeph all day," Elin was saying, "so I went to check on him. He was…" Elin took a breath and let it out in slow measures. Her hands were shaking.

"My goodness," Arwyn said, taking her by the hands feeling them tremble. "What is it?"

Elin's eyes glistened when she said, "He was wrecked. He was in his bedchamber, curled into a ball on the floor. Don't tell him I told you, Arwyn. Please."

"I won't," she said. "Why was he on the floor?"

"He wasn't lucid. I think he dreams. I don't think he's sleeping. When I saw him like that…" Elin shook her head, fighting back tears. "He looked like a child. It took me back to when we…to when we…"

"Shh." Arwyn pulled Elin in, giving her a warm shoulder to cry on. "It's all right."

"I can't abandon him. I can't. Not after learning that we're twins—that he allowed himself to be taken so I wouldn't be. I can't abandon him, Arwyn."

"I know. Neither can I. And that's the damnable thing of it, isn't it?"

Arwyn spared little time going in search of Zeph. After leaving Elin with Lochlan, she went to Zeph's room and stood outside his door, listening. She could hear him gently stirring about.

She had no notion of what to say to him. No clever sayings. No witty remarks. All she had was herself, and if history was a lesson to glean from, she had never been enough before.

Still, here she was.

She knocked.

"Go away."

"Zeph."

"Not now."

"If not now, then when?"

Silence greeted her.

"Zeph."

"Go. Away."

She opened the door, stepped inside, and closed it behind her. Zeph's eyes widened and then sharpened like blades as he stood bare-chested, in the act of undressing.

Neither spoke, both staring at the other. A cruel smile pulled at Zeph's lips. Arwyn flushed all over, though she refused to cower from him. She lifted her chin high, holding her body in an awkward pride, suddenly conscious of her own skin.

"Well, you are inside my chamber now. What are you going to do with me?"

"I haven't yet decided."

"May I offer suggestions?"

"No."

"But darling, I have so many ideas."

"You wouldn't know what to do with me if you had me."

"Shall we test that theory?"

Arwyn forced herself to show no fear. Zeph would never hurt her. He *wouldn't*. She moved forward slowly, nearing him with caution. Sunlight from the window slanted across the room like sweet honey. Her gaze fell on Zeph's exposed skin where scars dominated his torso, some like fishbone, others were wide and jagged. Some were obvious burns, puckered and unsightly. She had noticed them the night he'd first arrived, but she had not allowed herself to truly look at them. Not like this. Because she had recalled a time once…in Shadowland. She had just watched Zeph battle the Unseelie King and had suffered a wound, a gash in his side. She had tried to heal him, and he had been rather stubborn about taking off his tunic, and when he did, he held the tunic close to his chest. The lighting had been poor. She couldn't see anything other than the wound he had allowed her to see, though she knew he had been hiding something from her.

But now she was looking and now she had to ask, "Oh, Zeph, what did they do to you?"

His throat bobbed nervously when her fingertips touched him, fluttering like ribbons as she traced the line that zigzagged over his heart. An external voice to an internal anguish.

Their gazes locked. "Tell me," she begged.

His hand fit over hers, and for a moment, she thought he would remove it, say something glib. He did not. He held on to it, though he did not answer. She brought her other hand up where she traced more scars before he caught up that hand, too, and held it just as tightly.

"Don't," he rasped.

"Someday," she said, "you will tell me."

"Arwyn—"

"You will tell me, and I will listen." She placed her cheek against the warmth of his chest, listened to the beat of his heart, a wild, erratic tempo, and closed her eyes. "I will listen," she murmured.

He said nothing. The room, instead, filled with unspoken words and unformulated guilt, a brittle silence that felt absolute. And yet, it was the most they had ever said to one another without having to say anything at all.

9

"Why did you take Arwyn to the village?"

Zeph had been waiting patiently in Favián's bedchamber for hours while everyone else had been eating supper and doing whatever it was they did before retiring for the night. He had heard Favián's footsteps approaching and had barely waited for him to close the door, sealing them both in the darkened room, before asking the question. A smile danced on Zeph's lips when he heard Favián's startled breath.

"Wh-where are you? I cannot see a bloody thing."

"Afraid of the dark? My apologies." Zeph called back his shadow, vanishing like wisps of vapor. Zeph had wanted total darkness when Favián entered his own bedchamber, just to be a trite dramatic. Pale moonlight trickled in through the window, a long strand of silver glistened and scattered in a pearly hue. "Better?"

"What do you want, Zeph?"

Favián remained by the door, his posture stiff, untrusting. Zeph observed him closely as he stepped out of the corner and into the silvery beam, allowing Favián to see him for the first time, his white hair hanging loosely around his face.

"I want you to answer my question. Why did you take Arwyn to the village today? Are you trying to harm her?"

"No!" Favián said, stepping forward. "I wanted to take her away from here for a while."

"She's not your concern."

"Is she yours?"

"Yes."

"Does she know that?"

"Stay away from her."

"No."

Zeph's mouth twisted, his eyes narrowed. "Stay away from her."

Favián lifted his chin. "If I don't?"

"Are you trying to provoke me?" Zeph was behind Favián in a blink, one arm banded around his throat. "Very well, I'll oblige."

But if Zeph had planned for a surprise attack, Favián had been prepared for it. In another blink, Zeph was flat on his back with Favián standing over him.

Bloody hell.

Zeph grabbed Favián's ankle and brought him down. Hard. A struggle for dominance ensued. A table was shattered. A lantern as well. Fortunately, Zeph had chosen not to light it.

Through pants and grunts, Favián hissed, "I'm not going to take her away from you! But I'm not going to stay away from her either."

"What do you want from her?" Zeph demanded, pulling the churl up by the scruff of the neck and shoving him against the wall. Zeph held him there firmly, grinding Favián's cheek against the pitted stone.

"What do *you* want from her? Do you even know?"

Zeph opened his mouth for a retort. Nothing came out. He tried again.

Words he'd wanted to say somehow got lost between his brain and his mouth. He closed his eyes in frustration.

"You don't know," Favián said. "You have no idea what you want from her."

"I want *nothing* from her," Zeph grounded out.

"Liar. You are a miserable coward. You do want something from her."

"Are you an oracle? Some sort of seer? You know nothing about me."

"You see me as a threat."

"I see everyone as a threat."

"You hate me because I *like* her. Not because you think I'm out to harm her."

"I hate you because I hate everyone."

"And if you wanted to kill me you would have done so already."

"I like taunting my victims before I go for the kill."

Favián struggled to turn his head to eye Zeph. "Is that so? That is not so much a good strategy."

Zeph tilted his head. "Oh? And why is—"

Zeph's words were bit off when Favián did some odd footwork, tucking his boot around Zeph's, causing Zeph to lunge forward while Favián ducked beneath him, coiling around his body like a deadly viper, and somehow maneuvering his way behind him until they had switched positions.

Favián shoved Zeph's cheek into the stone wall and said, "Because you allow your opponent time to outwit you."

"I could still kill you."

"With magic, *sí*. Of course I am no match. But you have yet to use magic on me. I'd like to know why that is."

Zeph thought about using magic *now*. He grounded his teeth together so hard, he nearly tasted dust. Ignoring Favián's question, Zeph said acerbically, "If something had happened to her, make no mistake, I would rip you apart, limb from limb, and feed you to the wolves. Nothing, *nothing*, would stop me from killing you."

"Make no mistake," Favián said soberly, releasing his hold on Zeph. "I would cut my own vein before I would allow harm to come to Arwyn."

They eyed each other with speculation, their chests rising and falling from exertion.

"Why did you take her to the village?" Zeph asked again.

"I wanted to help her." He spread his arms out. "She's shut in this place. When does she ever get to go anywhere? Do anything fun?"

"Maybe next time a poisoned arrow will strike her heart! Did you think of that when you took her on an adventure?"

Favián inhaled deeply, walked to his bed, and sat like a lump of lead. He scrubbed his hands over his face, and then rested his forearms on his knees. "I was sure I could protect her. I wouldn't have let her go otherwise."

"What makes you think you could protect her? You are a *human*. The hound that attacked us was from Faery, which means it possessed magical powers you do not own. I fail to see your logic."

For the first time, Zeph saw remorse when Favián's eyes lifted to his. "You are right. I wasn't using logic. I see your point."

Hell's bells. Zeph wasn't expecting Favián to capitulate. He massaged his jaw and moved toward the window and stared out. His spark of anger had dampened, leaving behind only smoldering ashes and a faint scent of sweat.

"I only wanted to help her," Favián murmured. "You didn't see her face. The way she cried—"

"Why was she crying?" Zeph asked in a whip-like fashion. Then, because Favián did not answer quickly enough, he asked again, this time louder, "Why was she crying?"

Favián spoke slowly, each word emphasized with a kind of uniformity that made them stand out against his normally clipped, furious pace. "She was missing her family. She spoke to me of her brothers."

Zeph nodded. He turned his gaze back out the window. He appeared almost somber, like an important statue in a formal setting, but inside his heart cracked, a fissure running the length of him, and any minute he could shatter right where he stood. Arwyn had never spoken to him of her sorrows. Never. Not once. And Zeph realized he was jealous of Favián, even though he knew very well that Zeph had never given Arwyn any reason to come to him with her sorrows.

"She thinks of me as a brother."

Zeph's head swung in Favián's direction. "Beg pardon?"

A tiny grin pulled at the churl's lips. "I thought that might get your attention. She told me she thinks of me as a brother. Although you can go on being sulky and bitter if you like. You certainly have that mastered, though jealousy looks very odd on you, if you don't mind me saying."

Zeph opened his mouth for a blistering retort, but once again, what he wanted to say lost its way to his mouth. When he did find his words, his voice sounded curiously strangled, with gaps between his sentences. His feelings and thoughts, words and phrases, all battled inside of him, getting in one another's way, coming out in stuttered syllables. Favián looked on as though he was mildly entertained.

"What?" Zeph spat the word out like an orange seed.

"I have no idea what you just said."

Zeph's tongue finally stilled. The two men stared at the other, mute as gargoyles. The gray night shimmered through the window, casting just enough light that Zeph could not miss the rather annoying superior look on Favián's face.

Zeph's fangs itched to drop.

"She doesn't fancy me," Favián said. "Much to my disappointment."

Zeph smiled like a condescending relative. "Pity."

Favián smiled back, though his was secretive. "You love her."

This time Zeph chose silence. He certainly didn't trust his mouth to cooperate. Though he had to say *something*. He couldn't allow that sentence to stand—to let it permeate the air. Words held power. They held meaning. He had to say something to diffuse them.

"I don't. I—*can't*."

"You already do, *compadre*. Whether you want to or not…whether you can or can't…" Favián shrugged. "It does not matter. Because you already do."

Favián broke off a piece of bread, chewing it slowly while looking around the refectory. The faces of the monks were long, their expressions brittle. Favián looked down into his bowl of unsavory oats and forced himself to take a bite. He wasn't hungry, or rather he just couldn't stomach the unpleasantness of his surroundings. No one was speaking, everyone moving about in a haze. Favián felt as though he was on an island unto himself, sitting alone, eating his meal in solitude, even though men sat on either side and across from him. One fellow bumped his elbow. He mumbled an apology. Favián acknowledged with a nod. He didn't bother using words. He could sense when someone didn't want to converse, and none of these men, most assuredly, wanted to converse.

Favián forced himself to finish his oats and his bread and left the table. He took care of his own bowl, cleaning it himself, and placed it back where he'd found it. Then, he left the kitchens and breathed a full breath of air once he was outside the door.

He had risen before sunrise, unable to sleep, dressed in a woolen tunic belted at the waist, and slipped on a pair of woolen breeches. He put on his cowl, laced up his boots, and left the sanctuary of his chamber. He had been roaming around ever since. He had thought repast with the monks would have been an occasion to become acquainted with one another. It had been the first real opportunity since his arrival to do so, but their energy had been unwelcoming. Or perhaps, that may be a bit unfair to say. However, their energy had most certainly not been inviting.

He did ask Xavier at one point if his presence offended them, and Xavier had assured him it did not. They were all just dealing with Zeph being among them as best they could and, for now, they needed a bit of time to…deal with the situation.

Favián had not bothered with idle conversation after that, trying to put himself in their place as best as he could, and he let them be.

When he exited the refectory, he ambled back the way of his cell and was nearly there when he heard voices. He smiled. He liked these voices. They were friendly and pleasant, and he was just about to round the corner to say his greetings when he heard the friendly lilt strain into something else—something pleading.

"I want to make you my *wife*, Elin."

Favián froze mid-step, careful not to alert Elin and Lochlan to his presence.

"Are we to have children?"

"What?"

"Zeph would be their uncle. I am not turning my back on him. Are we to have children, Lochlan? And if so, how do you feel about Zeph being in their life?"

"Bugger me," Lochlan mumbled.

"See?" Elin said. "You need to think this through. I know you love me. I know you do. But—"

"I don't need to think this through! I know what I want. I want you!"

"Lower your voice," Elin whispered.

"Elin," Lochlan entreated. "Do you want me to beg? I'll beg. Do you want me down on one knee?"

Favián heard scuffling.

"Lochlan, what are you doing?"

"I'm on bended knee."

"I want you to be sure," Elin said gently. "I don't want you to wake up one morning regretting having ever married me. I want you to be certain that you want me for the rest of your days. And no one else. What? Why are smiling?"

"Are you finished?"

"Oh, hush," she said with false haughtiness. "I just want—"

"I am sure. I am absolutely, positively certain that you are the woman I want for the rest of my days and no one else."

Favián's lips tilted upward into a smile. He knew he shouldn't have stayed and listened to their private conversation. His *tío* would give him a good scolding if he knew he was eavesdropping. But he had to hear Elin say yes. He *had* to. He leaned forward, his ears straining to hear.

"What are you doing?" a female voice asked from behind him, causing Favián to jump.

"Shh," he said, clamping his hand down over Arwyn's mouth and whispering, "Lochlan is proposing to Elin."

Arwyn's eyes widened and Favián released his hand from her mouth, still feeling the warmth of her breath on the palm of his hand.

"Has she said yes?"

Favián shook his head. "Not yet."

"I'm on my knees, Elin." Lochlan's voice had grown over-rough. Arwyn gripped Favián's hand. Their gazes locked. "Marry me. Be my wife. I don't care who your brother is. We'll figure it out—together. He could be Satan himself and that would not stop me from marrying you. Say yes. Please."

Arwyn and Favián pressed themselves flat against the wall and waited with bated breath for Elin's answer.

"What are you two doing?"

Favián's hand shot out in hasty, jerky gestures before sealing it over Searly's mouth. "Be quiet," he mouthed. Slowly, he withdrew his hand. Searly's eyes widened under the brim of thick brows. "Lochlan just proposed to Elin," Favián explained quietly.

His *tío's* face split with joy. Now, three bodies pressed flat against the wall.

"I'm in love with you," Elin said softly. "That is the only thing that remains constant. Of course I'll marry you."

"Oh, thank Heavens!" Searly shouted, extracting himself from their hiding place and rounding the corner to where Lochlan and Elin stood. The both of them stared at him with matching startled expressions.

Favián held still, letting his breath out slowly, shutting his eyes in relief. Arwyn wrapped her arms around him and he couldn't help the blessed feeling of contentment in that moment.

"Finally, something to celebrate," Searly announced. "It has been too long. You two, come out and wish our newly betrothed couple congratulations."

Arwyn and Favián exchanged glances before stepping around the corner, each holding equally guilty smiles. "Congratulations," they said in unison.

"How long have you all been standing there?" Lochlan asked, his tone peremptory.

"Oh, I only just arrived, milord," Searly said, looking the picture of innocence. "Those two were here long before me."

Lochlan cast Favián and Arwyn a speaking glance. Favián's head fell forward, guilt pinching his gut.

"My apologies," Favián said with haste. "I-I did not mean to overhear. I was walking back to my chamber when I heard you and Elin and I-I did not want to interrupt and I-I…" Favián's words trailed off as he rubbed nervously on the back of his neck. "My apologies," he mumbled again.

"Well, I make no such apologies," Arwyn chimed in, beaming ear to ear. She rushed to Elin's side and hugged her. She then turned to Lochlan. "I know you don't like to be touched, Lochlan. But may I?" Her arms were extended out to her sides wide in an open invitation, one she hoped he would accept.

Lochlan's lean body went stiff as stone. Obvious to everyone, it was difficult for Lochlan to accept, but his long lashes swept upward to look Arwyn in the eye. "All right," he said.

Arwyn bit back a smile and stepped forward. She embraced Lochlan gently. His arms swept around her waist like she would crumble beneath him. He barely held her, but she held on to him without fear. "Congratulations," she said in his ear. "I couldn't be happier for you. You deserve this. You both do."

"Thank you," Lochlan said, watching his newly betrothed walk over to Favián, who was still a bit reticent about eavesdropping, not knowing quite what to say.

"Don't worry, Favián," Elin said, "I'm not mad at you." She lifted her hand, brushed her fingers gently against his left brow. "When did you get this scar?"

"I fell from a tree," he answered, "when I was a little boy."

A delicate smiled pulled at the corner of Elin's mouth. "Your mother fussed over you incessantly when this happened, cleaned you up, and after, she made your favorite dish, and together you lay on a quilt by the fire and she told you stories late into the night until you fell asleep."

"How did you know that?" Favián asked, instinct prompting him to capture her hand.

"I have the ability to see a person's happiest memory. This is one of yours, though it is not the only one. You have many happy memories, Favián. You are one of the lucky ones."

Favián couldn't help feeling the tightness in his chest. He missed his *mamá*.

"*Sí*," he said. "I suppose I am."

"A celebration it is!" Searly declared with a clap of his hands and a gleam in his eye.

"When?" Lochlan asked.

Searly slapped a palm on Lochlan's back. To Lochlan's credit, he did not flinch. "Tonight, my friend. Tonight."

Zeph stared at the two graves. The names on the wooden crosses were unfamiliar, yet he knew who they were.

His parents.

They had changed their names when they had fled Faery with his sister. He let his head fall against the bark of the tree. What a sad, twisted tale this was. Memories assaulted his vision: screams, pleas for mercy…

"Don't do this, I beg you"

Those had been the words of his father. Zeph had grown too cold, too callous, for his father's words to have any effect on him.

That was then. Looking back on it now, the look in his father's eyes, the pain in his voice, filled his lungs with air that felt too thin to breathe.

He had knocked on their door, pretty as you please, relishing the looks on their faces when his parents recognized their long-lost boy had come knocking. Oh, it had been quite the spectacle. His father had been joyous— in the beginning, albeit paralyzed from the shock of seeing his son standing before him.

"Son, is it…really you?"

For the first time in so long, looking upon the face that resembled his own, the lost child longed to grab hold of his father and hold him tightly and tell him all the things that had happened to him. *They hurt me, father. They hurt me so much.*

But he had driven the child's voice out of his head and out of his heart, and in its place, a malevolent smile had crept lazily over his lips instead. "So, you haven't forgotten me after all," Zeph intoned. "Neither have I forgotten you."

Not waiting for an invitation to enter, he'd pushed past his father. His mother, still lost for words, eyed him with wonder or with sheer shock. He couldn't be sure. He walked past her with a casual greeting, with no inflection in his tone. "Mother."

He looked around at the modest home, a direct contrast to the home he had shared with them in Faery. He looked for anything familiar, a figurine, an heirloom, a portrait, *something,* when he spotted the drawstring pouch, the one with the stones. The ones he now kept with him at all times. He had slipped the pouch into his pocket, not taking time to analyze why at the time, just acting on a whim, taking something back that had once been his. It felt like he was taking back his life—one stone at a time, and everyone responsible for robbing him would be punished. Only he, at least, would kill them. If he truly wanted them to suffer, he would let them live...the way he had been living.

"You're going to kill us," his mother had said with a gasp.

Zeph had laughed. It was cold and chilling. He had never been very good at hiding anything from his mum. His mother always had the uncanny ability of reading his mind. Clairvoyant. He had forgotten that. "A fine greeting. No hello, son? No...how have you been?"

"I can see very well how you have been...what they have done to you."

"As if you and he..." Zeph's gaze snapped toward his father, who looked like he'd aged in the moments since he'd stepped back into their lives, "had nothing to do with how I turned out?"

He wanted to ask them why—why had they left him there? But the longer he waited, with them offering no explanations, the angrier he became. Why should he have to ask? Surely, he deserved answers without having to beg for them!

"You don't understand," his father had said, "they lied—"

"About what? That my family ran off and hid? I'd say that was accurate. You left one child behind, though. Speaking of children, where is my dear sister? Will she be along soon?"

Zeph had known exactly where Elin had been, but he was playing a game with his parents, and with Elin, and thinking on it now...

He drove his fist in the dirt.

The rest, he just couldn't bring himself to recollect. He had refused to listen to anything they had tried to say. They were dead now because of him. Guilt was a monster of its own. It was a wall that trapped him, held him prisoner, too big to go around, too mountainous to climb over. It pressed upon him until he was crushed underneath the weight of it, stealing his air and taking his hope.

He hurled a rock he'd found beside him, lobbing it as far he as he could. He wanted to commit violence—against himself. Against the world...against...

A dark figure skirted past Zeph in his periphery, and even though his spine tingled with awareness that he was being watched, he remained still, controlled. He had spent his entire youth under watchful eyes. He had learned not to react, startled though he was. He had thought to be alone.

"Well," he murmured, standing back up. "No time like the present to find me a bit of trouble."

He eyed the markers of his parents one last time, his brows drawing tightly into a V. The words *I'm sorry* on his lips, but he didn't utter them. Words wouldn't bring them back. Nothing ever would.

"*You love her,*" Favián had said.

Love was not in Zeph's future, and he would not trap Arwyn inside this prison with him.

He looked past the graves, where he'd seen the dark figure slip into a grove of trees. A shiver ran over his skin, a strange feeling in the air. A muscle flickered in his jaw as he steeled himself and marched toward it.

The only thing in his future was war.

It had been a trap.

Zeph knew it the moment he had set out to following the dark figure. Still, he went.

He went because he wanted a fight. He wanted a reason to draw blood. He wanted a reason to unleash the power that crawled underneath his skin since he'd awoken from his death nap. And now he had one. But somehow, he had gotten lost and he wasn't quite sure where he was anymore.

Zeph looked to the left, and to the right. Majestic oak trees stood silent, casting shadows like black lace. Birches, with their slender, skeletal frames, arched like craggy old men. The evergreens were blackish-green silhouettes and the red maples looked more like burnt-out torches. The sky was neither light nor dark. Some flowers were in bloom, though most were not. Those that were, however, were muted, a faded lackluster assortment of nothing special. No vibrant hues of violets and pinks, reds and yellows. Just dark clusters, like each flower bore a sad name. And not the slightest breeze swept through Zeph's hair.

He let his eyes roam, taking in what was once a beautiful forest, pulsing with a heartbeat. There was no heartbeat now. It lay dormant, taking not a single breath.

He swallowed thickly. This was wrong. This was very, very wrong. Sieves of mist covered the lichen-covered bark. Nothing stirred, nothing sang.

"Find me," a small voice said.

Zeph spun around, his robe twisting around his feet. "Who said that?"

Something crunched to his left, a twig underneath a boot. Zeph twisted around again, finding nothing and no one but rolling fog. "Who's there?"

Silence.

Then a scream. A child's scream. Off in the distance.

Zeph ran toward it, his heart thumping a wild tattoo. A familiarity prickled at his senses. Running, chasing, falling, getting back up, and running again— this all seemed very familiar. He stole a glance over his shoulder, feeling like *he* was the one being hunted now.

Then he felt hands on his back, meaty fists hooking onto his clothes, and being jostled off his feet until he hit the wall of someone's chest.

"Hold still." The smell of burnt spices hung on the breath of his captor. Zeph thrashed about, trying to pull free, but it was like fighting against air. "Hold still," his captor said again.

Zeph's vision blurred and the scene flashed to something different. Unseelie stood around a fire, a wicked tempo of drumbeats sounding all around them. A boy, stripped of all clothing, save for a bag over his head, was being escorted to the middle of the circle. The boy fought against the shackles that bound his wrists and feet, but it was a useless endeavor. Unseelie laughed and sneered at his efforts.

The hand gripping Zeph's neck tightened, holding him there, and Zeph realized this was the past. He had somehow stepped back in time, when he, himself, was a boy.

What was happening?

He looked down at his body. He was a boy again, wearing only a thin cloth covering the most private parts of him. Tears formed in his eyes like chipped glass.

He remembered this. Oh God, he remembered this.

One of the Unseelie stepped toward the boy in the circle.

Zeph's insides twisted. His hands shook, and violent rage surged to the fore as he leaped forward, prepared to defend the child against the cruelties of these animals—these Dark Fae who preyed on the weak and the unprotected. Because here, children were stripped of their powers, with no way to defend themselves.

He was stopped by an invisible barrier, a shield.

"NO!" he yelled, pounding his small fists on the barrier he could not see. "Leave him alone! Don't touch him! Leave him alone!"

No one heard him. The scene unfolded before him as if he wasn't there at all. He looked away when the Unseelie each had a turn at the boy. He raised shaking hands to his ears and shut his eyes tight. "No," he murmured as Zeph rocked his thin body in short, quick fits. "No. No."

Time seemed to fold in on itself, and at times, he could almost hear his sister's voice punching through the pleats. But that wasn't right either. *What was happening? Why was he here?*

The boy screamed and Zeph cried out, too, remembering the pain of it…when it had been him. The hot burn in his backside…the pressure, the grunting, the sweat of his tormentors falling in his hair, dripping on his skin, as they ripped his body inside out. His mind tumbled like rocks down a sloping hillside. One by one, they climbed on, holding him down, using his body, and then discarding him like trash. When they were done, they left him in the dirt.

Some kicked him in the ribs, the stomach, the face. Some just laughed at him. Only one would pick him up and carry him back to the cell where he was kept, held prisoner, until he gave in, until he vowed to be one of them. As long as he held out, not give in, he would suffer the abuse. At twelve, he had still been able to hold on.

The boy continued to cry out. How long it went on, Zeph did not know. Time stuck to him like a damp tabard. It seemed endless.

Then, Zeph heard a rasp. "You found me."

Zeph's head snapped up, his eyes darting toward the monsters who were making merry around the fire now, ignoring the boy they'd tossed aside, the bag still over his head.

"You can see me?" Zeph asked.

"I-I've been w-waiting for you."

Zeph reached out to help him, but the barrier prevented him. "Can they see me?" he asked.

"N-No."

Zeph's pulse beat in his ears. "How did I get here? What's happening?"

"The sp-spell."

"What spell?"

The boy lifted his head, removed the bag, his hands a bloody mess, and looked Zeph in the eyes. Identical eyes to his.

An audible gasp escaped Zeph's mouth.

"Our spell." The boy wheezed as he rolled over to spit blood from his mouth. He was so thin, so frail. If you shook him, his bones would rattle.

Zeph tried to think, his thoughts going backward and forward, weaving time together, knitting them into a pattern that made sense. Then one of the Unseelie lumbered toward them and Zeph stood, his body the mirror image of the boy on the ground. "Leave him be!" Zeph yelled. "Don't take him!"

"Don't," the boy replied. "I-I'm the only one who can see you."

"What am I supposed to do?"

The Unseelie scooped the boy up, slinging him over one shoulder like a sack of oats.

"What am I supposed to do?" Zeph yelled.

The boy lifted his head, then dropped it. "Re-mem-ber me."

Zeph's tears fell like a veil, glinting and silent, obscuring his vision. He didn't want to see what was in front of him anymore.

Turning his head, he whispered, *"It hurts to remember."*

The celebration had just begun. Everyone wanted to congratulate Elin and Lochlan on their betrothal. A celebratory feast had been prepared, and together they gathered underneath a starry sky around a warm fire. Searly made a toast to the happy couple, and all in attendance, which included every monk, raised their chalices.

"To Lochlan and Elin."

"To Lochlan and Elin," everyone repeated.

The music started. Xavier, as it turned out, was quite good on the pan flute. Another played the lute.

Favián sat off by himself, close to the light of the fire, to finish what he'd started working on that afternoon: a poem to give to the happy couple. At some point, Arwyn sat down beside him.

"What are you working on, Favi?"

He arched a brow. "Favi?"

"Yes, do you like it?" She smiled, but it reminded him of the moon before the sun had fully set. Barely there.

"*Sí.* If it pleases you, then I like it."

He waited for her to smile again, but her eyes were distant, like she was seeing something no one else could see.

Putting aside his task, he reached for her hand. "Arwyn, what is the matter?"

She shook her head. "Something is wrong."

Taking her by the chin with his thumb and forefinger, he turned her face to his. "Tell me," he said.

She looked down and brushed her fingers across the fabric of her dress. "It's Zeph." Her forehead puckered. "He's..." She looked up with wild eyes and then promptly stood. "He's coming. Lochlan!" she shouted, pointing to Zeph, who was running toward them, looking half-crazed. "Stop him!"

Lochlan orbed into shimmering lights, and got behind Zeph, grabbing him by the neck. "Hold still," Lochlan said, trying to keep him from advancing on the group. "Hold still."

Zeph tried to wrestle free and then he...stopped...like he had simply given up...his eyes narrowing, focusing on the flames of the fire. Arwyn followed his line of sight, trying to understand what was happening. It was like he was somewhere else entirely. He spoke to someone who wasn't there. Said things... reacted to things no one else could see but him.

Silence fell like snowflakes around the celebration and everyone stood around like shadows, shaped only by their thoughts, yet unable to comprehend any of them.

Zeph seemed so small, so helpless. He fell into a heap on the ground, and when he began to cry, Arwyn cried with him.

Favián stayed with her. Every move she made closer to Zeph, he made as well.

"It hurts to remember," Zeph whispered.

"Zeph," Elin said softly, approaching with caution. She touched his arm and he howled like she had burned him.

"Don't touch me!"

"All right, I won't touch you," she said.

"Don't touch me. Don't touch me. Don't touch me." His hands shook as he wrapped his arms around himself. Then his red-rimmed eyes shot to hers and he blinked. He looked around, his eyes widening in disbelief. "How did I get here?"

"Zeph," Elin said, trepidation in her voice.

Everyone stared at him as he crumbled in on himself like he was made of paper.

"Don't let them touch me," he said when he found his sister's eyes. "Please." Tears fell, like silver drops of dew, down his cheeks. "Don't let them touch me."

Elin knelt before him, her own hands trembling to comfort him, to touch him, but she didn't, she couldn't. "I won't let anyone touch you. I promise. No one will touch you." Elin glanced at Arwyn, her features contorted like she physically hurt. "What do I do?" she whispered.

Arwyn's chin quivered. "You're doing it. He feels better when you're near. Just stay with him." Then she turned to Searly. "Please, if you will, we should leave them alone. I know Zeph, and he wouldn't want everyone staring at him when he realizes…" She swallowed. "He wouldn't want an audience to this."

"Aye." But Searly seemed to fight the instinct within him to stay, to nurture. "If you need me," he said, looking at Lochlan and Elin, and then to Arwyn, "come get me." Then Searly turned to Favián, "You coming?"

"Sí," Favián said. "Arwyn? We need to talk."

Arwyn sucked in a breath. "Can we talk later? I-I need to lie down."

Favián's hand shot out and grabbed Arwyn by the elbow. "Do you feel faint? Do you need me to walk you to your chamber?"

"Our bedchambers are across from each other, Favi. You may walk with me if you wish."

Favián kept stealing glances at Arwyn as he walked with her. He wanted badly to ask her how she knew about Zeph. What her powers were. He held back from asking, however, but he couldn't hold back from worrying, from caring.

"You will be all right?" he asked as he deposited her outside her door.

"Of course," she said.

"Arwyn," he hedged. "Talk to me."

"I'm really tired. We'll talk tomorrow," she said, slipping into her room with haste and closing the door behind her.

Once inside, Arwyn sat on the bed, curled her knees up to her chest, and cried as quietly as she could, unable to hold herself together a moment longer. She had felt Zeph's hurt. She had felt his sorrow. The agony of it…

Oh God, the *agony* of it.

Arwyn quickly reached for the chamber pot and heaved her supper into it. She cried through the heaving, then she heaved through the sobbing.

"I have you," came a low, friendly voice, pushing back her hair and running a cool cloth over her face. "There, now, I have you. Shh. It will be all right. Just lean on me. I have you."

"Favi," Arwyn said, her voice but a whisper of itself.

"Shh, *mi corazoncito.*" He rocked her gently, back and forth, with her cheek resting on his chest. "I'm here," he murmured. "Try to rest. I won't leave you."

Arwyn closed her eyes, but there would be no rest. Her heart kept whispering…*who is holding Zeph tonight?*

And the answer was no one.

Because she knew that Zeph would never let anyone hold him.

"My God," she breathed, her fist knotting Favián's tunic as a fresh new wave of grief crashed over her. "*My God.*"

Now she knew why. Tonight, she had caught a glimpse of Zeph's past.

And it was horrifying.

10

For a long minute, Elin just watched her brother. He was no longer fitful and restless, at least

for the moment. He was still, quiet. *Utterly beautiful* rang in her head as she stroked his cheek with the back of her fingers. His face smooth, angular, precision-made, like he had been sculpted by hand. His skin the color of alabaster. She hadn't had a moment to really look upon him until now, never in one place long enough, or if he was, he was in constant motion. She may never have an opportunity again to study him, to *know* him. And oh, how she wanted to know all the things that made up the man he was.

She closed her eyes, hoping to see a memory of his. Her gift was seeing happy memories of others. From Zeph, all she saw was darkness. And then… tiny dots appeared, flickering, like lamps just lit. She concentrated harder, trying to pull the image closer. Not dots. Stars.

"Zeph," she whispered, lying down beside him, curling herself protectively around him. She began to gingerly stroke his hair.

"Elin, what are you doing?"

"Letting him know he's not alone," she said.

"You promised you wouldn't touch him," Lochlan said. Her eyes shot to his. "I know you mean well, but if he wakes, he may not…you don't know how he will respond," he said, treating his words ever so delicately, like they were made of eggshells. Or maybe he was treating her that way.

Her eyes drifted back to her brother, where her fingers continued the slow ministrations through his ivory hair. "Do you know," she said, "how many times I wished to touch you before the curse was broken? How many nights I lay awake thinking about holding you, comforting you?" She closed her eyes, biting back the sting of tears…her nose tingling, and her throat burning. "I couldn't comfort you, Lochlan, for so long. I can comfort my brother. He needs me. I can feel it in the marrow of my bones."

"Yes, he does. And you will be here for him. But you must not do what you promised him you wouldn't. If you want him to trust you."

"I want to hold him."

"I know," Lochlan said tenderly.

"He will never let me hold him when he wakes. This is my only chance."

Lochlan moved to the edge of the bed, the side where Elin lay. As she stroked her brother's hair, he stroked hers. "Honor, Elin," he said, quietly. "We must honor our promises. Even when it hurts us to do so."

A beat…and then… "I can't make myself move," she said.

Lochlan bent down and scooped up his love. "You can hold *me*," he whispered in her ear. He carried her to a chair in the far corner of the room and sat her on his lap, his arms wrapping securely around her. "You can hold me."

Zeph opened his eyes. His sister's presence was a palpable thing. He was thankful for it and that thankfulness drew him up tight, and for the briefest of moments, Zeph held his breath as he listened to hers.

Slowly, Zeph turned his head toward her. Her back was to him. She stared out the window while he stared at her. Her voice had been the one to cut through the fog of his visions the night before. Or was it still the same night? It was dark out, not a sliver of light, save for the moon and one flickering candle on the windowsill. She stared at the pearl in the sky, fixated on it, as though it was the one firm object in a chaotic, disordered world. Perhaps it was. All Zeph knew was that he was glad for her presence. He had hoped she would be there when he awoke. His heart ached, like a tiny fist had squeezed it. He didn't deserve her, and yet here she was.

"Do you feel better?" she asked without looking back.

He turned his head and stared at the ceiling. "I don't know how I feel." *But I feel better with you near. Why?*

"I'm so sorry," she murmured, her back still facing him.

"Why are you sorry?" he asked, his voice rough and a bit raw.

She shook her head, folding her arms across her chest as though she were hugging herself. "Where to start? I'm sorry for whatever happened to you—for what happened to you as a child. I'm just…so sorry, Zeph." She turned to him then. She looked so young, so hopeless. "Tell me how to help you now. Tell me what I can do, and I will do it."

He felt a sharp poke in his chest.

He sat up slowly, bringing his legs to the floor, and pressed the heels of his hands onto the bed. "You being here is enough."

"Is it?" she asked, facing him.

"Yes. More than I deserve."

"I am your sister."

He nodded. "You are."

"I will always be your sister."

He nodded again.

"And you will always be my brother."

"I am not the brother I once was."

"No," she said. "You're not. Nor am I the sister I once was. But siblings we still are. *Twins*, even."

"Good and evil," Zeph said remotely.

"No," she said. "I don't think of it as that."

"You should," Zeph said. "It is what we are." It was what he had become. Evil. Through the night, he had walked through his memories, the spell forcing him to go where he had not wanted to venture. He swallowed, nearly choking on his emotions.

He remembered all of it, even why he had cast the spell, what had prompted a child to do something so desperate. Why it hadn't worked until now was the mystery. When it was too late.

Zeph stood and began careful steps to the door. He felt worn, frayed at the edges, and if truth be known, he felt the lingering effects of his memory. He paused at the door, laid his right palm against it and pinched his eyes closed.

"Where are you going?"

"To the bathing room," he croaked. He felt dirty. The need to wash the filth from his skin was all too familiar.

"Can we please talk?"

"I need to be alone." He opened his eyes and then he opened the door.

"Zeph—"

"Don't," he said. "Don't ask me to tell you what happened." He couldn't bear it.

"I...all right," she said. "Shall I wait for you here?"

"No. Go to bed, Elin. I'm fine."

"Zeph."

"I'm fine," he said once more, and left to find the bathing room before he risked falling to pieces in front of her all over again.

Once he entered the hallway, he made it only a couple of steps before his knees went weak. He caught himself by bracing his hands on the wall. As a child, he had endured so much abuse for so long. And when he could no longer endure it, he had finally given in to the Unseelie. He had known when he pledged himself to them that he would lose himself, forget himself; even most of his powers would be forgotten. The Unseelie would mold him to their legion. He would become a monster like them. He had known this. So, at a moment when he was alone, before his pledge, he had cast a spell. If he could hold on to a sliver of himself…his innocence would call out to him through *reality, shifting,* and his memories would return and hopefully, *hopefully,* his soul would return as well. He had thought he would be strong enough. He had just wanted the torture to stop.

An internal scream lit within him like a fuse and he ignited into a flame of grief all over again as two images formed in his mind.

Two graves.

His parents.

Dead. By his hands.

He had not been strong enough.

"Put your arm around my shoulders," a female voice said.

Zeph blinked, confused, feeling soft hands band around his waist. He should have felt repulsed by the touch. He didn't. He knew the voice. There was nothing repulsive about the owner of it.

"Arwyn," he croaked, letting her drape his arm around her slim shoulders. He leaned into her, feeling guilty about doing so. She was so small, and he was much larger than she. Surely, she couldn't hold him up.

"Let's get you to that bathing room."

His feet seemed to move on their own accord even as his mind fought to stay put. "How did you know that was my destination?"

"I lived in your keep for quite some time. I know you. When you are upset, that is where you go."

The corner of his mouth tipped up a fraction. Whenever she was upset, she liked to shoot her arrows. She likely did not know he knew that.

Once they made it to the bathing room, he expected her to depart, to leave him. She did not. She closed the door behind them, surprised to see the tub had already been filled, ready for him.

He blinked once, then twice. She cleared her throat and moved past him and repositioned the folding screen around the tub.

"What are you doing?" he asked.

Once the screen was where she thought it best, she smoothed her hands over her skirts. "Giving you a bit of privacy."

He pointed toward their point of entry. "I would have plenty if you were on the other side of that opening. It's called a door. Marvelous thing, a door."

She jutted her chin forward. "I'm not leaving."

One dark brow rose. "No?"

"No."

"I am capable of taking a bath by myself."

"I never said otherwise."

"Then why are you staying?"

"We need to talk."

"While I take a bath?"

"Yes."

"This is entirely inappropriate."

"I do not wish to make you uncomfortable. Hence the screen."

"Hence the screen," he repeated.

"Yes."

Frustration bloomed. Not for the reason he *should* be frustrated: her being in the bathing room with him—alone. But for her insistence that they talk. He did not want to talk.

"No," he said.

"No?"

"I do not wish to talk."

"Well," she said, "I do."

"Arwyn—"

"Take your bath." She turned her back to him. "Go on," she said. "The water will get cold."

He stood there, staring at her back, the moment pulling at him, irritating him, like a loose thread against his skin.

"Devil take me," he mumbled, stepping behind the screen, removing his tabard with a hard pull over his head. Once completely divested of all his clothing, he sank into the water, submerging himself, luxuriating in the feel of it. His eyes instantly drifted closed, his head finding purchase against the side of the tub, and for a full five minutes, not a single word was spoken between them.

But he could feel her—feel the residual warmth of her from when she had held her body close to his. And he could still smell the scent of her hair, sweet and earthy, like wild berries. His nostrils flared. He ducked his head underneath the water, staying there until he needed to breathe. When he emerged, he brushed back his hair with his fingers and reached for the soap, wishing the scent of wild berries did not suddenly consume his thoughts. He supposed he should be thankful for the distraction, at least.

"I have a secret to tell you," Arwyn said, cutting through the sound of sloshing water.

Zeph paused lathering soap over his left arm. "Pardon?"

"You won't like it, I'm afraid." Her voice sounded less sure than it had only moments ago.

"I'm listening," he said, uncertain.

"Finish washing. I need to get my thoughts together."

Slowly, Zeph returned to his task and finished lathering his arm. Then he lathered the other. He washed his torso, neck, face. Then he started on his legs. He washed his entire body before he responded to her. Setting the soap back where he'd found it, he leaned against the tub once again and closed his eyes.

"Tell me your secret, Arwyn." He didn't care what her secret was. He was just glad she chose him to tell it. And if her secret would give him a moment not to have to think on his own, then more reason for him to listen.

"Please don't be mad," she whispered.

Zeph's eyes opened. He sat up, finding her shadow behind the screen, sitting on a chair, her spine curved, not straight and sure, as was her usual way of sitting.

"Why would I be mad?" he asked, feeling nervousness settle underneath his skin.

"Because I never told you."

"Did I ever ask?"

"No."

"Then why would I be mad, Arwyn?"

When she didn't answer, he prompted again. "Arwyn?"

"I'm an empath."

Zeph swallowed. "So you—"

"Internalize the feelings and pain of others."

He let that sink in. *Internalize the feelings and pain of others…the feelings and pain of others…the feelings and pain.* His eyes followed her as she stood from her chair, a silhouette behind the screen.

"Your heart is racing," she said so softly. If he hadn't been Fae, he probably wouldn't have heard her.

Zeph's hand covered the thumping organ. "You know my heartbeats?"

Arwyn laid her palm flat on the screen. "Sometimes," she said, "I don't know if they are yours or mine."

"What does that mean?" he asked. She was confusing him. And maybe scaring him a little. *How much about him did she know?*

She turned away from him. His eyes stayed fixed on her silhouette. "Zeph, I…"

"What do you know, Arwyn?" he hedged.

"I know you are not a monster."

"Then you know nothing."

"I know what they did to you."

He started to stand, to go to her, to turn her around, make her look him in the eye, and then remembered he was naked. He wasn't sure he could trust himself to stand anyway. "*What* do you know?"

"Zeph…" she said, her voice thick as porridge. "I'm so sorry."

"What do you know, Arwyn?"

She was quiet for so long that Zeph thought she would never answer. Finally, she spoke. "Remember when I said that one day, you would tell me how you got those scars? And when you did, I would listen?"

"Yes," Zeph said, his eyes fluttering with emotion.

"Tonight…" She paused, her voice cracking on the word. "I listened to every single word."

Zeph's head was spinning. "I told you nothing. I said nothing."

"Somehow," she said, "I could see it all through your eyes."

"What?" Zeph felt ill. Violently ill. He wrapped his left arm around the lip of the tub, brought his left leg up and over, and tumbled onto the floor.

Arwyn startled. "Zeph!"

"Don't…" Zeph croaked. "Don't come near me."

Zeph reached for the linens neatly folded and stacked beside his head and wrapped one around him haphazardly.

"Zeph, please…"

"No, stay where you are." He pushed himself up, slipped on the water puddled on the floor, and caught himself with a funny twist of his arm. He suppressed a growl in his throat, but he could not suppress his fangs from descending. Panic blackened the edges of his vision. "Don't come anywhere near me."

She knew?

She knew?

Zeph wanted to scream. She had no right knowing his secrets—his *shame*.

"Stay away from me," he said, feeling betrayed. Then he did what Zeph always did. He let the shadows take him away.

Arwyn bit down on her trembling lip while she stared at the puddle on the empty floor. *I'm sorry. I'm sorry for knowing. I'm sorry for telling you.*

She had made a hash of her confession.

She had to tell Zeph, though. He had to know. It was not something she could keep from him. And part of her had hoped he would have been relieved that someone knew—that he wouldn't have to say the words— and that someone else in the world had known what he'd been through—that he wasn't alone.

I'm sorry you had to suffer it.

She should have known how much he would hate her knowing.

11

*I*n another land, once home to Zeph...to Elin...to Arwyn...another son bowed his head and stared down at two marked graves. Light cut through the hazy vault above like icicles. A sinuous mist caressed the ground.

The son smiled, an ugly twist of his mouth, as he heard footsteps approaching from behind. Not waiting to be greeted, he asked, "Did you find them?"

"Yes, Your Highness."

"And?"

"The hound attacked as you instructed."

"And how did our Zeph react?"

The Unseelie grinned. "Exactly as you suspected. He defended and protected the elf girl. He killed our hound soundly."

The son turned sharp eyes on the Captain of the Unseelie Army, who had been his father's captain. "My parents were fools to think they could make him one of us. I want Zeph dead. And I want his sister dead. As long as they live, Faery will never be mine to rule." He gave his focus back to the two *empty* holes in the ground. "Their graves have already been dug."

"That won't be easy, Your Highness. Their powers—"

"Have been weakened," the son interjected. "Now is the time to strike."

The captain was uncertain, though he dared not question his king. "What is your plan, Your Highness?"

"We set a trap."

"A trap?"

A wicked smile stole across the son's mouth. "Yes. We have been much too quiet. It is time we make some noise."

"What about the others? The half-breed and the elf girl?"

The son shrugged. "Kill the half-breed. But I want the girl. I want Zeph to know that I will make her mine." He bent down and ran a blunt finger across one of the markers, the one with Zeph's name. "Just before I kill him."

12

On the fourth day after Arwyn's confession to Zeph, she sat in the garden, watching the sun rise, sleepy and pink, as it yawned its way across the meadow. After Zeph had left her alone in the bathing room, she had kept to herself. As Zeph had kept to himself. Neither seeking out the other. They were two souls, clinging to the edge, white-knuckling the jagged protrusions of their emotions that cut too deep and left more scars behind.

But what were a few more scars?

She closed her eyes, but all she could see was the night she had glimpsed the unspeakable violence done to Zeph when he was a boy. She was swarmed with his rioting emotions when she had told him that she knew. All she had wanted to do was *reach* for him—comfort him. And he had left her…alone. She couldn't blame him. She felt his confusion, his heartache. Even now, she could feel him. She leaned forward, bracing her elbows on her knees, and pressed the heel of her hands into her eyes, her breath shaking with every exhalation.

"Arwyn?"

Arwyn abruptly sat up and turned in the direction of the voice, clasping one hand over her breast. "Elin," she said breathlessly. "You startled me."

Elin apologized. "I didn't intend to." She pointed to a spot on the bench beside Arwyn, unoccupied. "May I sit with you?"

"Of course," Arwyn said, dabbing at her eyes, hoping Elin didn't notice. She had purposely avoided everyone since that night, needing to distance herself from their emotions. Zeph's were more than she could handle—exceedingly more.

"I haven't seen you for days," Elin said, watching the sun crest over the horizon.

Arwyn could feel Elin's sadness. Ordinarily, she would want to mend the rift. As it was, all she could manage was a feeble, "I'm sorry."

"Don't be sorry. I'm just worried about you."

"I am not the one you need to be worried about."

"Are you certain?" Elin asked, casting Arwyn a side glance.

"I don't know what you mean."

Elin turned to face her, softness in her silver eyes, and something else. Understanding? Then Elin smiled, and it was reminiscent of the sunrise: a quiet, slow, pink expanse across the plains of her face, unhurried and quite beautiful. But there was a sadness underneath it.

"Is there anything you wish to tell me, Arwyn?"

Arwyn shifted in her seat. "Tell you?"

"Yes. Anything you wish to say? Confide? Friend to friend?"

Arwyn looked toward the sun and closed her eyes once more. It felt like a warm palm against her face. She allowed its warmth for a moment before standing and turning away from it, feeling like she didn't deserve the comfort. She had told no one of her ability—that she was an empath. It was too much of a violation, and she had already hurt Zeph with her truth. She couldn't hurt Elin, too. She couldn't lose another, and she most certainly would if Elin knew how often Arwyn had tapped into her emotions without consent. She fought the tears that threatened to spill and shook her head.

"You forget," Elin said. "I can see a person's happiest memories, and I have seen yours."

Arwyn turned to face her. "What?" She searched her memories, trying to capture a happy one.

"Surprised?"

"I am, rather." The only ones Arwyn remembered were the ones that brought her grief. "Tell me what you have seen."

Elin lifted a brow. "All the days your father taught you *Nyokou*."

Arwyn's legs felt wooden. "You...you know about that?"

"I have no more control over the memories I capture than you do over the emotions that you feel from others. We are not all that different, you and I."

"I didn't realize that was a happy memory. I..." Her voice trailed off, her eyes skimming over the tops of trees. There was a warm breeze at her back, blowing her lavender hair forward, obstructing her view. She thought about all the hours her father had spent with her, instructing her, teaching her strength and control. Her mouth curved into a smile. Of course it was a happy memory. It was time spent with her father. Time she would give anything to have back.

"You haven't had anyone tell you how special you are in a long, long time, Arwyn. I want you to know, I think you are truly special indeed."

"Don't," Arwyn said, remembering the look on Zeph's face, *feeling* the betrayal he had felt. She had robbed him of his mind, stripped him of his emotions. She took that which did not belong to her. "Don't say that."

What she had done was infinitely more personal than knowing someone's happiest memory. She had seen his deepest, darkest secrets. And for the life of her, she didn't know why or how. Although she had done it before—when he was on the mountain and he had poisoned himself. Both times had been when Zeph was in utter despair...defenseless...ravished with grief and pain. Arwyn had been ravished with it as well and had somehow fallen in with him, pulling her under, until she was drowning in his agony. She could no more pull herself out of it than he could.

A cold sweat trickled down Arwyn's spine. *Nyokou* had not prepared her for this. This was…

"Love…" Elin said. "It is the power behind your powers. It is what propels you. It is what moves you. And you love my brother."

Arwyn's eyes snapped to Elin's. "What?" she asked with a rasp.

"I see how you look at him." Her voice lowered. "And I see how he looks at you."

Arwyn shook her head. "I think he hates me now."

Elin closed the distance between them and took Arwyn by the hand. "Zeph is capable of many things. Hating you isn't one of them."

"I wouldn't be so sure."

"What happened?"

"Oh, Elin," she said, "I wouldn't even know where to begin."

"That night with Zeph. You…know what happened to him, don't you?"

Arwyn looked away from Elin's prying eyes. "Why would you say that?"

"I spoke to Favián."

Arwyn swallowed. "I see. What did he tell you?"

"He told me what happened in your chambers, how you became ill. He's quite worried about you. And you're avoiding him, as you have avoided us all for several days."

"I'm sorry."

"I'm not looking for an apology. I just want to know how I can help. I know your abilities, Arwyn. Do you know what happened to him?" When Arwyn didn't immediately respond, Elin pressed further. "Do you know what happened to my brother?"

Arwyn shook her head. "I can't tell you."

"Why?"

Arwyn squeezed her eyes shut and whispered, "It is not my story to tell."

"I can't help him if I don't know."

Visions of a little white-haired boy screaming shot through Arwyn's mind and she pulled away from Elin. Clutching her arms around her middle, she said, "I cannot be the one to tell you. I cannot betray him twice. I cannot."

"Betray him? You haven't betrayed him."

"Haven't I? He did not want me to know. Yet I do. I didn't mean for it to happen." A sob escaped before Arwyn could call it back.

"No, luv, you didn't betray him," Elin said. "I think because you are—connected—that you are able to read him, *see* him, on such a deep level that—"

"It doesn't matter," Arwyn said. "I hurt him." Tears welled in her eyes and brushed down her cheeks. "I feel it. Right here," she said, hand over her heart. "And it hurts *me* to know that I did that, because I had promised him that I would *heal* him."

"Oh, Arwyn," Elin said, pulling her into a hug. "You carry the world's emotions on your shoulders. Who is going to carry yours for you?"

Long minutes passed with neither speaking. Instead, they watched the sun rise high into the sky, the pink fading into a warm yellow glow, shining down as if there were no death, or evil, or heartache. How nice that would be if it were so.

Sometime later, they got up and walked off together. Their problems had not been solved, though perhaps their friendship had been strengthened.

Zeph waited a few more minutes before stepping out from behind the bushes. He stared in the direction Elin and Arwyn had gone, his sister's words whispering in his ears.

"You carry the world's emotions on your shoulders. Who is going to carry yours for you?"

Elin had stared directly at him, over Arwyn's shoulder. She had known all along he was there. Elin hadn't just been speaking to Arwyn. She had been speaking to him as well.

He sat on the bench and thought about what had been said. Arwyn was an empath. How had he never known? He leaned forward and scrubbed his hands over his face.

How had he never known?

Zeph journeyed the grounds around the monastery, keeping his head down, hair tied back from his face in a neat queue, hands behind his back. He had not spoken to anyone since the incident, the one that lingered on everyone's mind and filled them with questions never asked aloud. He passed several monks, who gave him a wide berth, but he noticed they did not avoid looking at him as they normally did. Once or twice he caught a sympathetic eye, a polite nod, though no words were ever spoken. Not to him. There was still fear among them. He frightened them. For that reason, Zeph maintained a respectable distance. He did not blame them for their trepidation. He had earned it, after all.

For the duration of the afternoon, Zeph walked in silence, trying not to think about his parents, unable to keep them from his thoughts.

Don't do this, Son. Please. You don't know what you're doing!

When he found himself at their graves, his knees hit the dirt. "Mother. Father. I'm so sorry." The words were an inelegant, strangled sound. "If I could go back…" He tried concentrating on the names on the crosses as he spoke, but they became a watery blur in front of him. "If I could just go back, I wouldn't have done it."

He wouldn't have pledged his fealty to the Unseelie. If he had never done so, his parents would still be alive. He may be dead instead, but he rather thought that was how it should have been. Perhaps he should have never been born at all.

"You cannot change the past."

Zeph closed his eyes as Searly came around and sat beside him on the ground. Searly's tone had been neither confrontational nor judgmental. Simply matter-of-fact.

"No, I cannot," Zeph answered.

"The fact that you want to undo your misdeeds gives me great hope. You may not have the power to undo your sins. You do have the power to change, Zeph."

"It is too late for me."

"As long as you breathe, it is never too late."

"Spoken like a true man of the cloth. You, who have never done a misdeed in your life."

Searly turned to face Zeph then, sadness brushing the edges of his brown eyes. "I came mightily close to breaking my vows once. The temptation was so great, so overpowering, I would have done anything to have one moment..." Searly looked away, breaking off his words with a hiss.

"Lolith," Zeph whispered, remembering the moment of which Searly spoke.

Searly gave a curt nod. "So consumed with lust I was that I cared not a whit about my vows."

"Nothing happened," Zeph said. "You didn't—"

"*Not* because I was strong enough to resist. As I recall, I was bound by a magical worm that prevented me from being able to move."

Zeph didn't want to talk about Lolith. He knew all too well the spells she wielded on her victims, for he, too, had been her victim. He hated her. *Hated* what she had done to him. Zeph looked away, staring off into the forest beyond. "I wouldn't have let her touch you," Zeph said quietly.

Zeph could feel Searly's eyes shift toward him. "Indeed, you did not."

A moment passed where neither spoke. The sun was beginning to set. Soon it would be dark, and Zeph was anxiously anticipating it. Darkness was his friend. His home.

"What are the things you care about, Zeph?"

Without even thinking, Zeph answered, "I care about my sister. I care about Arwyn." He smiled wanly. Betrayed or no, he cared for Arwyn. How could he not? Elin was right. He was capable of many things. Hating Arwyn wasn't one of them.

"Is that all?" Searly asked.

Zeph chuffed, "They are everything."

"You're leaving someone out."

"Who?"

"Yourself."

"I'm not—"

"What is your story, Zeph? How will it be written?"

Zeph chuffed again and came to a stand. He pointed to the graves. "This is my story. It's already been written."

"No," Searly said, coming to a stand as well. "Those are crosses you must bear. And you will bear them. But they are only a part of your story. What is the rest of it?"

Zeph stared at the monk, blinking. "I-I don't know."

"Aye. Because it hasn't been written yet. Go write it, Zeph. Give yourself the story worthy of your parents. If you owe them anything, you owe them that."

"Zeph," Favián said, his mouth twisting into a wry smile.

To his credit, Zeph didn't startle, though it was easy to deduce the anger that snaked along Zeph's veins to see Favián in his bedchamber in the dead of night.

"Let yourself in, did you?" Zeph asked as he closed the door behind him, not at all gently.

Favián shrugged, relaxing in a chair next to the bed. "Thought perhaps I'd repay the visit. You don't mind, do you?"

Zeph did mind. It was as plain as the nose on his face, but he wouldn't give Favián the satisfaction. "Of course not. I hope I didn't make you wait long. I know how you fear the dark."

Favián grinned, like a cat who got the cream. Hand to chest, he said, "He's worried about me. Wait until I tell *Tío*."

It was hard to see—it really was rather dark—but Favián would have wagered everything he owned that he saw Zeph smile...just a little.

"What do you want?" Zeph asked, removing his robe, discarding it at the foot of the bed.

Favián was surprised to see simple clothing underneath: white tunic, white breeches, white boots with sharp, pointed toes. He watched Zeph fill a cup with water at a side table before he answered. "I am here because of Arwyn."

The cup hovered at Zeph's lips. "What about Arwyn?"

Favián leaned forward, all joking aside. Like Zeph, Favián had learned how to skirt the edges when he didn't want to be seen or noticed. And no one noticed Favián lurking in a monastery full of shadows. Over the past days, he had watched over Arwyn like the brother he had promised her he could be. He had to, for she was not accepting his visits. She left her room in wee hours to avoid him, to avoid everyone. She was growing paler, and everything about her seemed so...fragile. Something needed to be done. "You need to talk to her."

Zeph drank the water. He put the cup down then opened the door. "Get out."

Favián stood, met Zeph eye to eye. "Talk to her."

"Is there something wrong with your human ears? I said get out."

"Is there something wrong with your big Fae ears? I said *talk to her*."

Zeph's jaw twitched.

Favián shook his head, forcing back his own irritation. "She's not eating. I doubt she's sleeping. I know you care about her. Forget about me, *compadre*. This has nothing to do with me. Talk to her because *she needs you to talk to her*."

Zeph's eyes fluttered and then fixated on a spot somewhere over Favián's right shoulder.

Favián gritted his teeth. "She needs you."

13

rwyn shivered in her bed. She pulled the coverlet tighter around her, hoping to chase the chill away. She couldn't find warmth. She needed a fire. Yes, a warm, toasty fire was what she needed. Wrapping the coverlet around her, she exited her chamber and ambled down the barely lit halls toward the communal room where a fire burned low in the hearth.

No one was about, everyone abed. Except for her, of course. She couldn't sleep. The one time she had drifted off, she had awoken drenched in sweat and tears, reliving all that she had seen that fateful night. She had not dared to try for sleep again. Not so soon after. Not yet.

She curled up into the chair closest to the fire, bare feet tucked neatly underneath her chemise, and she concentrated on the tepid warmth the fire provided. Still, she shivered.

"You should eat something," Zeph said, his voice as cool as water over lichen-covered rocks.

Arwyn's heart lurched at seeing him standing in the doorway, holding a bowl of thick stew. Her stomach rolled, nerves most likely the cause. "I'm not hungry," she said, having lost her appetite days ago.

He walked toward her, stopping directly in front of her. His eyes were unreadable. "You should eat something anyway." He extended the bowl to her, expecting her to take it, and for a minute, all she could do was stare at it, the steam licking over the top in an elegant dance. It was warm, and her hands were cold, so she reached for it, instantly appreciating the heat.

"Thank you," she said.

For a moment, Zeph stood over her, observing.

"What?" she asked.

"Eat," he said.

"I'm warming my hands first."

"You're cold?"

"Yes."

Zeph turned to the fire and waved his hand at it. The fire hissed to life with a whoosh. Arwyn felt the heat on her skin immediately.

"Now eat," he said, finding purchase in the chair beside her.

Arwyn ate tentatively, chewing slowly, sopping the bread, which Zeph had made sure to include, into the warm bisque. When she'd had her fill, she placed the bowl on the table beside her.

"Better?" Zeph asked. He had remained silent while she ate, keeping his eyes on the fire.

"I think so," she answered. He was speaking to her. She felt better about that anyway.

"I was raped." Zeph's voice was low, quiet. Honest.

Arwyn turned to face him, surprised he had said the words aloud. She had made it so he would never have to say them, at least not to her. But here he was...saying them anyway. Her eyes misted. "I know," she said, just as low, just as quiet, and just as honest.

"For years," he continued, still staring into the flames. Then he looked at her briefly before focusing on something just over her shoulder. "By monsters." His eye twitched, like he felt the memory and he was doing his best to hold himself as regal as a king. "They even looked like monsters."

Arwyn remained where she was, afraid the slightest movement would set off Zeph's defenses. But oh, how she wanted to dive into his arms and hold him. She would never ever let him go.

"Sometimes I wonder..." He paused. "...if I had just died—if the world would have been better off."

"No," Arwyn said with certainty. "I, for one, would not be here without you."

His eyes found hers then. He looked at her like she was the one bright spot in all the world. "I am glad for that, my sweet. The world certainly needs you. It would be cold and empty without you in it."

"Do you?" Arwyn asked.

"Do I what?"

"Need me?"

"I would be cold and empty without you, too." His lips quirked. "Rather, colder and emptier than I already am."

"Zeph—"

He held up his hand. "It took me quite some time to gather the nerve to say this. Allow me to finish. Please."

Arwyn nodded. "All right."

He stood and wandered over toward the window and stared out. He did that a lot, Arwyn realized. He had done so for as long as she'd known him. She sat quietly and waited for him to speak. Aside from the faint glow of the moon and the sprinkling of stars, the crackling fire was their everything: their heat, their light, and the only sound in the room.

"I held out for as long as I could. I swear it," he said. "They were relentless." Zeph placed his palm flat against the glass pane. "I knew I would die there. It was just a matter of time. There were days when I hoped it would be my last.

And then…there were days when I wanted to live to see all of them brought to their knees…by my hand. I wanted to live so I could avenge myself. I knew that unless I pledged fealty to the Unseelie, I would not live long enough for that to happen. I knew I would lose myself. I knew I would become one of them. I knew that I would be susceptible to their lies. I knew it. But I thought…" He paused. "I thought I had figured out a way to save myself." He glanced at Arwyn over his shoulder. "I cast a spell." He went back to staring out the window, his fingers idly drawing on the pane. Arwyn wiped the stray tears that had fallen. "Obviously, something went awry. I didn't do it right. I don't know. But I lost myself. I think we can all agree to that. I became a monster." He dropped his hand and backed away from the window. "And I killed my parents. It's a miracle I didn't manage to kill my sister, too."

Arwyn was up and out of her chair and embracing Zeph before he had time to comprehend how an elf had wrapped herself around him so thoroughly. She held him as tightly as she could. His arms were at his sides, unsure what to do with them. When she realized the awkwardness of the moment, she pulled back and stepped away.

"I'm sorry," she said, dabbing her eyes with the cuff of her sleeve. "I'm sorry I ever called you a coward. You are not a coward." She shook her head vehemently. "You are brave. So, so brave. You were just a boy and y-you did the only thing you could do. They tried to destroy you, but they couldn't. I-I…" Her voice trailed off as her eyes caught his. He was staring at her…as if he'd been thunderstruck. "What?"

For a moment, Zeph was still, motionless, like a tree rooted in the ground. He took in the sight of her, in her chemise, backlit by the fire. "I think you could destroy me in an entirely different way, Arwyn."

She took in the sight of him, too. Without his robe, she could see the shape of him, broad shoulders, slim waist, long, lean legs. He was beautiful. He had always been beautiful to her. But now that she knew his past, knew what had made him what he came to be, how life had molded him, he wasn't just beautiful to her. He was everything she thought he could be. "I can't destroy you, Zeph."

He closed his eyes and exhaled deeply through his nose. "Ah, my sweet, I believe you already have. Piece by piece."

She moved then, until she was standing only inches from him. "That's not destroying. That's rebuilding."

His eyes popped open, and in them, she saw flames. Desire. *He desired her.* Suddenly, she was overwhelmed by it. "Your heart is beating so fast," she whispered.

"You know my heartbeats." This time it had not been a question.

She nodded. "Sometimes...I don't know if they are yours or mine."

"You should finish it," he whispered.

She tilted her head, confused. "Finish what?"

He cradled her face, his thumbs drying her wayward tears. "Tear me down, build me back up again. Make me something new. Something else. Something other than what I've become."

"Tell me how and I will do it."

That's when he kissed her. Arwyn gasped at the suddenness of it. His lips were hard, demanding. *Desperate.* It was the kiss of a man grasping for something. He ate at her mouth like he was starving for affection, and when he coaxed her to open for him and felt the stroke of his tongue against hers, Arwyn was swarmed once again with emotion. Hers. His. And she met him, stroke for stroke, until she knew not her own name. She was caught up in the storm of him, tumbling and rolling and then he was—gone.

He was across the room, cursing himself, fists at his temples. It was a feat for Arwyn to stay upright, for she was disoriented. She tried to calm the fluttering in her chest, to no avail.

"Zeph," she rasped.

He marched toward her. Stopped. Reached for her. Stopped. He shook his head. "I'm sorry. I shouldn't have done that. I'm sorry."

"You're apologizing?"

"Yes. No. I…bloody hell! I don't know what the right thing to do is."

"Well, don't apologize!"

He clamped his mouth shut.

"Why did you stop?" she asked.

Zeph scrubbed his hands over his face, then settled them on his hips. "I don't know. The last thing I want to do is hurt you. I've hurt enough people in my life."

"You weren't hurting me."

"But I have," he said softly. "In the last few days alone. Look what I've done to you." Arwyn shook her head, but he continued. "You weren't eating. You aren't sleeping." He slapped his hand over his chest. "That's my fault."

"Zeph—"

"I'm sorry." He backed away. "I care too much for you. What just happened between us—it will never happen again. Goodnight, Arwyn. Get some rest."

"Zeph!"

"If you care about me at all, please, try to sleep. I need one less thing on my conscience. Please."

Arwyn bit back words and tears and looked away from the haunted look in Zeph's eyes. She gave him one magnanimous nod.

"Thank you."

Then he left the room. But why did it feel like he was leaving her too?

14

Zeph had run from the communal room—from Arwyn—from himself. Mostly he ran from the things he felt when he had kissed her. Things he had never felt before. A cacophony of zings and flutters, and the distinct feeling he was falling—heart in his throat and fear in his gut. He had broken the kiss, separating himself from the source of his discomfiture, and immediately swore upon doing so. His heart only pounded harder at the loss.

But he was bad for her. Surely, she knew that. And if he hadn't left that room posthaste, he wasn't certain he would be able to.

So he ran. With every slap of boot to stone, Zeph grunted another curse. He cursed his past, his choices, all the rotten, evil things he had ever done. It would have been easier to dissolve into shadows, but he wanted the pain of exertion, his muscles and lungs screaming in protest. He ran so fast and so hard, the need to cast up his accounts became central to his thoughts.

When he came to a set of double doors, he burst through them, shoving them closed with his body and letting the weight of his troubles sink him to the floor. He lifted his knees, rested his forearms on them, and let his head fall back on the unforgiving wood. He took deep, gulping breaths and closed his eyes. Arwyn's face immediately came into sharp focus. Her pert nose, her brilliant, blue eyes, and pink, swollen lips that had been thoroughly kissed. He had thought he could run away from her, but here she was, buried in his thoughts and coursing through his veins.

"You realize you are in the chapel?" came a low, whispered voice.

Zeph's eyes opened, surprised to find he was not alone. For the first time, he took in his surroundings. He stared down an aisle, bench seating on either side, that led to an altar. Candles were lit and incense burned, emitting a cloying aroma of woody, earthy smoke with an undertone of sweetness. It filled his head as if he had swum through thick plumes of it. A pleasant scent, he realized. Ethereal in a way. He closed his eyes again, trying to breathe as silently as possible because, for the first time since bursting through the doors, he felt a calming effect take hold.

He had almost forgotten someone else was there until he heard the rustling of a wool habit and near-quiet footsteps coming toward him. Zeph looked up. Xavier was observing him, a few steps away, with suspicious eyes. Zeph remained still, unthreatening.

The suspicion shifted to anger. "I followed you. Yesterday. You were heading into the forest and I wanted to know what you were doing. You didn't walk far. You came to a tree and sat underneath it." Xavier's voice was low and bitter. Zeph had done nothing the day before, so he was unsure what the monk was going on about. Zeph's lips remained closed nonetheless. He had earned Xavier's scorn. "I thought about killing you." Zeph lifted two dark brows at that. "You don't think I can?" Xavier asked.

"No," Zeph said. "I do not." It wasn't blustering that made him say it. It was honesty. Because he hoped Xavier wouldn't attempt to try it. He didn't want to fight him.

Xavier laughed. There was a bit of darkness to it, and Zeph found himself observing Xavier more closely. "I'm not daft. I know I can't kill you. But that was the thing of it. If I attacked you, and you killed me fending me off, they would only know that you killed another monk. Would they believe you, do you think, if you told them the truth? That I attacked you first?"

Zeph was a master at hiding his thoughts, his feelings. His countenance remained neutral. But inside, he bristled like someone had just walked over his grave. "No," he answered, "they would not believe me. Why didn't you attack?"

The anger in Xavier's eyes morphed into frustration. "I was about to. I gathered up the nerve to do it. I took the first step toward you and then a baby bird fell out of the tree and landed next to you. It startled us both, I think."

Zeph's mouth twitched at the corners. It *had* startled him. Who expected a baby bird to nearly land on one's head?

"You looked up," Xavier said. "Realized its mum had pushed it out of the nest. You looked back at the bird on the ground. I held my breath."

"Why?" Zeph asked.

Xavier looked away, staring down the aisle to the altar. "Because I had been praying for a sign," he said quietly. "Of your compassion—if you had any. Searly and Arwyn, they believe there's something in you worth saving. Even your sister believes that. They didn't see what I saw when you killed Thaddeus that day. I saw pure hate in your eyes. There was no compassion for Thaddeus when you spilled his blood."

He couldn't dispute Xavier's words. He was right. He had been filled with hate. He did spill the blood of an innocent. He couldn't undo it. Regret pressed upon him, heavy as a stone. Another cross he must bear. Another wrong he could never right.

He opened his mouth to say *something*, but anything he said at that moment would be futile.

"But then you picked up the bird, cradled it in your hand, talked to it, whispered to it, a few minutes later, you opened your hand and the bird flew away. It was practically dead before. You healed it. You healed one of God's creatures—showed it *compassion!*" Xavier hissed. And then his face fell, contorting like he'd been struck by some elemental force. "Why couldn't you have shown Thaddeus that compassion?"

Zeph swallowed thickly. *Why couldn't he indeed?*

"Nothing to say?" Xavier croaked.

Zeph closed his eyes, hating who he was…*is*. "There is *nothing* I can say. Is there?" he whispered.

Xavier shook his head. "No, I suppose not." He moved slowly, like a man who still grieved, before sitting on a wooden bench.

Long minutes went by with the two of them sitting in utter stillness, lost in their own thoughts. Zeph breathed in the incense, trying to capture that calm it had first brought him. It evaded him. Rightfully so.

"Why did you save the bird?"

The question echoed off the walls of the chapel. Or perhaps they were just echoing in Zeph's head as he searched for an answer. He recalled the scene quite vividly in his mind's eye. A tiny little thing, sickly. A castaway. A creature no one wanted. Perhaps he saw a little of himself in that bird. He had not really studied the why of it. Maybe to prove to those who had not wanted it that it could survive—thrive, even. So with a few whispered words he'd healed the bird and off it went. The feeling he had done something good for once was—even now, made his chest expand with something akin to joy.

"I don't know," Zeph answered. "It just felt like the right thing to do."

Xavier studied Zeph for a long minute. And then he rose to his feet. "I'm going to bed."

Zeph stood, removing himself from the large doors so Xavier could pass. As he was crossing the threshold, Zeph couldn't help asking, "Why didn't you attack me, fulfill your plan?"

Xavier looked him in the eye. Sadness and anger were still present in his gaze, but there was something else, too. Something that made all of Xavier's sharp edges appear a bit softer. "I don't know," Xavier answered. "It just felt like the right thing to do."

With that, Xavier walked out the door and Zeph released a long, slow breath.

Back in his chamber, Zeph lay prone on his bed, fighting sleep because sleep was not his friend. Sleep brought dreams and dreams quickly turned into night terrors. It had been this way for as long as he could remember. But even Zeph had to lie down occasionally. And yes, even sleep. Though, he fought it for as long as he could. He had tried the usual—sitting in the hard, unforgiving wooden chair in his tiny room until his backside was sore, then he stood and gazed out the window until his legs and back screamed in protest.

His eyelids started to droop, so he shifted on the bed that felt too small, forcing his eyes back open and picking a random spot on the ceiling to stare at. His eyelids pulled closed again and Zeph was unable to pry them open.

At first, Zeph was dreamless in his slumber, untroubled, his breaths slow and even. Tranquil. And then he was sitting in the communal room—Arwyn by the fire. Her lilac hair fell down her back, loose and wavy. He reached to touch it. It felt like silk in his hands. She turned to face him, her eyes sparkling like blue flames. She was so beautiful. Everything about her was beautiful to him. He knew he was dreaming, and he couldn't be bothered to care.

"Arwyn," he rasped.

"Kiss me," she whispered.

He obliged, of course. Bending over her and taking ownership of her mouth, wanting to devour every part of her. She tasted so sweet, so achingly sweet. He deepened their kiss, pulling her closer, holding her tighter.

He released her mouth long enough to worship a path to her neck only to realize he was no longer holding Arwyn in his arms, but Lolith.

He jumped back, startled, angry, confused.

"Darling," Lolith purred. *"It's me you want."* The scene changed and Zeph was

on a large bed. No longer a dream, a memory, a nightmare he'd lived. Lolith had started her seduction when he was only fifteen summers. Anger rose above the confusion. Now. But when he was a boy, he had just been confused and unaware why someone as beautiful as Lolith was seeking him out, though he had never cared for her advances. Never wanted to be touched by anyone ever again. And here she was…touching him in ways that made his insides turn to rot.

"Don't touch me," Zeph hissed.

"You like it when I touch you," Lolith said, running a long nail down his naked torso.

He tensed and gritted his teeth. "Stop."

"I taught you pleasure, young Zeph. After years of abuse. I don't hurt you. Do I?" She continued her gentle caresses and Zeph continued to hold the scream inside that threatened to rip its way out. He was powerless to stop her. Lolith was not only evil. She was a succubus and she had targeted Zeph for her own power and gains. In the end, it was her undoing, though not before she effectively ruined Zeph and everything he had ever hoped to be.

Her fingers were in his hair. She had always loved his hair. "Grow it longer," she whispered, twisting a strand around her hand and tugging on it. Hard. "I love pulling on it when I make you scream my name."

Zeph sat up with a gasp and rushed to the table in the corner that held a wash basin. He splashed water on his face several times, his hands shaking.

Lolith was dead. Lochlan had killed her. It was just a dream. She couldn't hurt him anymore.

He told himself this several times, hoping it would take root and his anger would settle, and perhaps a small bit of him still held a remnant of fear, though he pushed that down. Way, way down. He lit a lantern and picked it up, thinking of taking a walk. With it still being dark out, he caught his reflection in the window. He edged closer, noticing not his face, only the white locks that flowed gracefully over each shoulder. Setting the lantern aside, he touched his hair, like he was seeing it for the first time, letting it fall through his fingers.

He looked at his reflection again and a decision was made. Conjuring a small blade, he began to slowly saw off the locks, white strands of silk falling at his feet.

Zeph stayed behind closed doors the next day, dozing off and on. When he wasn't nodding off, he was gazing out the window, watching the world go by, hoping to catch a glance of Arwyn once…maybe twice. If he was lucky.

He was not.

By nightfall, Zeph was a restless thing, so he decided to leave the confines of his room. Hugging the thick stone wall of the uppermost floor of the monastery, he kept to the shadows, not wanting to be seen, as he made his way through the corridor, down a flight of stairs, to the second floor, pausing for a breath, listening for activity, before venturing down to the lower level and out the door. Once outside, he took in a lungful of air, pungent with the scent of tree sap and mossy earth, then he exhaled and sagged against the austere structure he was currently calling home.

Home?

No, the monastery was certainly not his home. So why was he still here? He shook his head. He was going quite mad from all the thinking he was doing. He was *here* because his sister and Arwyn were. He couldn't leave them. He had a bad feeling in his gut. Something warning him to stay, telling him to protect them. His eyes searched the landscape, seeing little under the inky-night sky, but there was always a prickle of unease just underneath his skin.

What he wouldn't give to know peace, to have just a moment's worth of it. He took another deep breath—the kind where his nostrils flared, and his head fell back, his chest expanding. In Faery, before he'd been stolen from his family, the air always had a sweetness to it. Shoals of honeysuckle and bluebells and all the rich mosaic wildflowers perfumed the land. A tonic he longed to drink so he could taste its dewy flavor. After he'd been stolen, he'd only smelled decay, wet earth, sweat, and blood. Apart from Lolith. She smelled like an overripe fruit.

His stomach rolled at the thought and pushed her from his mind. Lolith was dead. She was dead, and he was alive, and she would never touch him again. As for the Unseelie, one day, he would get his revenge. He breathed in again. This time, he caught the faintest hint of wood smoke. Pushing off the wall, he followed the scent to the southern side of the monastery where the stables and workshops were located. Lochlan sat on a stump in front of a fire, alone.

Zeph had every intention of turning around and going whence he came, but before he knew it, he was within speaking distance. "Did you and my sister have a quarrel?" Zeph asked, curious why the half-breed was alone and outside at night.

Lochlan glanced in Zeph's general direction, his eyes lifting no further than Zeph's knees. The light of the fire cast dancing shadows all around—on his hair, face, and hands, where he was busy shaving the bark off a piece of wood with a knife. "No," Lochlan answered.

"Mm, pity," Zeph replied, taking a seat on a felled tree that had intentionally been placed there for seating. Yes, he was intentionally provoking, the corners of Zeph's mouth slipping up a fraction. In truth, he perhaps liked the half-breed, though he would never admit it. "I was hoping she would have come to her senses by now."

Lochlan did not rise to his bait, though he was almost certain he heard Lochlan grind his teeth. "She is with Arwyn. I am giving them time together."

Just hearing Arwyn's name caused Zeph to lose his grin. A bruised, achy feeling came over him. Something alive and feral crawled around inside his chest, tripping over his heart, making him catch his breath. He rubbed at his sternum, wondering when this feeling would ever subside.

"What did you do to her?" Lochlan asked, still paring down the piece of wood in his hand.

Zeph closed his eyes, feeling the heat of the fire, reminding him of the previous night—the kiss he had stolen from Arwyn. It had been...*everything* and not enough. How odd that he could feel this way after all that had happened to him—that he could want another's touch. But he wanted hers, because her touch held him in place, somehow, when all he wanted to do was disappear.

"Saints in Heaven. You cut off your hair."

Zeph looked up as if he wasn't startled in the least, though inwardly he frowned, dismayed. He had been taken by surprise. He should have heard Favián approaching. His jaw flexed, then he gathered his wits and shrugged his shoulders. "You're beginning to sound more and more like your uncle."

Lochlan stopped his whittling, looking up for the first time. Favián stood at the mouth of the brew house, holding a pitcher in his hands, the two of them staring at Zeph with expectancy and surprise.

Again, Favián spoke. "Why did you cut it?"

Zeph waved his hand dismissively. He hadn't thought how he would explain chopping off his locks, so used to being on his own, it never occurred to him that someone would speak on it.

"Thought I'd try something new," Zeph quipped. "It was getting tedious." It wasn't a lie, precisely. It *had* gotten tedious at times and he *had* thought he'd try something new. It was all a play on words, really. His Seelie birth disallowed a true ability to lie. He could evade, distract, avoid, which was what he mostly did to avoid telling certain truths, although he could get away with white lies—lies that involved only his feelings, like telling Elin he was fine when he wasn't, but nothing outside the scope of that.

"Tedious," Favián repeated, rolling the word on his tongue, tasting it, his eyes narrowing, as though he was peeling back the layers of Zeph's response.

The hairs on the back of Zeph's neck stood on end. He didn't like nor appreciate the scrutiny. "Perhaps I should have checked with you before making such a decision? I hadn't realized you had become so attached to my hair. My apologies."

Lochlan muffled a laugh under his breath and returned his attention back to shaving and paring the wood in his hand.

"Would you do that for me?" Favián asked with a lopsided grin. "Next time…" He winked. "I would like advance notice. I need to prepare myself for the shock."

"You'll be the first to know," Zeph retorted. "Wouldn't want you to get the vapors like some fair maiden and embarrass yourself."

"You wouldn't? See Lochlan, I knew he cared for me." Zeph shot Favián a sardonic glance. Favián's grin split into a blinding smile, and he held up the pitcher in his hands. "I found this in there." He tilted his head at the brew house. "It's not wine. And it's not ale. But it smells potent. I say we drink it and come what may."

Zeph raised one dark brow.

"What?" Favián said. "It's not poison. And if anyone could use a drink, it's you."

"I'm fine," Zeph said.

"And I'm the Virgin Mary." Favián closed the distance between them and offered him the pitcher. "It's just a drink, Zeph."

All three of them were deep in their cups, completely fuddled. Even Lochlan, who had claimed alcohol wouldn't affect him. "It never has," he had said. That was before partaking in whatever this fruity-tasting brew was.

Favián hopped onto the felled tree Zeph was sitting on, and with arms extended out on either side for balance, he began to place one foot in front of the other to walk toward Zeph. "This is how I learned to fight," Favián slurred. "*Papá* would have me balance on a log while teaching me how to dodge a fist. Then we moved on to weapons, dodging and weaving knives, daggers, poleaxes. I daresay I never learned a single maneuver on solid ground. '*Balance and the smart application of force,*' he would say, '*is how you defeat your opponent.*'" Even inebriated, Favián was steady on his feet as he made his way across. "He wanted me to fight with him…in his army. I…did not."

"What did you want?" Lochlan asked.

Favián shrugged, his eyes drifting to his feet. "I do not know. Just…not that. If I could be sure that I was to fight for a noble cause then I would be happy to do so, but not every war is noble or just." He shrugged again. "If I fight, I fight for the causes I deem worthy of dying for."

Zeph nodded, if only to himself, the tiniest bit of envy bubbling to the surface.

"Did your father accept your wishes?" Lochlan asked.

Favián lifted his head and stared off at nothing. "No. He did not understand." He blinked and jumped off the log. "He stopped speaking to me."

"Your father is Searly's brother," Lochlan stated rather than asked.

"*Sí.*"

Zeph watched Favián drink from the pitcher again, his back to them, then set it down clumsily on a warped stump.

"Does Searly know you and your father are not speaking?" Lochlan asked.

"No. I haven't told him." He turned to face them, looking Lochlan in the eye. "I ask you do not mention it to him. He has quite enough to worry about."

Lochlan nodded once. "It is not my place."

"Thank you." Then Favián turned to Zeph. They met each other's stare. "You will not mention it either."

Zeph held Favián's regard for several beats, not having a witty retort, his higher thinking muzzled. Finally, he settled with… "Do I owe you my loyalty?"

Lochlan shook his head, his jaw tightening. Then he picked up a rock and threw it sidearm, away from everyone, cursing under his breath. "Why?" he seethed. "Why does it have to be this way with you?"

Why indeed? Zeph regretted the words the moment they'd left his mouth. He was piling up regrets like stacks of stone, building a wall with them. How long would it be before his regrets came crashing down upon him and buried him? He stood, blood rushing to his head, and crossed over in an angry stride to where the pitcher was. He lifted it to his mouth, the cool liquid making his insides heat. He wasn't going to tell Searly anything. So why couldn't he just agree to stay quiet? Anger churned in his gut, but it was anger at himself—for being this way—for being this impossible monster who couldn't have a normal conversation to save his life!

"I want to understand you, Zeph. Lord knows I try," Lochlan said through gritted teeth. "But you make it damn hard to care."

Zeph chuffed. "I don't need you to care." He took another drink.

"What do you need then?"

"Presently," Zeph mumbled, feeling unlike himself, "for you to stop talking." The alcohol was going to his head.

Ignoring him, Lochlan swayed as he pointed his finger at him. "Why did you cut off your hair? Truly."

"I'm not talking about this," Zeph hissed.

"You don't have to carry it around with you, Zeph," Lochlan said.

"What, pray tell, am I carrying?"

Lochlan looked at him with hard eyes. "You can tell me. You can talk to me."

There was something in the way Lochlan was looking—those unnatural, odd eyes cutting through to him, penetrating Zeph's cold, hard shell.

Zeph turned away, whispering, "No, I can't."

"You can. Why did you cut off your hair?"

"I wanted to."

"Why?"

"Because it made me feel dirty. I didn't want…" Zeph looked at Lochlan, the same way he had looked at him—hard and cutting. "Because of Lolith. I needed it gone. Now leave it be."

Lochlan opened his mouth, wanting to speak, then clamped his mouth shut. He waited a minute and pointed toward the pitcher Zeph still held in his hands. "My turn."

Zeph passed it over to him and took a seat. Favián kept quiet, though he watched and listened. The fire crackled, and crickets chirped. The wind played a melody with the leaves in the distance.

"I'm glad I killed her," Lochlan said. "I'm glad she's dead." He took a drink and handed it back to Zeph, watching as Zeph drank the last of the dregs from the pitcher, then said softly, "She'll never touch you again."

The way Lochlan had said those words…like he knew…like he had sorted it out…something inside Zeph wanted to cry. Maybe it was the little boy he had lost, but he wanted to weep at those words. *She'll never touch you again.* Zeph quickly got to his feet and blinked several times, holding the flood back. It was the alcohol. It was weakening his defenses. That was all.

That was all.

Lochlan sighed. "I wish you didn't hate me, Zeph."

"You hate me too."

Lochlan shook his head. "I did. Not anymore."

"You should."

He shook his head again. "I'd rather understand you."

Zeph was too tired to fight, to keep up the sarcasm he used for armor. He was weary down to his bones.

"Zeph—"

Zeph held up an open palm. "I don't hate you. I hate myself." He had failed everyone he had ever cared for and he would keep failing them, because the die had been cast, and when he had lived the life of a monster for so long, he didn't know how to go back, or turn the page, and begin anew. He was stagnated, unable to advance in any direction.

He sighed and stared at the night sky, his head unclear, his thoughts hazy. Part of him wanted to scream. Part of him wanted to beg for forgiveness. Part of him wanted to give up caring altogether. Caring hurt. It hurt so damn bad. He fisted his hands on his head, expecting the familiar feel of long, silken locks between his fingers. He wanted to pull it at the roots, to feel the pain. He had to settle for the much shorter locks instead and pulled at those.

"Stop," Lochlan said.

Zeph continued to pull at his hair, wishing the pain of it could overcome the pain in his heart.

"I said stop!" Lochlan said, coming toward Zeph.

"You logger-headed, fly-bitten, maggot pie!" Favián yelled.

Zeph stilled, lifting his head. Lochlan froze mid-step and glanced over his shoulder. "What did you say?"

He pointed a finger at Zeph, his face unreadable. "I called him a logger-headed, fly-bitten, maggot pie." Then his mouth twitched. "He's also an impertinent, toad-spotted dewberry. As well as a pribbling, dizzy-eyed pigeon egg."

For a moment, Zeph just blinked at the human, taking him in, dissecting his words, as he let his hands slowly fall to his sides.

"Are you mad?" Lochlan asked, turning full body toward the young man, purposely putting himself between Favián and Zeph. "Are you trying to get killed?"

Favián leaned around Lochlan and winked, plainly in Zeph's view. "You wanted him to stop pulling his hair. Now he has." He shrugged. "Moreover, he drank the last of the brew. At the very least, he is a yeasty, sheep-biting, whey-face."

Lochlan mumbled, "sheep-biting" while scrubbing his hands over his face.

Zeph's mouth turned up at the corners. "Is that so?"

Favián smiled wide. "It is. Care to challenge me? Sheep-face."

Zeph had to turn his head, a laugh bubbling to the surface. He cleared his throat and straightened his posture, sliding his eyes in Lochlan's direction. He looked a bit pale and seemed to be calling up a prayer. Zeph caught Favián quelling a laugh of his own.

Zeph tipped his head to Favián. *I see what you're about. Well done, human.* Favián responded in kind.

Playing along, Zeph pretended to be offended. "Sheep-face, is it?" He realized he was about to embark on infantile name-calling, only he had no idea how to respond.

Then he heard footsteps behind him and Searly calling out, "I can't leave you three alone for even a minute." His tone was teasing, his countenance warm and friendly. Placing his hand on Zeph's shoulder, he said, "You can't let my nephew get away with calling you sheep-face, can you?"

"No, I hadn't planned on it," Zeph said with a wry smile.

"Well, what is your retort?"

"Searly," Lochlan warned.

"Oh, come now, Favián threw down the gauntlet. Zeph has to pick it up. Now, what is your retort?"

"Well," Zeph said. "I can't say I have engaged in childish name-calling before. What would you suggest?"

"Hmm," Searly said, giving it thought. "Has logger-headed been tried?"

"Aye," Lochlan answered, looking Heavenward. "And maggot pie, if memory serves."

Searly chuckled. "I do love that boy," Searly said quietly to Zeph. "Very well, here's what you answer with."

Searly whispered in Zeph's ear. Zeph drew back and stared at the monk. "Truly?"

"Aye."

Zeph blinked. "No one should ever doubt you two are related. Very well." He turned his attention to Favián, who still wore a blinding smile. Zeph did his best to relax his face, erasing all signs of amusement, but it proved to be more difficult of a task than he'd expected. He had to bite the inside of his cheek. Taking a breath, he said, "You are a…gleeking, earth-vexing flap-dragon."

Searly made a noise deep in the back of his throat and Zeph had to bite down on his lip to keep his stoic composure.

But Favián roared in laughter, doubling over. "Well done. Well done, indeed," he wheezed. "Now, Lochlan, you give it a try."

"Me? No. I'd rather not."

"Oh, don't be like that, milord. You don't have to be so serious *all* the time," said Searly.

"Apparently someone needs to be."

"No, you are participating," Searly insisted. "Now, insult us."

"What?" Lochlan asked, blinking, hands on hips.

"Insult us." He waved his hand impatiently. "We haven't all night."

"You are all mad," Lochlan mumbled.

"You'll need to do better than that," Favián said.

"Very well," Lochlan said, irritated. "All three of you are…are…" He paused, nostrils flaring. "Gor-bellied, spur-galled, apple-johns."

Zeph, Favián, and Searly looked at Lochlan like he was half-witted. Lochlan squirmed under their scrutiny.

"Gor-bellied?" Zeph asked.

"Spur-galled?" questioned Favián.

"What in Heaven is an apple-john?" asked Searly.

"I don't know!" Lochlan said, eyeing Zeph. "What the hell is a flap-dragon?"

Zeph raised his brows. "I was just repeating the lines Searly fed me." He tilted his head to Searly. "What *is* a flap-dragon?"

"I made it up," was Searly's answer.

"Well, I made up apple-john!"

"You're terrible at this, milord. You shouldn't participate anymore."

"I didn't *want* to participate at all."

"Now we know why," Searly quipped.

Lochlan gripped the back of his neck, mumbling words to the sky. Then he lowered his head, a smile breaking across his face, even though he was fighting to contain it. "All three of you are Satan's spawn."

"Much better. Though lose the smile next time. It would be more effective without it," Searly said, slapping his dearest friend on the back with all the love of a brother.

"I'll work on it."

Zeph planted himself on the felled tree once more while he watched the other three laugh and talk. Something settled within him, a calmness, like a morning after a stormy night. A sense of rest wrapped around him like a cloak. He found it easier to breathe now, so he did, and the smokiness of the fire seemed sharper and the air was crisper. More alive he felt than he had in quite some time.

Favián came over and sat down beside him. The two sat in companionable silence, listening to the soft cadence of nature and the lilting voices of Searly and Lochlan in their own conversation, and after a while had passed, Favián turned to Zeph and said, "I think I like you better this way…with your hair at chin level."

Zeph turned a skeptical gaze to Favián. "And why would that be?"

Favián shrugged a careless shoulder. "I can't say for sure why. But you seem more *you*, I suppose."

"I don't know what that means," Zeph said with brows drawn tightly together.

"Before, with your long hair, you seemed so Faery Prince-like. Untouchable." Favián grinned. "Very intimidating. Now you are more…how you say… approachable." He shrugged again. "You seem more like the rest of us."

Zeph cocked his head to the side, trying to read between Favián's words. *You seem more like the rest of us.* He had never been included in anything before, not with good people like them. He turned his head and closed his eyes as a breeze swept across his face. "You hardly seemed intimidated by me," he said, needing to respond in some way.

He heard the laughter in Favián's tone. "I wasn't. Well, I mostly wasn't."

Zeph couldn't help the chuckle that escaped him.

"I think you are finding yourself, piece by piece," Favián said. "One haircut, one drink, and…" He paused. "One kiss at a time."

Zeph's eyes popped open, his head whipping in Favián's direction. "Pardon?"

"Relax. Arwyn told me you kissed her. She treats me like a brother, remember?"

That didn't help Zeph relax. Not at all. "What did she…" Zeph closed his mouth. No, he would not ask the question. He didn't want to know.

"Say?" Favián supplied. "That you kissed her and immediately ran off." He shook his head. "I suppose I understand. But…"

"But?" Zeph prompted.

Favián met Zeph eye to eye. "It's not what I would have done."

Zeph narrowed his gaze, something fiery sweeping underneath his skin, warming his cheeks. "And what would you have done, pray tell?"

"I wouldn't have run off. I would have stayed, and I would have—"

"Enough!" Zeph said, spitting out the word like it tasted sour. He ground his back teeth and tried not to think of Favián and Arwyn together, his hands bunching into fists.

Favián chuckled. "It would never be that way between Arwyn and myself. I care about her, which is why I brought it up, but she…" Favián's voice trailed off. He brushed his hands over his breeches, pretending to clean them of dust.

"She…what?" Zeph asked, more calmly this time.

"She only wants you, Zeph. And you're the idiot who kisses her and runs away." He inhaled a tight, shallow breath. "Idiot," he mumbled.

Zeph observed Favián a moment, then leaned forward, forearms on his thighs, and bowed his head. "I'm not good enough. She deserves better than me."

"Mm, a woman like Arwyn doesn't come along every day. Smart, beautiful, and a heart *so big*. She looks at you and she lights up like the damn sun. She wants *you* and you think you are doing her a favor by rejecting her? You think she doesn't know her own heart? Her own mind? I find that insulting on her behalf."

"That is not what I'm saying. That's not what I mean."

"It is. As well-intentioned as you are, it is."

Zeph chewed on Favián's words. Was that how she had taken his departure? That he had rejected her? That he didn't want her? He suddenly felt very, very ill. "I need to fix this."

"Sí, you do. If you want my advice, I recommend finding her and kissing her madly." Favián was back to his broad smile, slapping Zeph on the back.

Yes! Zeph thought that was exactly the thing he needed to do. He stood rather quickly, and his head immediately began to spin, causing him to sway on his feet.

"Easy there, *amigo*. Perhaps not tonight, since you've been drinking."

"Tomorrow," Zeph said. "Tomorrow would be better."

"Come," Favián said, "I'll walk with you to your chamber."

Zeph stayed him with his hand. "No, I can make do on my own. You stay."

"Are you sure?"

Zeph nodded once. "Yes." He started to leave and then felt a thank you was in order. The words were there, on the tip of his tongue, but they weren't the easiest words to let go of, so what he said was, "I won't say anything to Searly." He said this low so only Favián could hear.

"I know."

"How do you—"

Favián cut him off. "Because friends know these things. You did not have to say it for me to know it."

Zeph blinked, then blinked again. "Are we friends?"

"Well," Favián said, altogether serious, "we certainly are not enemies."

"Going to bed?" Searly called.

Zeph looked over his shoulder to where the other two men were sitting. "Yes, I am."

"Sleep well, then," Searly said.

"Good night," said Lochlan.

Zeph's eyes slid to each of them, and that lighter, fuller feeling inside his chest expanded. Something had happened this night, between the four of them. Not that he could define it. This was a wholly new experience for him. Or maybe… maybe it had already been defined. He just needed to accept it.

He tipped his head. "Good night." And as he walked away, underneath his breath, he whispered, "Friends."

15

The old lady opened her eyes, as though someone had gently nudged her awake. It was quiet in her tiny one-room cottage, still dark, save only for the fingers of moonlight that slanted through the window. She knew it was time to rise, knew the hour was nigh.

She sat up, and placed her bare feet on the floor, her toes curling at the sudden coldness that greeted her. She shivered, pulling the coverlet around her shoulders for warmth, and inhaled a fortifying breath at what must be done this day. She had lived her life knowing this moment would come, and when it did, it would be the beginning of the end. It had been so from the moment the cursed child had been placed in her arms. She had known what she would be required to do to keep him safe, and she had. All these years, she had watched over him, helped keep his identity hidden. And she had done so by keeping her own identity hidden, even from him. For centuries. She had played many roles, been many people to Lord Lochlan. She was the one who had fed him from her breast and cared for him as a babe. She had watched him grow and mature from a boy to a man, mostly from afar as he had aged. But in this last century, she had allowed a closer alliance, a friendship of sorts. To him, she was Maude, a witch whom he had learned to trust. He had come to her, after all, when he had needed help with stronger protection wards, runes, around the monastery. There, the protection wards still lay.

But to others, she had been someone else. To Elin, she had been the woman who had come to her aid when she was some years younger, after drunkards had attacked her in the village. Then, she had been the lady who had helped give her a bath after her parents had been killed. She was also the woman who picked up a dying Zeph from a seaside cliff and brought him back to be saved. She had been known as Francesca, Maude, and a host of other names in her lifetime. Sometimes, she forgot what name she had been born with, for her life had not been her own for quite some time. In service to others, for the greater good was her life's work.

And now, her life's work was nearly complete.

She made a few preparations, got dressed, then made her way to the monastery under the cloak of darkness. She stared at the pitted stone exterior with humbleness, for she felt like she was a part of its history, though no one would remember her when time slipped by, when seasons changed, when the world changed. And it would. It would begin on this night, by this woman, for what she had seen through her visions would finally come to pass. And if by chance someone did remember her, would they know what she had sacrificed?

She sighed and lowered her eyes. Bending over, she picked up a protective rune. No, they would not. Likely, they would think she a betrayer. Better no one remember her at all.

She placed the rune inside her pocket. Then she collected the others, one by one. When she completed her task, she looked at the monastery one last time. "Ignis aurum probat," she whispered. *Fire tests gold.* "Igne natura renovatur integra." *Through fire, nature is reborn whole.*

She smiled a fragile smile. "Go well, my children. You are ready."

16

Zeph opened his eyes and immediately winced, the morning light stabbing its way through the window with acute accuracy—right in his face. He rolled away, but that only made the throbbing inside his head beat like war drums.

"Kill me," he murmured.

"I've considered it, actually," came the voice beside his bed.

He cracked one eye open. "Arwyn," he rasped. "Why...what..." He licked his lips. His mouth felt like he'd swallowed sand.

"Here," she said, "drink this." She thrust a cup in his face. "Sit up." He tried. He really did. But his head was protesting rather persistently. "Drink it," she demanded, "or I'll pour it over your head."

He cracked open his other eye. "You're angry with me," he said.

"Angry? Whatever makes you think that?"

He sat up slowly, resting his head against the wall. "An intuitive guess." He reached for the cup, sniffed it. "What is it?"

"Searly said you would have a headache this morning. That should help."

She got up from her seat and moved briskly toward the door. "There are some mint leaves beside the bed. Chew on those. It will help with nausea." She wouldn't look at him as she spoke. "You cut your hair," she said, though she made no further comment. She just stared at the back of the door. "I have things to do," she said as she pulled the door open a bit too hard. "Drink it all if you hope to feel better. I hope you enjoyed your merriment." She walked out without another word.

Zeph's head splintered at the sound of the slamming door. And the organ inside his chest—fractured.

Arwyn lifted her hands, spreading her fingers wide at the base of a giant oak, and listened to the gentle hum of nature. *"Let us take our hearts for a walk in the forest, Daughter, and listen to its quiet music."* She smiled weakly at her father's words, clinging to the memory of his wisdom, as she struggled to regain her temperament. She'd behaved poorly with Zeph this morning, and she would no doubt need to apologize for it. She hadn't even realized she'd been angry. She had only meant to bring him a remedy for his headache, something for his queasiness, and be gone. Because no matter how hurt with him she was, she still wanted to care for him. However, seeing him, being alone with him, after he had kissed and left her, had set her off-kilter. Only Zeph could do that, set her off balance. And she was beginning to hate it, and *that* had made her angry.

She sighed, knowing she needed to gather her wits before she made a bigger hash of things.

Closing her eyes, she tried to clear her mind, let go of her troubles. She breathed in, slow and steady, and breathed out, concentrating on the chirping of birds, the rustling of leaves on gentle breezes, and woodland creatures pitter-pattering along the floor of the forest. There was an enchanting harmony to it all, and Arwyn absorbed the energy the forest offered, allowing it to calm her, soothe her, until she was no longer plagued with the restlessness and the frustration she had brought with her.

She lingered a while longer, wandering further to the river where she sat on the edge of the bank for hours, thinking, remembering. It was here Zeph had taught her his childhood game with the stones he kept in his pocket. It was here where she had given him a little more of her heart. It was here where she had been struck with a poisoned arrow, and it was here where Zeph had protected her, saving her once again.

Then the sunlight started to shrink, and the forest seemed to tell her it was time to go.

Arwyn entered her chamber much later than she had expected to return—the sun had nearly set by the time she closed her door—and was surprised to find Zeph waiting for her, sitting on the edge of her bed, hands neatly folded in his lap.

"What are you doing in here?" she asked.

"Waiting for you," he said, coming to a stand, though not advancing in her direction.

He was watching her, she noticed, very closely, as though he was uncertain about the reception he would receive. Which was ridiculous. Zeph never cared about the kind of reception he received, least of all from her.

She moved casually across the room, untying her cloak along the way and removing it, draping it across the back of a chair. "For what purpose?"

"To talk."

Arwyn smoothed the fabric of her dress. "Feeling better, I take it?"

One corner of Zeph's mouth lifted. "Much. Thank you."

"It was no bother."

"It seemed like a bother," he said, his eyes smiling. "You have a temper."

She cleared her throat and averted her eyes from his. "About that. I owe you an apology."

"I don't want it."

"Yes, well, I give it all the same."

"I don't want your apology, Arwyn." He took a step toward her.

She took a step back, her eyes lifting to his. "You needn't be difficult about it. I'm telling you I'm sorry."

"The other night…I hurt you," he said gently, "when I walked away."

"Ran," she said. "You *ran* away."

He took another step toward her, his gaze never leaving hers. "I'm sorry I ran."

She folded her arms across her chest and looked down, saying nothing. She didn't trust she could speak without her voice wobbling. He had hurt her, and she tried not to be hurt by it. She understood why he'd left. But her heart had taken a spill nonetheless. *I am a river,* she chanted to herself. *A deep, flowing river.*

"I haven't stopped thinking about you," Zeph said, taking another step. "If I thought I could run from you, I quickly discovered I was a fool for trying. You're in my veins, Arwyn. You're in my thoughts." He spoke clearly, yet with hesitation, as though he feared to stammer. "I close my eyes and you're in my dreams. I can't run from you when I feel you in my bones."

"Stop," she said.

"Do you truly want me to?" he asked, stepping closer still.

"What do you want, Zeph?"

"Not your apology."

"What then?"

"Tell me what you feel for me."

"No."

"Why?"

"It wouldn't change anything."

"Say them. Let's find out."

"I can't. I've held them inside for so long, if I let them go now…" She shook her head. "They're all that's keeping me together."

"Say them."

"No!"

"Why not?"

"You'll just run again. I'll say them, and you will run." A tear slipped down her cheek.

He took another step and brushed her cheek with the pad of his thumb. "I won't run."

She turned her head.

"For years," he whispered, "I've had the words of monsters in my head. I need your words to drown them out. Give them to me. I need to hear what they sound like. Please."

A sob escaped through Arwyn's lips. She caught it with her hands.

"Tell me how you feel for me."

"I can't."

"Try."

"Zeph—"

"Damn it, Arwyn," he said, holding her face, his eyes imploring. "Tell me."

"I…"

"Say it!"

"I love you," she said through broken cries and blurry eyes, releasing her words like arrows, aiming them right for his heart. "From the moment you pulled me out from underneath my bed, I've loved you."

Zeph wrapped his arms around her, held her as close as two people could possibly be, and closed his eyes, inhaling the scent of her hair. He smiled a watery smile. "I'm not running," he whispered.

She shook her head and pulled away from him. "What does that mean?"

He swallowed, kissed the top of her head, and stepped away. He planted himself on the floor, back against the wall, and drew his knees up. She calmly sat on the edge of the bed and watched him, waiting for him to speak. His expression, at first, was unreadable. Typical Zeph. But Arwyn's talent wasn't reading expressions. It was emotions she could read. And Zeph's emotions were bubbling underneath, building and building. She could feel it happening, could feel her heart pounding, could feel *his* heart pounding with such heaviness that she wondered if their hearts could take the beating. He pulled the drawstring pouch from his pocket, emptied the colored stones into his hand, and for a long minute he just stared at them.

And then it happened. An eruption. He threw the colored stones across the room and his unreadable expression morphed, dissolved into inexplicable pain. A keening wail of utter sadness broke from his belly and burst out like a pot of boiling water. His hands covered his face as he sobbed into them. For every tear he shed, Arwyn shed one too. She was beside him on the floor, holding him, as he wept. She didn't remember taking the steps. One minute she was on the bed, the next she was on her knees.

Everything he was feeling, he was setting it free, letting it out, and all his hurt and pain, anger and guilt, fear and sadness, they felt like a whip and a lash against her skin. But she took it. She took it all. Because he had carried it inside him for so long—and it was killing him.

"I don't know how to find my way back," he cried. "I don't know how." He let his head fall against the wall and he lowered his hands. Opening his eyes, he looked at her, defeated. "I don't know how."

Arwyn crawled into his lap and held his face between her palms. "Where does it hurt?" She sipped at his tears. "Show me."

Zeph placed his palm over his heart. "Here," he said. "It hurts here."

She held his eyes for a moment before dipping her head and placing a kiss where she knew him best, his heart. "Where else?"

Zeph touched his temples with his fingertips, his gaze watching her closely.

"Here," he answered.

Arwyn grazed a kiss over each temple. "Where else?" she asked again.

He blinked, his throat bobbed, but he did not answer a third time.

She kissed the corner of his mouth. "Do you remember when you asked me if I could mend broken hearts?" He nodded. "You said you would let me have a go at it. Do you recall?" Another nod. "Zeph," she whispered, "let me try." Her mouth moved over the seam of his, hovering there, waiting for him to respond.

And then he did, slowly, carefully, working his lips over hers in gentle nips and tugs. One hand found the nape of her neck, the other found her cheek. Their lips parted, and their tempo increased, but it was not hurried or frantic. It was a longing that was unfurling with soft hands and soft breaths and rapidly beating hearts.

Arwyn knew what Zeph needed. She knew he would have to be the one to lead. So much had been taken from him. And she did not want to take anything. So she moved when he coaxed her to move, and she stilled when he coaxed her to still. She was his to instruct, his to cling to, his to pull, and when he rolled her onto her back, she was his to love.

Tears leaked from the corner of her eyes. He kissed each one of them. Arwyn thought her heart might burst. For so long, she had loved Zeph. For so long. "I love you," she said, knowing he needed her words. It didn't matter he couldn't give them back. She knew he was giving her more than words. "I love you," she said again. "I love you."

He sat up, removed his tunic, exposing his chest, and placed her hand against his heart, which was a drum against her palm as he kissed her. Then he lifted her off the floor and placed her on the bed, his body coming down over hers. She traced the lines on his back, the scars the monsters had left behind. She longed to erase them, but no magic could take those kinds of scars away. She could only soothe them, make them hurt less. "I love you." Now that she had said the words she couldn't stop saying them. They kept spilling out, filling the quiet of the room. She wanted to be sure her words were the only words he heard.

It was subtle, the change in him, but she saw it. His hair swept forward, barely touching his shoulders. She couldn't help touching it, marveling at it, running her fingers through it gently. She didn't ask him why he had cut it. She only asked, "Is this what you wanted? Was this your decision?"

"Yes," he said with more air than voice.

"It becomes you," she observed.

Zeph's eyes locked onto hers. They said so many things. *I'm scared. I'm lonely. I'm hurting. I need you.* "Arwyn," he whispered, her face framed between his forearms. "I…I don't know what I'm doing." He shifted to his left. "I'm sorry. I should leave."

"You said you wouldn't run."

"I don't want to ruin you with—"

"Shh," she said, another tear falling. "I am yours. I have always been yours."

"Arwyn." He looked at her, his eyes once again saying so many things. *I'm still scared. I'm still lonely. I'm still hurting. I still need you.* When he kissed the stray tear, there was a fragility to his efforts, like the act of doing something truly kind was completely foreign to him. Then when he kissed her long and deep, he surprised her by the things his mouth said. *I don't want to be scared. I don't want to be lonely. I don't want to hurt. I don't want to need you. But I do—I do—I do—I do.*

She tasted the salt on his tongue. She wanted him to taste the love on hers.

Her pulse quickened, "Zeph. I love you, Zeph," she said with quick puffs of air.

"I'm not running. I am here," he said. They were the only words he could give her. She knew. She felt it.

Then Zeph surprised her by rolling onto his side, bringing her with him, holding her tightly with one arm, pulling the coverlet on top of them. For a time, nothing was said. Night had fallen like flower petals, soft and silent, and Arwyn was grateful for the quiet. The world outside had stretched a deep, velvet curtain around them, sheltering them, hiding them away. If only for tonight.

"You were wrong," Zeph said, breaking the silence. "Your words changed everything." Zeph kissed the top of her head and breathed in the scent of her hair "Thank you, Arwyn. The monsters in my head aren't quite so loud anymore."

17

lin drifted through the library, perusing books. She came here whenever she needed to think or find solace. She'd been having strange feelings, a nervousness that trickled through her body, settling in her gut, leaving her perplexed and out of sorts. She tried to identify its cause, coming to no logical conclusion. It was making her rather on edge, and she'd hoped the library, the place she loved most in the monastery, would help ease whatever ailed her. It did not, for she had been inside the library for well over an hour, and still the ominous oppression loomed heavily over her.

Then, she felt a darkness at her back. She stiffened. Since learning who she was, the Faery of Light, Lochlan had trained her to become attuned to her surroundings. It was becoming easier for her, and as she evaluated the presence, she realized the darkness was nothing sinister. She took a measured breath and turned. Zeph was standing in the doorway, his mouth set in a straight line, and eyes so similar to hers watched her with worriment. Her heart raced at the sight of him and her mind thought her heart a betrayer because her heart was happy to see him. This was a constant battle she fought within herself. Loving her brother. But also thinking she should hate him.

She looked down and away, a painful knot forming in the cavity of her chest. She closed her eyes, trying to squelch the burn behind them. When she opened them, he was standing before her. She gasped at the unexpectedness of him being so near.

"What's wrong?" he asked.

"Nothing is wrong. You startled me is all."

He tilted his head, studying her, as though she was a window and he was looking right through her. "No," he said. "Something is wrong. What is it?"

Perceptive, her brother. Or perhaps it was because they were twins that he could read her so easily, but that thought caused an irritation to bubble underneath her skin because she could rarely read him at all. "Were you looking for me?" she asked, turning to pluck a book off a shelf and holding it to her chest, determined to redirect his focus. She didn't know what was wrong, and until she did, she didn't want to talk about it.

"I was, yes."

"Any particular reason?"

"I was hoping we could—talk."

"Oh?" She had not seen much of Zeph; avoiding her seemed to be something he did rather well. Surprised that he had sought her out, she asked, "Would you like to sit?"

His eyes shifted around the library, as though he was leery of it. When they settled on a spot by the windows, he flinched. It was subtle. If she hadn't been watching him so closely, she would have missed it. Realization dawned. He had killed a monk in this library. Thaddeus's blood had splayed the windows.

Zeph looked away. "Can we talk somewhere else?"

"Would you like to go for a walk?" He nodded. She placed the book back on the shelf and together they ambled out into the hallway. Her heart cried. Her mind screamed. And yet, she walked beside him with polite, sedate steps. She waited for Zeph to speak. When he didn't, she prompted him. "You said you wanted to talk."

Zeph focused on the path before them, hands folded behind his back. It was then she noticed the similarities in the way they moved together. His posture, the way he carefully held himself, like he wanted the world to see one thing, while hiding behind the illusion of it. She understood that all too well; she lived it every day. Perhaps she could read him after all. A tiny smile touched her lips.

"You look like her," he said softly.

Her mouth instantly turned down at the corners. "Mother, you mean?" He nodded. Her father used to tell her that. Her eyes drifted back to Zeph. She studied him. His build, his shape. The line of his jaw, the sharpness of his cheeks. Now that he'd cut his hair, she saw it so easily. "And you look like him," she said, just as softly. Granted, their father had to look human for most of her memories, but now that she was looking for it, it wasn't difficult to see the similarities.

Zeph turned his head toward her. "You think so?"

"Yes," she said. "I do."

A yawning fissure of quiet fell between them. Only the echo of their footsteps sounded around them. Then something nudged her, like a tap, a whisper. She stopped, turned, listened.

"What is it?" Zeph asked, stopping alongside her.

Again, she couldn't answer him. She didn't know. But she could feel something on the periphery of her mind.

Trust him, a voice whispered. *He will know what to do when the time comes.* She shook her head. "Did you hear that?"

His brows pinched together. "Hear what?"

She looked up and down the hallway. Silence greeted her. When her eyes flickered back to Zeph's, an odd sensation struck her. She felt as though Zeph held the answers, though she knew not the questions. They stared at one another, both seeking something from the other.

"What did you want to talk to me about?" she asked, inching forward.

He blinked, then bit down on his lower lip. "I…" He scrubbed his hands over his face, exhaling a long breath. His eyes skirted over her head as he spoke. "I want to tell you so many things, and every time I open my mouth…the words are so hollow, so empty. It feels insulting to even utter them to you."

Speaking quietly, she asked, "What things?"

His eyes fell on hers and held. Vulnerable, they were, and glistening. "That I'm sorry." His voice sounded like a rusty gate. "I would take it back if I could. All of it. I swear it. I would…" His voice broke and his throat bobbed up and down.

Elin's heart thumped a broken rhythm and then something loosened inside her, letting go of the last vestiges of whatever kept her from fully accepting her heart's appeal. "I have already forgiven you," she said. After hearing herself say the words, she realized now that she had forgiven him. It hadn't been all at once. It had been a process, a series of steps, and perhaps this conversation was the final act that allowed her to *breathe* the admission. "You need to forgive yourself," she said.

Frustration twisted his features. "Impossible."

"Nothing is impossible." She motioned to a bench in an alcove at the end of the corridor. Taking a seat next to each other, Elin said, "I'm going to tell you a secret." She glanced at him from the corner of her eye. He was watching her with rapt attention. "I saw Mother when I was Fading." His eyebrows shot up. She grinned. "That's right. And you know what she told me? She said, '*You must save him, Elin.*'"

Confused, Zeph asked, "Save who?"

"You," she said. "Though I wasn't sure who she meant at the time. But then, later, when I thought Lolith was going kill you, I heard Mother's voice again. It was you she wanted me to save. So I did."

Zeph abruptly stood, brushing the hair back from his face, and took to pacing back and forth in front of her.

"You're welcome," Elin added with a smile and a wink.

"What?" he asked, looking dazed.

"For saving you." She was only joking, but the way Zeph's countenance changed had her sitting up straighter.

"You saving me got you killed. You died in my arms! Did I ever tell you what that did to me?" His eyes welled up with tears. "It destroyed me. Why do you think I was up on that mountain trying to kill myself?!"

"What?" She stood. Her heart and mind were a cluster of thoughts and emotions she couldn't possibly catch up to. "You tried to kill yourself...*did* kill yourself...because of me?"

He reached for her, pulled her into his arms, and held her. "You're the only family I have," he breathed. "Yes, because of you."

"I didn't know," she whispered. "I didn't know." It felt like coming home, being in her brother's arms. A rush of energy flooded over her, making her head swim. Then anger flooded over her and she had to fight the urge to shake the ground underneath their feet. She shoved at his chest. He stumbled backward. "Don't ever do that again!" she said, pointing a long, slim finger at him. "Don't ever do that again!"

"Elin—"

"No," she said, shaking her head. "Did I ever tell you what it did to *me*... seeing you dead...on that table when Francesca brought you in? Do you know what it did to Arwyn?"

He blinked slowly. "No," he said, his voice low. "Don't tell me. Please." He walked back to the bench and sat, head bowed. "I'm sorry for that. I'm sorry for—so many things."

Elin let out a breath, and with it, she released her anger. She sat too and took his hand. It was soft and warm, and she relished that he allowed her to hold it. "I'm sorry, too."

"You have nothing to be sorry for, Elin. Nothing."

"I'm sorry for what happened to you. It changed you so much. I know that whatever it was..." She looked at him. His face was grim. "I know that it hurt you—in so many ways. And I know it would have been me had you not protected me that day, so I feel partly responsible—"

"No," he said, interrupting her. "You are not responsible for what happened to me. They are."

"All right," she said slowly. "Then, will you tell me what they did?"

"Unspeakable things. Don't ask me to tell you. I won't."

Elin rested her head on his shoulder, a tear slipping down her cheek. "Very well," she said, speaking around the lump in her throat. "I won't ask." He squeezed her hand. "But nobody hurts my brother and lives to tell the tale."

He let out a soft chuckle. "Is that so?"

"I cannot lie, so it must be."

They sat like that for a while, Elin and Zeph, getting reacquainted, reforming their bond, when something extraordinary happened. A light within Zeph began to glow, directly in the center of his chest, and then just as quickly it faded.

"What was that?" Elin asked, her quicksilver eyes wide.

Zeph, just as surprised, answered, "I don't know. That's..." He rubbed his chest. "That's never happened before."

"I thought you said—"

"Fae of Light," he said, pointing to her with his other hand, knowing what she was going to say. Hooking a thumb toward himself, he said, "Fae of Shadows. That's who we are. Light and Shadows."

"But..." She stared at his chest where the light had glowed. "How do you explain that?"

His forehead creased. "I can't."

Zeph needed to think. He walked Elin to the refectory where Lochlan was waiting for her, along with Favián, Searly, and by the looks of it, a good portion of the monks. They were all sitting down for a meal. He hadn't seen Arwyn, though, so on his way to his chamber, he knocked on her door. He missed her, missed the smell of wild berries, missed the way her lips curled into a smile, and he missed the warmth of her breath against his skin.

He placed his hand over his heart; it felt like it had grown twice in size. Heavy and full it was, and then he thought about the way light had shone from that very same place only—

"Come in," Arwyn said.

Smiling, Zeph opened the door. "Everyone else is having din—" Zeph stopped everything—his words, his steps, even the organ inside his chest stuttered to a halt. He was frozen, hand still on the door, his eyes fixed on the knife at Arwyn's throat and the one who held it.

"Ah, there he is. And you said he wouldn't come."

Zeph searched Arwyn's face. Her eyes were wide with fright, wet from crying, and they were begging, *pleading* with him, but he wasn't sure what she wanted him to do. Then Zeph looked to the one holding the knife. He smiled like a wolf ready to eat his next meal.

"Zeph," he said, smooth as cream, "you should probably see about your sister."

And then they were gone, like dust in the wind, and Zeph had to blink several times before realizing that he had just lost...

"ARWYN!" he yelled, fury coursing his veins, pain stabbing his chest. "ARWYN!"

The squall of shouts and battle cries reached his ears. *You should probably see about your sister.* Zeph left Arwyn's room in haste, retraced his steps from where he'd last seen Elin, the refectory. The double doors leading into the room were hanging off the hinges, and inside—war was taking place. Sparing one quick glance, he saw his sister inside Lochlan's protective shield, along with Searly and the other monks. She didn't look happy about it, but all Zeph could think was: Good. Safe.

Lochlan and Favián were left to fight the monsters on their own. Lochlan lobbed fireballs while Favián kicked, ducked, and twisted his way through the melee of Unseelie, holding knives in both hands. He was covered in blood, his face hard as stone, as he stabbed an Unseelie behind him without even looking back, while cutting the throat of another who attacked him from the front. Fireball explosions were going off all around them as Lochlan launched them in quick succession. Favián cut a path in Lochlan's direction. An Unseelie was coming up behind Lochlan when Favián jumped onto the back of a dead monster, propelling himself into the air, landing on the Unseelie, and stabbing it in the heart. But before Favián could right himself, another attacked from behind. Favián pitched forward, hoping to set the thing off balance, but another joined in and Zeph lost all sense of where he was, because for a moment, a memory of Unseelie monsters mounting him, ripping him open, tearing at his flesh, flashed before him. Cold sweat trickled down his spine.

Then a scream rent the air and Zeph blinked, bringing him back to the bloody, chaotic scene before him. Tumultuous rage lit through him as his fangs descended and his shadow grew large. Darkness spread like water. He could feel himself going dark, cold, and then…

He was standing in the middle of the room, pieces of dead Unseelie littering the floor and walls, blood splattered everywhere. *Everywhere.*

Then silver eyes were staring at him, glistening, her face stained with tears. "Are you all right?" Elin asked. She was touching him, patting him down like she was looking for something. "Please tell me you're all right."

Zeph felt listless, worn, confused, not at all himself. His eyes wandered lazily around the room, catching the faces of Lochlan, Favián, Searly, and several other monks, before they wandered back to his sister. "What happened?"

She shook her head. "I don't know. It was like you…" She looked over her shoulder to Lochlan.

"You scattered into little pieces," Lochlan finished for her.

"You killed them all in one savage swoop," Favián added. "I blinked, and it was over."

Zeph felt as though he would swoon. His knees buckled underneath him, but before he could hit the floor, Lochlan and Favián each had a hold of him, guiding him to the first empty chair they came to.

"Sit," Lochlan ordered.

Zeph sat with their assistance, Elin right there, staying close. "How did you do that?" she asked.

He wasn't sure *what* he had done, so he couldn't answer her. "I don't know," he said. He looked down at his body. He was whole. Perfectly whole. However, there were other pressing matters to worry about. He started to stand.

"Sit," Lochlan ordered again.

"They have her," Zeph choked.

"Have who?" Elin asked.

"Arwyn," he whispered. "The Unseelie King took her." He had hesitated. He had been in shock, caught unawares when he'd entered her chamber. He'd just *stood* there, doing nothing!

His hands formed into tight fists.

"What?" Elin bent to her knees, curled her hands over his. "The Unseelie King is dead. I watched him die."

"You watched King Savorin die. He had a son," Zeph explained, looking everyone in the eye. Then to his sister, he said, "He and Lolith had a son. And now he has Arwyn."

18

rwyn's throat burned and her neck hung at an odd angle. She moved—at least she tried to move, but she was unable, pressed against something hard and solid. Lifting her head, she pried her eyes open. Everything was a blurry haze of smoke and fire. She blinked, trying to focus, though her eyes stung from the smoke in the air, and finding it hard to breathe, she began to cough.

She tried to recall the last thing she remembered. The monastery. She had been taking a nap when the door to her chamber swung open. She jerked awake, startled by the suddenness of it. Then someone entered her room, with eyes like tunnels, dark and frightening. She had scurried out of bed and pressed herself against the furthest wall.

"Who are you?" she asked, voice trembling.

"Your soon-to-be king," he sneered.

Arwyn scanned the room for a weapon, her hip bumping the table, and everything on it teetered off the edge before crashing to the floor.

The intruder had made his move then. Advancing on her, he hissed, "Quiet.

I don't want to draw him out too soon."

"Who?" she croaked as he pinned her to the wall.

"Zeph, of course."

She shook her head. "He-he won't come."

"Ah, my dear, he will come. For you, he will come."

The king pressed the elf against his chest, held her close as they rode through Faery on a pale horse, smoke billowing all around them, having set fires along his route, wanting to leave his mark, to show where he'd been. His royal retinue with him. He chose not to use the hidden passageways, choosing to ride through Faery on horseback for all of Faery's creatures to see him, know him, understand that he would soon be their ruler, their king. He had been met with resistance, of course. Those who had been loyal to the Seelie Court would not want an Unseelie King ruling over them. He did not care. His parents had died trying to rule Faery with deception. He would not deceive. At least, in that, he was honest.

He hated Faery's radiance, its shine, its shimmer. It sent the wrong message—that Fae were malleable, weak, mere magicians that liked pretty things. Fae were like gods! They should be feared! He rather thought Faery should be dark, ominous, malefic. And they most certainly should not be kept behind a wall because of a treaty designed by humans!

His arms tightened around the elf. She moaned, coughed, and sputtered. He loosened his grip, trying to tamp down his fury that zinged through his veins every time he thought of the treaty. He would set things to right once and for all. Once he killed Zeph and his sister, Faery would go dark and the human realm would soon follow because he would destroy it. He could fairly taste it, and it tasted nearly as sweet as the berry-scented elf in his arms.

So, no, he would not pretend to be someone he was not or want something he didn't. If his parents had taught him anything, they had taught him that taking Faery by deception was not the answer. *This* was the answer—this plan he had set in motion, taking this elf, antagonizing Zeph, leading him and his sister into his trap, and he was ready, more than ready, to be underway with it.

The elf continued to stir in his arms, and this time he let her wake rather than putting her to sleep like he had been doing since he'd spirited her from the human realm. They were approaching the capital of Faery, and he wanted her awake for this part.

His lips twisted in delight. "Ah, she wakes," he whispered in her ear.

She went still. He chuckled in amusement. They were nearing the heart of Arslan, the city built into the mountains. His eyes glinted with pride as all of Arslan's inhabitants came out into the open and watched with terrified faces as he called to his minions to set fire to the city. The rumors had caught up to them, as he had hoped. For each town and village they had visited on their journey, he had made sure to leave carnage behind. Only enough survivors were spared to tell the tale of his coming and how forcefully he had squashed resistance.

Arwyn moaned again. It would take a minute or two for her to gain her bearings. The poison he had been giving her had been a powerful toxin, after all. He loosened his hold on her a bit more as she shifted in her seat. She was a beauty. Even he couldn't deny that. But oh, he was going to enjoy destroying her soul, turning it as black as his, as black as Faery was going to be. The very idea brought him a measure of joy.

"Did you sleep well?" he asked in her ear, his voice low as the screams started and all the different creatures of Arslan began clamoring about to either put out the fires or seek safety.

"What's happening?" she asked, her voice tight.

"We are in the capital city of Arslan. Now, I need to make this announcement. Be a dear and say nothing, or else I'll be forced to kill someone."

"What?" she gasped.

"You don't think I would kill you, do you?" He stroked a finger down the side of her neck. "No, Arwyn. I plan to keep you alive. But if you speak when I have asked you to remain quiet, I will kill an innocent, perhaps even a child. Do you understand?" She nodded. "Good." He inhaled a deep breath, then he blew a thin veil of ice over the city, cooling the fires instantly. A wintery cold fell hard and fast over the land and all the creatures ceased what they were doing. An eerie stillness settled, as well as fear and unease.

"Greetings!" he called, stopping dead center of the capital's square, feeling pleased with himself. "I am King Rolim, of the Unseelie Court, and soon to be king of *all* of Faery." He smiled viciously and victoriously. "And this," he said, pulling Arwyn close against his chest, "will soon be your queen."

Zeph stood inside Arwyn's bedchamber, taking in the scene left behind. A table had been overturned, and her things had been scattered about. A clear sign a struggle had taken place. Zeph lowered his eyes and walked sedately to the bed, where he sat, placing his head in his hands.

Elin went to him, sitting down beside him. "It's not your fault," she said.

"How did they get in?" Zeph asked, his voice warbling. "I thought the monastery was protected."

"I'd like to know that as well," Lochlan answered, gritting his teeth as he returned the table to its upright position. "I'm going to find out. Right now, in fact." He started back toward the door.

"Wait," Elin said. "I have something I need to say." Her voice quivered when she looked at her brother. When she returned her focus to Lochlan, she somehow regained her composure. "We need to get Arwyn back. And you are not going to trap me inside your shield again."

"No, I'm not," Lochlan agreed. "Because you aren't going with us when we go."

In a blur, she was up on her feet, and stood poised, looking like a figure of doom. Lochlan blinked in surprise. "I will say this once and only once. Arwyn is my friend and I *will* help in retrieving her. I am not helpless. You have trained me *not* to be helpless. I can defend myself against all manner of things, including against stubborn brutes who think they can tuck me away in a tower somewhere, thinking I will just wait for their return. If that is the kind of bride you seek, then you will be disappointed, milord, because I am not that girl. You either accept that, or don't. Either way, I will be coming with you to get back my friend. If you have difficulty accepting that, may I suggest you work that out with yourself, because that is not my problem. It is yours."

"I can't lose you." Lochlan's mouth worked, but no other words came out. He couldn't speak. Emotion clogged his throat. This was the woman he loved. The thought of anything happening to her…

"You won't," she said, her exasperation clear.

"You don't know that," was all Lochlan could force out. He struggled for composure. The room vibrated with the way they each held themselves tight as a bow's string.

Elin would be in danger, and even though he knew he couldn't keep her trapped in a cage, shielded forever, he would prefer if she *was* locked in a tower somewhere, until the evil was dealt with, but he also knew she would resent it, resent him, and he didn't want that either. He hung his head. What was he to do? Allow her to trollop into danger?

"You have to let her come with us," Zeph said quietly.

"She doesn't know what she could face," Lochlan retorted, trying not to shout, but it was a shout anyway, fear driving his missteps.

"Your lack of faith in me is something I had not anticipated."

"Lack of faith?" Lochlan moved toward her, eating the distance between them. Taking her by the shoulders, he said, "I'm afraid of losing you."

"I am a Fae," Elin said, lifting her chin in a regal gesture. "A powerful one at that. Perhaps they are the ones who should be afraid. Because I don't intend on just retrieving Arwyn." She turned her eyes on Zeph. "I intend on destroying the ones who took her."

Hell's teeth. Lochlan released her shoulders and stumbled back. She was a vision. The determined tilt of her head, her spine straight as an arrow, she was a warrior, his lady. With pursed lips, she practically dared him to challenge her. His heart was heavy against his ribs as he watched her grow more confident while he wilted at the thought of her fighting.

"You have to let her come with us," Zeph said again to Lochlan.

"I don't think I'll be *letting* her do anything by the sound of it," Lochlan said, his eyes never leaving Elin's.

"Good," Elin clipped. "I see you finally understand I wasn't asking permission."

Lochlan regained the distance he had lost and swept a piece of hair behind her pointed ear. "I love you and don't want to see you get hurt or worse," Lochlan said in a soft voice. "I won't apologize for wanting to protect you."

"I love you, too," she said, her words also softer. "However, it is time I stop hiding. I must do this. I have to."

Lochlan pressed his forehead to hers, not wanting to argue. After a moment, he said, "I need to find Maude." He kissed her cheek. "Can we resume discussing this later?"

"If you have hopes of dissuading me, it will be a fruitless endeavor."

Lochlan's jaw flexed. "I'll be back soon." He kissed her again on the cheek and quit the room before he did something rash he would regret later—like locking her in a tower.

Zeph had watched his sister rise like a sail on a ship, graceful and unwavering, snapping to attention when she had confronted Lochlan and expressed her anger, standing her ground. Pride swelled within him unexpectedly, for he had understood Lochlan and his decision to keep Elin out of the fight. But after watching her, listening to her, he found he agreed with his sister. Thus, it was what prompted him to interject, twice.

Now that Lochlan left and it was just he and Elin, Zeph didn't know what to say. Still, he watched her. She had sailed against the wind and kept her heading, and now she lowered her sails and drifted as she stared at the door Lochlan had exited.

"Come here," Zeph said, extending his hand.

Elin took it, sitting beside him on the bed. She rested her head on his shoulder, and for a stretch of time, neither spoke.

Zeph couldn't stop thinking of Arwyn, their last moments together. He closed his eyes, imagining all the ways she had told him she loved him. She told him with words, with actions, the way she touched him—the way she *didn't* touch him. He felt a pinch in his chest and his hand instinctively rubbed at the spot that ached, though nothing soothed it. He was going to go mad if he continued to sit here doing nothing. He had to get her back. That was all there was to it. He eased his sister's head off his shoulder and rose to his feet.

"Where are you going?" she asked.

"I can't sit here. I..." Zeph's words trailed off as something caught his eye, close to where Arwyn had been standing before the Unseelie King spirited her out of the room. He moved toward it, knelt, and picked it up.

"What is that?" Elin asked.

Zeph's thumb caressed its smooth surface. Where were the others? Zeph stood back up and began searching for the rest of his colored stones.

"What are you looking for?"

Zeph got down on all fours and searched underneath the bed. There they were. He grabbed the drawstring pouch, opened it, peered inside, noting all the other stones were tucked inside. So why was the purple one loose?

Then he remembered. He had thrown them across the room. Arwyn must have gathered them all up, missing this one. He sank back on the bed next to his sister.

"May I see?" she asked.

Hesitantly, Zeph handed her the pouch. She took it and dropped the stones into her open palm. Wide, silver eyes looked up at him. "Where did you get these?"

Zeph's fingers trembled as he tried to loosen his neckcloth. "I took them from your cottage. I saw them there and I—I wanted them."

Elin stared at the stones in her hand. "I remember how we would play with these," she said, smiling wistfully at her palm full of stones. Then she placed the stones back into the pouch, pulled the drawstring tightly, and handed them back.

"The purple one was your favorite when we were children," Zeph said, his voice sounding scratchy as he showed her the purple stone, setting it in her palm.

She picked it up. "It still is," she whispered.

"Keep it," he said.

"No. It should stay with the others."

"Keep it," he said again. "I remember how much you loved it." He took her fingers, curling them into a tight ball around it.

A tiny smile lifted on the right side of her mouth. "Very well."

Then, beams of light broke through the cracks between her fingers and his. Both startled as they stared at the light. It was then that a memory struck Zeph, transporting him back to a time when they were children. It had been their birthday. Their last birthday spent together, in fact. They had spent the day celebrating with their parents and had eaten their fill of all their favorites until their bellies ached and their bodies were exhausted from all the running and playing. They had turned out the lights in the room they shared and had just settled into their beds when a flicker of light caught their weary eyes and they both sat up.

A woman appeared, translucent and glittering in their darkened room.

"Hello," she said, her voice as beautiful as the lady herself.

"Hello," they said with a bit of trepidation.

"Do not be afraid. I have brought a gift."

"You have?" said Eliniana. "Why?"

"Because," the woman said, a smile playing at her lips, "you are the Fae of Light, a very special young lady indeed. And you, Zuriel, are special as well."

He frowned, not feeling very special at all. "I'm just the Fae of Shadows," he said.

The woman's head tilted in concern. "You do not realize your powers?"

Zuriel shrugged. "I can make shadows dance. Is that what you mean?"

"You can do more than make shadows dance. Come here, Zuriel, I want to give you something." He padded across the stone floor and climbed into bed beside his sister. The woman held out a purple rock, smooth on all sides. "This is a magic stone. I brought it straight from the Middle World. One day you will know how to use it and what to use it for. Until then, keep it, and when it is time to use it, the stone will let you know."

Zeph blinked. "By God's bones," he muttered, staring into his sister's eyes. "I had forgotten."

Elin nodded. "Until now, I had as well."

Lochlan entered the tiny one-room cottage belonging to Maude and paused. Turning in a slow circle, Lochlan scanned the room. There wasn't much to the place: four walls made of wattle and daub, a dirt floor, and one window. In the center of the room, a long chain hung from the ceiling, holding a kettle that hovered above a firepit that had been swept clean. A long, slim table rested against one wall with baskets on top that had once contained herbs and spices, now empty. And a bed near the back had been stripped of all bedclothing.

All of Maude's personal belongings were gone. Like she had never been there at all. Anger began to boil in Lochlan's blood as he stood in the center of the cottage, doing a slow turn of the room. He shook his head, not understanding how someone he had considered a friend could betray him so thoroughly and disappear from his life without a word. He spotted a note left on the back of the door, held in place by a knife. Marching toward it in a quick, angry stride, he wrapped his hand around the hilt, pulled the knife free, and unfolded the note.

Please forgive me, it read.

He balled the parchment in his hand and pitched it across the room. He had come to get answers and he would leave without them.

For a moment, he stood there, staring vacantly out the one window. He didn't understand. It didn't make sense to him. She was his friend. He hadn't had many friends. Searly was his friend. That was unquestionable, but Searly was young. Lochlan had lived for five hundred years. And because of his curse, the one he'd been born with, the one that wouldn't allow him to touch or be touched, he'd lived a life of seclusion.

Maude had been someone he had known, someone he had learned to trust—for a hundred years. Mostly, because she wasn't afraid. Like Searly, she had demanded his friendship, though she had been subtler, less aggressive. Granted, they may not have been as close as he and Searly. Still, he had grown to care about her. He'd had so few people in his life…

This act of betrayal crushed him.

He wanted to weep, but instead of weeping, he let out a thundering roar of rage, and after, he fell into a nearby chair that had once been cushioned with a thick hide of fox fur. Now it was just hard, demanding wood on his weary joints. Assaulted by a sudden case of lethargy, his eyelids pulled closed; so very drowsy he became, that he could hardly hold his head up.

"Lochlan," a voice said behind him.

Startled, he found the strength to get to his feet and spun around to face whoever called his name.

"Maude," he clipped, feeling his anger and hurt ignite once again. "I thought you left." He spread his arms out wide. "You left nothing behind."

"I couldn't leave without first speaking with you."

Lochlan raised a brow and pointed toward the door. "I got your note. What am I to forgive you for?"

"The little spell I cast on you just now."

"Pardon?"

"The one making you feel tired, sleepy. It will wear off soon. I just needed you calm while I explained a few things."

Lochlan looked at the old woman, noticing the drawing around her eyes, the tightening around her mouth. "Do you fear me, Maude?"

"What? No, never."

"Then why did you feel the need to cast a spell on me? I am not the betrayer in this room. You are."

A stiff grimace washed over her aged face. She smoothed it away. "You have a temper, milord, and I was afraid you would storm out without hearing what I had to say. And I didn't betray you."

"You removed your protection around the monastery. You allowed the Unseelie entry." He pointed a finger at her. "That is a betrayal."

"Please," Maude said, "sit and let me explain."

Lochlan wanted to yell at the woman. He didn't want to sit for conversation and pleasantries. But he was doing all he could to keep his feet underneath him. He sat in the chair he'd abandoned with a grunt, letting her know he was not happy about the circumstances in the least.

Maude eased into the chair directly beside him, her eyes every bit as wary as his.

"Speak," he snapped. "Do your explaining."

She let out an exasperated sigh. "Did you know that I have known you your whole life?"

Lochlan scoffed, leaned his head back, and closed his eyes. "It only seems that way. A century is a long time to know someone."

"No," she said. "Your *whole* life." Lochlan opened his unnatural pale eyes and turned his head slowly in her direction. She went on. "I was there the day you were born. It is one of my fondest memories, holding you in my arms. I swore to your mother that I would always take care of you, to look after you, and I have kept that promise. I would never, *ever* betray that promise."

Lochlan watched the old woman transform into Francesca. He stood abruptly. "Who are you?" Then he watched her transform into several other people he had been acquainted with throughout his five hundred years. He pointed a finger, taking steps away from her. "Answer me, who are you?"

"Your friend," she answered. "First and foremost, I will always be your friend. Though I am something *other*, too, sent from the Middle World to guide and protect, not just you, milord, but also, Elin and Zeph, and now Arwyn."

"The Middle World?"

"The Foundation, some call it. It is the realm of angels, elite servants, born of divine gifts and power. I was called the day you were born to watch over and protect you, and I have dutifully served as I was bid to do." She stepped toward him, and when she did, she transformed into a translucent woman that glittered, beauty so perfect he fell to his knees. She touched his cheek. "I have loved you as a mother would love a child. And I love Elin, Zeph, and Arwyn as my children as well. I…did not…betray you."

"Then why?" Lochlan asked. "Why did you let those monsters in?"

"I was bid to do it. But can you trust that I have seen things, been privy to things, far beyond your reasoning, beyond this time and space? It has been written, what must be, and everything must happen exactly as it has happened, for Faery to be saved. And it is not just Faery we are saving. We are saving the human realm as well. I have seen it. I know this to be true."

Lochlan shook his head, not knowing what to believe. He moved away from her, hoping to clear his head. He felt a lot like a pawn in someone else's game and he didn't like it. "All the suffering—you've allowed it," he croaked.

"Was this all a test? To see if we could survive all the pain we've each had to endure?" For the second time that day, emotion clogged his throat.

"A test? No. Although it could be argued that it has made you all what you are today."

"What are you saying? That we are better for having suffered? You said you were bid to do it. Who bid you? God? What kind of God moves his people around like game pieces on a battlefield while he sits back watching from a distance? What are we to Him?"

"You haven't been sent to the battlefield empty-handed," she said. "You have been given gifts, tremendous gifts, many of them. You all have. If you want to speak of battlefields, however, no warrior goes from womb to battle without first learning to crawl and then walk, and then he must learn all the things that come after. During that span of living, he falls...many times. Yet he always rises, because that is what warriors do. But, you and the others... you aren't warriors. You are *more*. Therefore, there was more you had to learn, more you had to endure." She poked him in the chest with a long, slim finger. "Because you are *more*. You may be battle-worn. You may be weary. But every one of you are fierce. You are survivors. You are *ready*. This is your war to win. Your sufferings? They will be the thing that saves you because they are what made you. In your sufferings," she said, "the world will be saved."

Lochlan scrubbed his hands over his face and moved to sit down again. He wasn't sure how to respond. He was too tired to think clearly. The flutter of wings drew his attention to the window. He imagined a beautiful, white owl perched on the ledge, watching him, instead of the small songbird that sat there. He swallowed. He wanted to see his mother. He wanted to hold her, hug her, hear her tell him how stubborn he was. He missed her more than he ever thought possible.

As if Maude, or whatever her name was, could read his mind, she said, "Your mother watches over you. She's always with you. You are never alone."

Lochlan nodded. Sometimes he could feel her, but it wasn't enough.

"Soon," the woman said. "You'll see her again soon."

Lochlan chose not to speak. His head felt like it was in the clouds, and he wondered how much of this he was going to remember. "Will I forget you... this conversation after you leave?"

"Do you want to forget me?" she asked.

That was an awfully good question. Did he? Lochlan turned to her. "What you have told me...was I supposed to know?"

She shook her head. "No. After I leave, you will not remember I was here. You will fall asleep for a very short time and wake to an empty room."

"Then why did you tell me?"

A sad smile tilted her lips up. "*I* will remember this conversation." Her eyes began to glisten. "I will remember how you looked at me—when you saw the real me. And I will remember, for a moment, that maybe you believed me."

Lochlan let go of the remaining hesitation he held on to. He saw the truth in her face—her heart was right there, on her sleeve. "I believe you." Then he tilted his head. "What is your real name?"

She burst into tears and laughter. "Would you believe that I no longer remember? Maybe when I return to the Middle World I'll be reminded." She shrugged.

"Is that where you're going?" he asked. "Back home?"

"Yes, though not just yet. I still have some overseeing to do." She winked and dried her eyes with the back of her hand. "I just can't stay *here* any longer." She waved her hands around the tiny cottage. "I'll be watching over you all, though, make no mistake about that."

"Thank you—for..." He trailed off, not sure what to say.

"I have time to grant you one parting gift," she said, smiling fondly.

"What kind of gift?"

"One that will help with your quarrel with Elin."

"Pardon?" he asked, sitting on the edge of his seat.

"You should trust your betrothed," she said. "Lean back, close your eyes."

He obeyed and sat back up. "Wait," he said. "What are you going to do?"

"Give you answers you already know in your heart of hearts. Ease your worry."

"What do you mean?"

She placed her hand over his heart. "Do you feel that? That sense of peace?" Lochlan nodded. "That comes with knowing that Elin is powerful. She must be given the opportunity to let her light shine. She can do this, milord. You already know it. Now, let this peace take hold, and do not let your worry come between you again."

He cupped his hand over hers. "Thank you."

"You are quite welcome. Now, it is time for me to go. When you awake, I will be gone, and you will not remember—"

"I wish it didn't have to be this way."

"And I," she said, touching his cheek. "Sit back, close your eyes," she said quietly. "I must go now."

He did so with a bit of reluctance. Lochlan succumbed to sleep so quickly, he didn't even have time to say goodbye. He wasn't asleep for long, however, and when he opened his eyes, he sat up with a start. The room felt remarkably empty. A wave of loss washed over him, for he felt incredibly bereft, and he didn't know why.

Sitting up, Lochlan looked around. Confusion set in as he eased onto his feet. He spotted the wadded up note he had thrown when he'd read it and how he had felt drowsy shortly after. He must have fallen asleep and was feeling disoriented. That must be it.

He started for the door, and when he reached it, he turned to stare at the empty cottage once more. His visit had been fruitless. He shook his head, angry with himself. And frustrated. And if he was honest, he was feeling the pain of heartache from Maude's betrayal.

A swell of emotion began to rise to the surface, so Lochlan threw open the door and marched out. He needed to get back, prepare for their journey to

Faery, and hope his own protection wards would be enough to keep the monks safe.

He refused to look back.

Maude watched Lochlan go, her heart bruised and aching. He may never remember their conversation. But she would. She would always remember. A tear slipped down her cheek, because even angels needed to cry.

Go well, my child.

Go well.

Favián wrung out the blood-stained cloth for what was probably the hundredth time and began wiping down the wall again, trying to rid the refectory of the massacre that had taken place there. He wasn't the only one trying to clean the blood and gore from the room. He was surrounded by monks, all working tirelessly to put things to rights. Some were cleaning the floors, while others rigged a system of stacked barrels to reach the ceiling. Favián scrubbed until his muscles screamed, though he turned off his mind and did what needed to be done because the alternative was thinking about Arwyn, and he couldn't think about her yet. He would come undone.

The refectory was mostly quiet as everyone worked. Monks weren't ones for wasting words. He thought once or twice about speaking. When he opened his mouth, he didn't know what to say. Their grim faces said enough, so he kept his head down and concentrated on his task, scrubbing hard, using both arms, pressing deep into the pitted surface of the stone walls.

He bent over to rinse out the blood-stained cloth once again into the pail of water by his feet when a gentle hand landed on his shoulder. He expected it to be his *tío*, but when he looked up, he found Xavier instead.

"I've drawn a bath for you. Go and get yourself cleaned up," Xavier said, his voice sounding tired and strained. "We can finish in here."

Favián looked around at what was left to be done. "No, I can stay. Let me help."

Xavier looked at him with sympathetic eyes. "You've done enough. Truly. You helped save us." He tilted his head toward the doorway. "The water will get cold. Go on. Go clean yourself up. And then rest."

Favián looked down at his clothes. He was still covered in blood from his battle with the Unseelie monsters. He frowned. "If you insist."

"Indeed, I do." Xavier took the cloth that Favián had been using and started wiping the blood from the wall without looking back, effectively dismissing him.

Favián headed for the exit, and when he got to the doors hanging off the hinges, he turned back to look at the carnage left behind. None of the blood had been theirs. It was all Unseelie blood. He wanted to smile at that fact, and yet his hands formed into fists as he stood stiffly in place, like a page in court, wondering when justice would be served to the one who took Arwyn. Tears gathered like small pools. He closed his eyes, opened them, turned on his heels and took the corridor that led to his chamber to fetch a change of clothes, then made his way to the bathing room. All the while, tears fell down his cheeks like wax down a candle.

He discarded his clothing immediately, placing them in a pile to be burned, then climbed into his waiting bath. The moment he sank into the hot water, he wanted to moan in gladness and sigh in relief. Resting his head against the lip of the tub, he finally let himself take in a full breath of air. Never had Favián fought so stout-heartedly and never had he felt so much fear, although the fear hadn't come until after the battle had been fought and won. The fear hadn't come until Zeph had uttered the words that Arwyn had been taken. That was when the fear had set in. Even then, he pushed it down, not wanting to experience a world where Arwyn wasn't in it, so he refused to think about it.

Until now.

In the quiet quarters of the bathing room, his thoughts were exceptionally loud. They crowded his mind like a pack of unruly dogs trapped behind a gate. His body began to tremble.

Where was she? Was she being mistreated? Was she hurt? Scared?

He fisted his hair in his hands. A gut-wrenching sound erupted from his throat. He wanted to howl and snarl and growl. For the first time in his life, Favián didn't feel human. He felt savage.

Then, the sweet words Arwyn had said to him when they first met whispered through his mind.

"You and I," she declared, "are going to be good friends."

"We-we are?"

"Yes!" She beamed. "We are."

He smiled tentatively at the memory. She had been absolutely correct. They were good friends. The best of, even. Favián would move Heaven and Earth to help get her back.

He nodded resolutely. Yes, he would help get her back.

He finished his bath quickly, put on clean clothes, and padded back to his chamber. He needed to get a few things in order.

In his room, his *tío* had provided him a place to sit and compose his letters and poems, complete with all the instruments and materials he would need. He sat at the writing table, and taking a piece of parchment out, he dipped his quill in the inkwell and began to write a missive. Well, two missives. One to his *mamá*. And another to his *tío*. He was just putting the finishing touches on his last letter when his uncle knocked once and opened the door. Favián put the quill back in its proper place and covertly moved a few things around to cover what he had been writing.

Turning toward his *tío*, he waited for him to speak, for he knew he most likely had something to say.

"Are you well?" Searly asked, his countenance and posture appearing sad and fatigued, but he also glanced curiously at the pages on the table.

"*Sí.* Are you?"

"I am not harmed, though my soul is crushed." He edged toward the bed and sat, shoulders slumped, head bowed.

Favián stood from his chair and came over to sit beside him. "*Sí,* I, as well."

"They will be leaving soon—Lochlan, Elin, and Zeph," Searly said, his eyes cutting toward him. Favián looked away. "I know what your intentions are. You're planning to go with them."

Favián had never lied to his uncle. He wasn't about to start now. He nodded in confirmation. "I have to," he admitted. "I cannot stay here and do nothing."

"You assume I wouldn't understand?" Favián looked at the man beside him, the man he loved as if he was his own father. "Of course you want to go. You love Arwyn."

"I…" Favián swallowed the words he wanted to say and began again. "She is like a sister to me. I love her like a sister."

Searly raised one dubious brow. "You can lie to yourself. Refrain from lying to me, if you please."

"*Tío,*" Favián said, "it does not matter how I feel. What matters is I am going to assist in retrieving her and bring her back." He stood and proceeded to gather the things he thought he may need and stuffed them into a pack. He glanced at the table where his letters were and said, "If you don't mind, I need a few more minutes. Where shall I meet the others?"

Searly stood. "The library is where I believe they agreed to meet. Don't dawdle long. Lochlan returned not long ago. They'll be ready to leave soon. He's checking the wards around the monastery, and then—"

"I will be there momentarily," Favián said, cutting him off.

"Aye." Searly stared at him a moment, like he was holding on to something valuable, something precious, before he let go. "I'll see you soon, then."

Searly left his nephew, closing the door softly behind him, his heart breaking like glass. He didn't want Favián to go with the others to Faery. For one, Favián was human and he didn't know what kind of chances he had entering a world where he'd be fighting those who possessed magic, those who were evil. Searly may be a man of letters, rather than a man of numbers, but he understood odds like that.

However, he also couldn't be prouder of the boy. He had seen with his own eyes how valiantly Favián had fought when the monsters had stormed into the refectory. He had not delayed acting. One minute, he had been laughing, enjoying his meal, and in the very next, Favián was up and over the table, knives in hand, and running toward the very monsters he and the other monks were running from.

Searly moved from his nephew's door, silent and miserable, and ambled down the sallow corridors until he came to the library. Zeph and Elin were already inside, waiting. He wasn't looking forward to this—seeing them all go, not knowing when they would return. But Arwyn was out there, somewhere, and his heart lurched thinking what she must be going through, and when he thought of her, he wanted them all to leave as soon as possible so they could bring her home posthaste.

Home.

Was this their home? Did they think of it as such? He'd never thought to ask; however, to him, it would be their home for as long as they wanted it to be. Zeph included, although, looking at Zeph now, Searly knew he wasn't thinking of anything except Arwyn.

He looked to be in misery. Absolute misery.

"Zeph," Searly said, walking toward him. Zeph looked up, his eyes glassy. "Are you all right?" he asked.

Zeph was seated in a chair beside his sister. His eyes flitted toward Elin, then back to Searly. "No, not until I have Arwyn back. No," he said again.

"We will get her back," Elin said softly, placing her hands on Zeph's.

Searly smiled. He didn't know what kind of reconciliation had taken place between them, though it was obvious they had reached an understanding.

"I'm here," Lochlan called as he entered the library. "I've done my best with the wards. I hope my best will be enough."

"Do not worry about us, milord," Searly said. "Just do what you must to save Arwyn."

"What?" Elin asked, coming to a stand, staring at Lochlan. "Why are you looking at me like that?" She jutted her chin forward. "If you think to keep me here, let me tell you—"

Lochlan held up a hand, interrupting her speech, his eyebrows drawn tightly together. He looked at Searly, at Zeph, at Elin again.

"What is it?" Searly asked. "You seem discomfited."

"I just…" He studied Elin, his head tilting in consternation. Then the lines on his face smoothed, and the clouds behind his eyes dissipated. He walked toward her, held her like she was precious, and pressed his forehead to hers. "I'm sorry," he said, "about earlier. I trust you. I do. I trust you to fight because I know in my heart that you are made for this moment. I worry because I love you, but do not doubt that I believe in your abilities. And I will be there, fighting by your side. Every step."

"Lochlan," Elin breathed. "Thank you. I-I did not know how much I needed to hear you say that—that you believe in me."

"I should have said it before."

Searly couldn't help the smile that slid across his face. He tried to remember this moment, something he could recall later when he couldn't rest, when he was missing them so.

"Am I too late?" Favián asked, entering the room.

Zeph stood. "Too late for what?"

"I'm going with you," Favián answered. "I am ready to leave whenever you are."

Elin sidestepped Lochlan. "Favián, do you know what you're saying? You have no powers, no magical abilities. Do you truly want to go into a land where everyone dwelling there does?"

Searly watched his nephew adjust the strap of his bag over his shoulder. The sight of him standing there in the doorway of the library brought a tear to Searly's eye. It was reminiscent of when Favián had first arrived, all smiles, his expression so innocent of a boy his age. Now, as he stood before him, that innocence had all but been wiped clean. The person before him now was no longer a boy. He was a man. A determined man.

"I do," Favián said. "And I know exactly what I'm saying."

"What you did today," Lochlan said, "was honorable, and I am so grateful to you. But this isn't your fight. Let us handle this."

Something akin to anger flashed behind Favián's eyes. He turned those heated eyes to Searly. "*Tío*, I didn't want to tell you this because I didn't want to upset you, but *Papá* and I are not speaking. He's angry with me because I didn't want to join the king's army and fight alongside him as father and son. I wanted to decide on my own which battles to fight and die for." Turning to Zeph and Lochlan, he slapped a palm over his chest, and said, "I choose *this* battle. *This* war."

Elin had already walked the distance to him and touched his cheek tenderly. "You could die," she said softly.

"I would rather die young saving Arwyn than die old living with regret. Don't make me live with regret."

It was a moment before anyone spoke, then Elin was the one to break the silence. "All right, Favián. All right."

"We'll watch over him," Lochlan assured Searly. We'll keep him safe. We'll—"

"Of course you will," Searly retorted. "You have the Kiss of Life. Bring him home." Searly felt his chin quiver. He looked down and away, fighting to steady it.

Lochlan stood directly before him. Toe to toe. "Look at me." Searly forced his head up to meet Lochlan in the eye. "We'll bring them both home."

Searly could only nod, his heart breaking at the thought of watching them leave.

Zeph moved toward Favián and placed a hand on his shoulder. "Thank you," was all he said. He moved past him and headed for the door. When no one moved to follow, he turned toward the room. "Well," Zeph said, "let's go kill some monsters, and bring our Arwyn back, shall we?"

19

"I will *not* be your queen," Arwyn hissed, trying to wrestle her arm free. "Unhand me."

King Rolim's answer was to laugh at her, his hold on her arm tightening, bruising her, as he escorted her through the abandoned palace once belonging to the Seelie Queen. More recently it had belonged to his mother, Lolith, the false queen. The one who had deceived everyone into believing she was their queen by using glamour, a magic unique to Fae, to look like the Seelie Queen. The one Lolith had killed.

Now that his mother was dead, the palace was uninhabited. Rolim had come back and killed everyone who'd remained after her death, down to the last scullery maid. It was his palace now. He brought with him his own servants. And since no one remained on the Seelie Royal Court, having killed them as well, he had free rein to do as he pleased.

His lips twisted into a nasty smile. "I am going to give you a choice, Arwyn," King Rolim said, stopping in the great hall, stripped of all things elegant and grand and beatific, and replaced with all things dark and heavy and oppressing.

But somehow the elf, standing in his great hall, made it appear slightly less dark and slightly less oppressing, which made him hate her even more. "I can give you a room above-stairs where you can enjoy comfort during your internment here—or—I can throw you in a cell underneath the palace where I can assure you there will be no comfort. It does not matter to me which you choose because if I want you to be my queen then you will be. I am not asking for your hand. I am simply telling you in advance what you can expect. A courtesy, if you will." He grinned, like a serpent who had tricked its prey, and waited for her reply.

"*What* room above stairs?" she asked.

Ah, she had thought to ask the particulars before making a decision. He shrugged. "Mine, of course."

She clamped her teeth together, her eyes burning like torches. "Put me in the cell."

"As you wish." He gave her a little shove. She stumbled backward into the arms of one of the servants. "You heard her. Put her in the cell."

King Rolim left her then, his laughter echoing off the walls. One night in the cell, and she would be begging to share his room.

The shimmering beams of light that had once warped and bent around low-hanging trees were now a sickly gray, twisting around blackened bodies and charred bones of what remained. Gaunt skeletons rooted in barren soil reached skyward like gnarled hands as if they were attempting to latch on to a miracle, whole again. Big trees, bare as gallows, black like silhouettes. They had once appeared like mystical giants, rising like cathedral spires. Now they stood like a wounded army, tired and reticent.

Lochlan was the first to slip through the seam between the human realm and Faery, and as he stood where he had once stood with his mother, he could not reconcile what he saw.

Faery had been laid to waste.

The others slipped through the seam, one by one, and each stood beside Lochlan staring at what lay before them.

"A crude welcoming," Favián said without inflection. "Not what I expected."

"Nor I," said Lochlan, sorrow in his tone. Faery was not his home, and yet, he felt a profound loss.

Zeph stepped forward, one step, then two. With his back to them, Lochlan could not see his face, nor read his expression, but he could see how his shoulders stiffened, how his spine straightened. "I know what he's doing," Zeph said.

"Who?" asked Lochlan.

"The king. I know what he's doing." Zeph knelt, scooped up a handful of ash, and let it fall between his fingers. "He's telling us he owns Faery now, that he rules it." Zeph stood, dusted off his hands, and turned to his sister. "He owns nothing unless you give it to him. Do you give him Faery, *Fae of Light*?"

Elin had been quiet. She had not uttered a sound when they had crossed through the seam. Lochlan glanced at her and then he had to take a second look. Because even through watery eyes, she had a look about her that would send the hounds of hell running.

"No," was all she said.

Zeph grinned. "I didn't think so." He tilted his head just so and held out his hand. She took it, and together they walked a short distance, coming to a stop where a dried-up stream once flowed over lichen-covered rocks, now covered with soot. Zeph whispered something in her ear, took a step back, and came to stand next to Lochlan and Favián.

Elin kneeled and pressed her hands on the ground.

"What is she doing?" Favián asked in a hushed voice.

"Watch," Zeph answered. "She did this once when we were little."

Elin's hands glowed a soft, blue light. Pale flowers bloomed around her, pushing through the ashes.

Lochlan gasped, matching the quick intake of breath from Favián beside him.

Faery gasped, too. It could be heard and felt, like a pulse and a heartbeat. Elin's light spread like roots, sprawling like a silent sentinel underneath the ground. The gnarled tree limbs that had reached skyward as if asking for absolution, a second chance, were being granted a pardon. Fresh new bark replaced the dehydrated crust of the old, and diamond-shaped leaves began to sprout in thick clusters. A sap-sweet fragrance saturated the air, replacing the scent of decay. Vibrant green grass sprouted underneath their feet, thick and lush. And the tinkling sounds of water once again flowed as if it had never been silenced. A honeyed light spread above their heads like owl wings, chasing away the gray.

The festered wounds of the land had been healed.

"How?" Favián murmured.

"My sister," Zeph said with pride, "is the life force of Faery." He turned to Favián, looked him in the eye. "It is why the Unseelie King wants her dead."

Favián's features turned hard. "He'll not get the chance."

"No, he won't," Lochlan said quietly, still watching Elin breathe life into Faery. "No, he won't."

But the honeyed light that feathered over their heads darkened once again when a thick misty fog rolled in. Lochlan loped to Elin's side and took her hand. His protective instincts were what they were; no apologies could be made for it. He would always seek to protect her, especially now, when they knew not what they faced.

Shadowy figures emerged before them. Lochlan tightened his grip on Elin's hand. A distinctive scraping sound to his right let him know that Favián had unsheathed his sword from his scabbard, but his eyes never strayed from the living wall of creatures before them. It was only when one of them spoke that Lochlan released the air in his lungs.

"We meet again," Tabris said, a rumble in his voice, standing on hind legs.

Yes, they had met before, this living wall of cat-like creatures, and they were exactly how Lochlan remembered them. Black-furred, long-limbed, thin-bodied with white spots across their chests. They had helped him once—when Elin was in Shadowland, and they had stood with him to fight the Unseelie.

Lochlan took another fortifying breath. "Tabris," Lochlan said. "I'm happy to see you are well."

Tabris's cat eyes skittered to Favián, who held his sword as though he was readying to strike. "Tell your friend, if you please, to put away his sword."

"They are not the enemy, Favián. Put it away."

"Are you certain?" Favián questioned, lowering the blade, but not sheathing it.

Had Lochlan not been betrayed by Maude, he would have answered with a definitive yes. As it was, he *had* been betrayed, thus he couldn't be certain. Not anymore. "Mostly certain," Lochlan answered. Then, looking at Tabris, he said, "Once again, I find myself in Faery because someone I care about was stolen from the human realm." Lochlan's eyes cut to Zeph's, who stood close to Favián, still as a statue, his expression unreadable, except for the tiny tick of an eye twitch. Lochlan returned his focus back to the Caits, to Tabris specifically, and said, "Do you know anything about Arwyn, the elf girl, who you helped bring back with us when we returned through the seam? The new Unseelie King took her."

"Yes," Tabris said. "It is why we have come. To help. We assumed you would be coming same as before." His cat eyes looked over Lochlan's companions. "I see you aren't alone this time."

Lochlan hadn't been alone the time before. He had been with his mother, though now was not the time to remind him.

"Who is the human and why have you brought him?" Tabris asked, more curious than insulting.

"Searly's nephew," Lochlan answered, certain Tabris would remember Searly. "He's loyal, honest, and he cares about Arwyn a great deal. He's also adept at fighting. And he wanted to come."

Tabris eyed Favián head to toe. Favián lifted a brow over the scrutiny. "I wasn't aware I needed your approval," Favián sniped.

"My apologies," Tabris said. "'Tis not what I meant by my examination. I am truly standing in admiration of you, being human in a land of magic." Tabris bowed his head, then turned his focus to Zeph. "However, I do find it hard to understand why *you* are here."

"He is my brother," Elin interjected before Zeph could respond, knowing her brother's sharp tongue. "I daresay no one cares more about Arwyn than he does. Please, can you help us?"

Tabris was still eyeing Zeph when he answered. "Of course." Then he turned to Elin. "King Rolim has taken the elf girl to the City of Arslan. You would have found her without my help, however. He has carved a path of destruction from here straight through to the city. I do believe he intended for you all to find her with ease. He wasn't trying to hide her, or himself for that matter. In fact," Tabris paused, his cat eyes finding Zeph again, "the king announced your friend…will be his queen."

If Tabris expected an outburst, he didn't get one. Not from Zeph. Zeph looked at Tabris as though he was looking through him, to some distant memory. Nor did he get one from Favián, Lochlan or Elin. However, the quiet that befell the group was sudden and heavy, like the sharp slide of a guillotine, cutting off their conversation. The deadliness of their silence was louder than any words they could have spoken.

"We can take the shadow roads to the city," Tabris said after a beat. "We will get there faster that way." Tabris turned, and the living wall of Cait Sidhe followed suit. "This way," he said.

Lochlan had forgotten to warn Favián of the effects of the shadow roads.

It had been a while since his first experience with the icy, airless swaths of nothingness, and after they emerged from the first road, Favián cast up his accounts.

"No one told me I wouldn't be able to breathe," Favián heaved, bending at the waist, one arm pressed against a tree to hold himself upright.

"Again, I must apologize," Tabris said. "I forget how it affects those who aren't used to traveling this way. We don't normally take others with us who aren't Caits." Tabris eyed Lochlan then. "How are you holding up, my friend? You were ill the first time as well, if I recall."

"I am fine," Lochlan answered, surprised that he was. He remembered having to stave off the feeling of nausea and beg off to right his equilibrium before taking another road on his first journey through Faery. Sympathetic to Favián's plight, he rested a palm on his back. "Elin, can you heal him?" She nor Zeph didn't seem to have difficulty from this form of travel.

"I-I've never tried to heal a person before." She looked down at her hands. They still glowed. She hadn't stopped glowing since they'd arrived. "But I will certainly try."

"I can do it," Zeph said, his voice sounding over-rough.

Favián's head shot up, and even though he looked green, he grinned. His voice was weak when he said, "See, Lochlan, I told you Zeph loves me."

"It's a matter of getting to Arwyn quickly," Zeph said. "I don't want to waste any more time."

Favián sobered. "You're right. I am slowing everyone down. If you can heal me, please do. I want to get to her as badly as you do."

Zeph was already at Favián's side before he had finished speaking. He placed both hands on Favián's fevered head and closed his eyes, his lips moving, though Lochlan couldn't make out his words. Then Zeph removed his hands and stepped away. "Better?" he asked.

Favián stood to his full height, his countenance no longer green. "*Sí.* Thank you."

"Then let us go," Zeph said, looking around. "Where is Elin?"

Lochlan felt his heart quicken. He hadn't been watching Elin, he'd been watching Zeph. "Tabris," Lochlan said, throwing the name like he was throwing a weapon. "Did you see—"

Tabris held up a paw. "I've not let her out of my sight, my friend." He jutted his chin to his right. "She saw them and went to them. Look." He smiled a cat-like grin. "The Faery of Light. I should expect no less."

Lochlan, Zeph, and Favián followed his line of sight. Elin was walking among wounded creatures of a wrecked village. It had been destroyed by fire, same as what they had witnessed when they had crossed through the seam. And everywhere she passed, the land became anew, same as before. Lochlan had seen her do it with his own eyes, and yet he still had trouble believing it. But that wasn't what Tabris was referring to. He was referring to the aid she was giving to those who had been hurt.

Zeph was the first among them to approach her. "Elin, what are you doing?"

"They're hurt. They need our help."

Elves, gnomes, goblins, hags, dryads, satyrs—all had been affected. Fae, lesser fae—it hadn't mattered to the Unseelie King. He cut down anyone who had dared confront him.

Anger simmered in Lochlan's blood like a tempest, something that was becoming too common, too familiar. Searly had spoken to Lochlan over the years about anger, and he had always listened, but as they were leaving for Faery, Searly had felt inclined to deliver these parting words to all of them:

"Anger can be fatal, my friends. It will steal your soul if you allow it. A man without a soul is no man at all. Do not become the very thing you hate."

"We need to help them," she said again to her brother. "Will you help me?"

Zeph looked away for a moment, to collect his thoughts perhaps. He wanted to get to Arwyn. Desperate for it. The set of his jaw, the tightness around the eyes, was something not even Zeph could hide. There should be no shame in that. Lochlan understood being desperate to save someone he cared for. Someone he loved.

"Please," Elin pleaded.

For a moment, Zeph closed his eyes. When he opened them, he said, "We'll heal the worst of them first and move on from there."

"This one," Elin said, quickly calling Zeph to a gnome who appeared to have a serious head wound.

"You can heal him, Elin," Zeph said. "Better than I could. Here…place your hands on his head…like this."

Lochlan walked away. He couldn't help them with that particular task. After some time, Favián came over and sat beside him on a stump, neither knowing quite what to do. Elin was busy healing an ogre's arm while Zeph mended a gnome's broken leg when a little girl with eyes yellow like the sun and hair blue like the water came up to them. She was Fae, and without her parents. Alone.

She looked up at them, clutching a poppet in her hands. Her face was dirty, her clothes torn. Her yellow eyes should have been shining, but the light had burned out behind them. Lochlan felt his heart crack.

He knelt before her. "Hi," he said. His unusual pale eyes shone. He looked away from her—to Favián, who was now crouched beside him.

"Hi," she murmured.

Lochlan cleared his throat. "My name is Lochlan. This is Favián. What is your name, little one?"

"Gretchen," she murmured shyly.

"That's a lovely name," Favián said. "Does your poppet have a name?" The little girl shook her head. "No? Why not?"

Tears filled Gretchen's eyes like a cup. "Mother had just given it to me. Then the monsters came."

Lochlan and Favián glanced at one another. "Where is your mother now?" Lochlan asked, hoping she wasn't dead, though somehow knowing she was.

Gretchen clutched her poppet tighter. A teardrop dripped from each yellow eye. "She died."

"May I?" Lochlan asked, holding out his arms. A man who had gone centuries without touch suddenly forgot he didn't like to be embraced. "I could use a hug. What about you?"

The little girl nodded, then dove into his arms.

"This isn't right," Favián said quietly. "What do we do?"

Lochlan held the little girl, let her tears soak through his cloak. His eyes drifted to Elin and Zeph where they continued to heal cuts and bruises and broken bones. Maybe he and Favián couldn't heal wounds, but they could hold crying babies, hug children who had lost their mothers and fathers. They could let the people of Faery know they cared, that they weren't alone. By doing that, they could hold on to their souls until they reached Arwyn, until they could right the wrongs.

Lochlan swallowed the knot and the ache and said, "We do this. For now, we just do this."

Arwyn was carelessly shoved into the dank cell, and when the door closed with a heavy bang, darkness pressed down on her, thin and worn, like an old widow's dress, letting the cold through to her bones. She shivered, rubbing her arms to gain warmth. She had only time enough to see she was surrounded by four solid walls and a patch of dirt floor before the light was cast out. She knew she was alone, and yet, she was afraid to move from the center of the room. The hairs on the back of her neck raised as she listened to the *drip, drip, drip* of water falling from somewhere around her. The squeak of a rodent echoed and Arwyn hugged herself tighter, afraid to move or make a sound, her toes curling inside her leather boots. Something wet splashed on top of her head and Arwyn squealed, jumping to her left, her heart beating like a snare drum. Reaching up, she felt for whatever had splashed her, but in the dark, all she could feel was that it was cold and wet.

"It's just water," she said, her voice sounding young and frightened. "It's just water." But fear was a cloak that wrapped around her until she was unable to move. She tried to imagine herself in another place, in another time. She pictured Zeph, the last time they were together. She tried to hang on to that memory, the way he had looked at her, the way he had held her, the memory still so new, she could still feel him on her skin. She swallowed the burn in her throat. Did he know how to find her? Was he searching for her?

She twisted around at the sound of scraping behind her—fingernails against the wall. "Who's there?" she asked, voice trembling.

Scrape.

Scrape.

Scrape.

Hot breath whispered in her ear, saying her name. She twisted around again, her hand instinctively going to her ear. "Who's there?" she shrieked, backing away.

"*Arwyn...Arwyn...Arwyn,*" voices whispered.

She clamped both hands over her ears. "Stop. Leave me alone," she cried.

"*We're coming for you,*" they sang. "*We're coming for you...coming for you... coming for you.*"

"No," she said. "Stop."

Disembodied voices cackled, and something touched her, gooey and sticky. She skittered backward until she hit the cold, slimy wall behind her. The undeniable feeling of a rat running over the toe of her shoe had her shrieking again.

Scrape...scrape...scrape sounded to the right of her head. She lunged off the wall, her arms stretching out in front of her, feeling her way around, stopping when she felt she was at the center of the cell again.

Fear consumed her. She hadn't been this frightened since the day she saw and heard her family being slaughtered. This time, she had nowhere to hide. No one to come save her. No one to pull her from underneath her bed and take her someplace safe.

She was alone.

This time she was completely on her own.

Zeph and the rest of the group stopped just outside the walls of the City of Arslan, the seat of the kingdom. Hiding in a copse of trees, they gazed up at the homes, halls, tombs, turrets and domes, all carved from sandstone, built into the face of the mountain, towering high above the valley below. A palace in the clouds, a magnificent sight it was—or would have been—if the peaks had not been crowned with a headdress of ice. A city standing in defiance, even as it shivered. Above it, the sun lulled in the sky, looking through the mist, like a bruise on the belly of Heaven. Zeph put his ear to the city. It was as though the entire kingdom was holding its breath.

Too long, he thought. It had taken them too long to get here. He and Elin had worked quickly on the wounded. There had been so many. Every village seemed to have more than the last, and they had stopped at every one on their way to the city. He hadn't wanted to stop at any of them. He had a singular mission—to get to Arwyn. He was beginning to feel the familiar pang of resentment in regard to his sister as she insisted they tend to the afflicted. The resentment as familiar as his own shadow. Not long ago, Zeph would feed on that resentment, let it stoke the flames of his anger. Now, it left him feeling ill—sick in a way he could taste the rot until he was queasy with it.

"Just one more child," Elin had said, "then we can go." She had pointed to a little boy sitting off by himself, bloodied, dirtied, and bruised. "I'll go let the others know we'll be ready to go soon while you heal him." She placed her glowing hand on his shoulder, gave him a look that thanked him before he'd even done her bidding, and off she went to find their companions.

Zeph had walked over to the boy, taking careful steps so as not to scare him, and crouched before him. "May I have a look at you?" Zeph asked softly.

The boy raised his head. His eyes were swollen almost shut, his lower lip cut, his right cheek most likely fractured, his nose broken. Zeph's eyes fluttered, though he tried not to react to the boy's trauma. Memories plagued him all the same. Because memories didn't die. They lived. They lived inside of Zeph and they always would.

Zeph spoke to the boy again in soft, dulcet tones. "I'm going to put my hands on your head—"

"No," the boy said, scooting away. "Don't touch me."

Zeph's hands had frozen in midair. He looked at the boy again, evaluating him in a different light, deeper than the wounds he could see. Zeph lowered his hands and sat on the ground. "As you wish. I am not here to do you harm, young one. I only wish to heal you."

"I don't want anyone to touch me."

"I understand. I wish I could heal you without touching you. Are you in much pain?"

The boy shifted his bruised and broken body away from Zeph. He was fighting back tears, his chin quivering, but only slightly before he regained his composure.

Zeph looked over his shoulder. Elin was watching, though she turned away quickly and pretended to be busy with…something.

Zeph frowned. He was not at all sure what to do. How could he help someone who didn't want to be helped? He looked back at the boy. Thin, frail, abused. Zeph had been this boy. Some parts of him still were.

"I'm sorry," Zeph said, shaking his head. "I'm so sorry."

"Why are you sorry?"

"I'm sorry for what you're feeling. I know what it's like. I've…" Zeph's words stopped like they had fallen off the page of a book. He had never told anyone his story except for Arwyn. But she had known without him having to say a word.

"You what?" the boy asked.

"I was a boy…like you when they took me…the monsters, I mean." Zeph lowered his eyes. He didn't want to talk about this. He never wanted to talk about this. "I just…I know how you feel."

The boy said nothing. Perhaps he didn't need to. Zeph peered over his shoulder again. Everyone was waiting. Again, Zeph frowned. If Arwyn were here, she would know what to say. She always knew what to say. Zeph stared at his hands. They itched to heal the boy, maybe because if someone had healed him—had rescued him—before he lost himself to the darkness, things would have been different for him. "Tell me where it hurts," Zeph whispered, feeling his heart had been pinched as he repeated the words Arwyn had said to him. "Tell me."

"My face will heal on its own."

"I wasn't talking about your face," Zeph said. The boy looked up through swollen eyelids. "I was talking about the pain I can't see."

The boy looked away as though he was ashamed. Zeph waited, hoping he would talk. When it became apparent he would not, Zeph stood. "You're right. I can't heal your wounds. Not the kind you have. I would know. But I can still help you." Zeph turned and headed for the group. It was time to go.

"Where are you going?" the boy called.

Zeph stopped and faced the boy one last time. With a grin, he said, "I'm going to slay the monsters who hurt you and the king who rules them."

"You don't know which monsters hurt me."

"I suppose I'll have to kill them all, then."

A slow grin crept across the boy's face, an exact replica of the grin Zeph wore. "Kill them all," he said.

"It will be my pleasure."

Zeph felt a careful hand rest on his shoulder, stirring him from his reverie. Elin was at his side, looking at him with uncertainty. "I'm all right," he said, though his voice sounded odd to his own ears. The truth was he wouldn't be all right until he had Arwyn back in his arms, away from the king, away from the evil that surrounded her. His heart was a war drum pounding a ritual cry every second she was away from him.

"It's a good plan," Elin said, trying to reassure him.

They had received word from Tabris's retinue the moment they'd arrived that Arwyn had been taken to the catacombs underneath the palace. Cait Sidhe were sly creatures, able to hide in the most unusual places, unseen. It was part of their magical abilities. Once they had been given all the information, they were able to learn the layout of the palace, even sketching out a map of it in the dirt. They had come up with a plan to get Arwyn out, and as they were discussing the details, Zeph's heart had grown heavier and heavier. Because he had finally realized something he hadn't bothered to give any consideration to.

Zeph's eyes drifted to where Lochlan and Tabris stood, talking. Turning to his sister, he said, "It is a good plan, I agree." He patted her hand, hoping he appeared more at ease. "Excuse me a moment."

Zeph approached Lochlan and Tabris with measured steps, his boots crunching the ground underneath, and as he neared, they paused their conversation. "Pardon the intrusion," Zeph said, looking at Lochlan. "I need to speak with you." His eyes darted toward Tabris. "Alone, if you don't mind." Tabris took his leave with just a bob of his head and Zeph silently thanked him.

"What is it?" Lochlan asked, his brows furrowing.

Now that he and Lochlan were alone, he didn't know how to say what he'd wanted to say. He gestured with his hand for them to move further away from the others. Lochlan didn't argue, though his eyes narrowed a fraction.

Zeph stopped when he felt they had gained a bit of privacy. He didn't face Lochlan. Instead, he faced the others, his eyes resting on his sister. "I owe you an apology," Zeph said without preamble. "I..." He swallowed, his eyes never leaving his sister.

"What is the apology for?"

Zeph could feel the heat of Lochlan's stare on his right cheek. "I understand now," he said, trying hard to keep the emotion from his voice but unable to do so. "When I took Elin from you." He shook his head. "If you felt anything close to how I'm feeling in this moment…" He looked Lochlan in the eye then. "You should have killed me the moment you clapped eyes on me in Shadowland. I would have."

"You begged me to heal Elin because she was dying. Pleaded with me to spare your life long enough to heal her. We were both desperate in those moments. When she died in your arms, you vanished, and I was left with…" Lochlan's voice trailed off. "I don't want to discuss this anymore."

"I ran off to kill myself. And I did. But you brought me back. I still do not understand why you would do that." Zeph shook his head again. "I don't know if that makes you better than me or—"

"I brought you back because Arwyn begged me to. Because Elin begged me to. Because Searly demanded that I do it."

"Searly?" Zeph asked, not understanding.

"Yes. He was quite adamant."

Zeph had to look away from Lochlan, his eyes falling to the ground. Zeph had not deserved a second chance, yet he had been granted one all the same. As they stood there, Zeph was determined that he would earn this second chance, deserved or not. He owed his *friends* that much of him at least.

"Do not make me out to be a saint, Zeph. If it had been up to me, you would not be standing here today."

Zeph smiled down at his booted feet. "Good. I could not abide feeling inferior to a half-breed." He glanced up at Lochlan, his eyes glittering with mirth.

Lochlan's countenance was blank at first and then crinkled into a soft chuckle.

In Zeph's periphery, he caught Favián move away from the group and sit down with his back against a tree. "He's well trained," Zeph said, recalling how he had handled himself in the refectory against the Unseelie.

"He is indeed," Lochlan agreed.

The look on Searly's face as they were leaving the monastery flashed in Zeph's mind. Searly had tried so hard to appear stoic, but his eyes blazed bright with fear.

"We have to keep him safe," Zeph said. "For Searly."

Lochlan turned toward Zeph, full body. He observed him openly, honestly. Zeph didn't much care for being studied so thoroughly.

"What?" Zeph asked.

It was as if Lochlan was looking at him anew. "Nothing," Lochan answered. Then he refocused his attention back to Favián. "We'll keep him safe. We must. For Searly."

Zeph nodded, looking up at the darkening sky. They had been waiting for the sun to sink behind the mountain, for the shadows to fall across the land like spilled ink. Now that the moon hung above them like a lantern, Zeph asked, "Are you ready?"

"Quite," Lochlan replied. Stepping forward, he called to the others, "Everyone, it is time."

20

The whispered voices grew louder, and the scraping sounds would not cease. Arwyn felt like a frightened child as eddies of fear swirled around her feet. She had not moved from the center of the dank, dark cell in quite some time. The voices seemed content just scaring her, so she refused to move, afraid to make the tiniest sound.

Until something behind her made a terrible grinding sound, like the wall itself was moving, shifting from its place. Slowly, she turned. Cold, stale air hit her in the face, and she could taste the dust and debris flying in the air. The whispered voices grew quiet and the scraping sounds hushed. Then something stepped out of the wall with red, glowing eyes and fetid breath.

Arwyn opened her mouth to scream but fear had paralyzed her.

"*You're dead now*," the disembodied voices chanted. "*Dead, dead, dead, dead…*"

Arwyn's heart thundered in her ears. This was it. She would die here, in this cell. Tears pricked her eyes. There was nothing for it.

As she stood there, shaking like turning leaves, she looked death in the eye and accepted that this was how it would end for her. She only hoped her life had mattered, that it had meant something to someone.

Then she thought of Zeph and how his childhood must have been this terrifying. She thought of all the things these monsters had done to him—of the many dungeons and dank cells he had slept in—of the many times he had been violated—of the many times he had been terrorized. As a child.

When she thought about Zeph and what he had endured, a little bit of her fear subsided, and anger took root. She allowed it to fill her up and up and up.

"You're dead, you're dead, you're dead..." the whispers chanted.

"Shut up!" Arwyn hissed.

The voices went mute and the red-eyed beast tilted its head, as though it was surprised she had spoken. Arwyn welcomed more anger. She had kept it buried, not truly allowing herself to feel it. The anger over what had happened to Zeph—the anger over what had happened to her family—she had let herself feel only a tiny fraction of it, until she had swept it away and let grief see her through. This time she let the anger build and build and build until she felt like her skin would boil with the fury that raged underneath it. Maybe Arwyn had never been a river, because now she felt like she had been silently simmering for most of her life, like a volcano, her wrath patiently waiting like lava deep below the surface until she was ready to blow.

Arwyn tilted her head in the same manner as the hideous beast, and stared back at it, like a dare, a challenge. Being an empath had always been a burden she had learned to temper, but at that moment, it felt like a slice of Heaven.

She smiled. "Not so certain, are you?" The beast huffed a frothy breath. Arwyn let the emotions of the world, the ones she'd carried with her every day: hers, Zeph's, Elin's, Lochlan's, Searly's, Xavier's, every monk she'd encountered at the monastery—every emotion of every person she'd ever known since the day she was born, she pulled them to the surface, let them fuel her, consume her. Feeling emotions wasn't her only power. She could also inflict them on others.

When Arwyn was ready, when she was saturated with hate, loneliness, pain, betrayal, despair, sadness, fear…until she felt mad with it, she said, "Come get me."

The beast growled low, fell on all fours, then launched at her.

Zeph and Favián moved in the night like twin snakes, both cloaked in darkness and shadows. Surefooted and soundless, they made their way into the city, onto the cobbled streets that were deathly quiet. Homes were lit by candles, bodies came in and out of view through windows, but the city itself had gone to sleep.

Something rattled in the distance, a muffled cry, a monstrous laugh. A laugh that Zeph wanted to crush, destroy, mutilate. With his blood burning in his veins like fire, spreading to his limbs and branches, he followed the sickening sounds of a laughing monster on an eerily quiet night.

There, behind old wooden crates, tucked between two buildings, a monster had a young Fae girl trapped. Before Zeph could decide how he wanted the monster to die, either by fire or with Zeph's bare hands, Favián had already made the decision, whistling once, getting the monster's attention to turn around, then releasing his knife, and sinking it into the monster's chest. It crumpled to its knees before falling over, face first.

Zeph blinked. "All right. That's one way."

Cait Sidhe slipped out of the shadows and Zeph ordered one of them to see the Fae girl home safely. The rest took care of the body after Favián retrieved his blood-soaked knife.

"You remember where to find the entrance to the catacombs?" Tabris asked as Zeph and Favián prepared to rescue Arwyn. There were two ways in. One from inside the palace and one from outside, through a cave at the base of the mountain, though they had to go through the city to get there.

"Yes," answered Zeph.

"I will follow. Once you get to the cave, I will guard the entrance to make sure no one comes in behind you."

"Thank you," Zeph said. "For your help. I—we—appreciate it."

Tabris's cat eyes appeared feral when he looked directly at Zeph. "I want this king dead as much as anyone. Let us not make any mistakes this eve."

Zeph nodded once. Lochlan and Elin would wait for Zeph and Favián to return with Arwyn, but Zeph needed to be assured of one final thing. "The other Caits, they are keeping watch?" They had rescued one Fae girl. They didn't want to spend the evening rescuing others. Monsters broke into homes, killed families, just for the merriment of it. Zeph knew all too well. And with the city under their siege, he was—worried for them.

"No monsters will be breaking into homes tonight," Tabris said. "Concentrate on saving the elf girl."

"Arwyn," Zeph hissed. "Her name is Arwyn." He wondered if he looked a little feral, too. He felt feral, ready to pounce on the next creature, man, or beast who referred to her as anything other than by her name.

Tabris's tail swished slowly behind him. "My apologies—again," he said, his voice lowered, contrite. "I meant no disrespect."

Zeph's nostrils flared as he took a deep breath through his nose. He could feel Favián's blunt stare and was grateful he had chosen not to interject. "I'm sorry," Zeph said, like he was reading from a difficult text. "I'm not myself."

Favián barked out a laugh. "*Sí*, he is usually more of an arse. He is being unusually polite."

A proper mute stare...and then... "Thank you, Favián, for coming to my defense."

Favián smiled that annoying, too big, too bright smile of his. "Of course. We're friends." He shrugged. "That's what we do."

"Let's be off," Zeph grumbled.

They made it to the entrance of the catacombs, and once inside, they lit the lanterns they'd acquired from Tabris. The passageway was narrow, smelling of old wet earth and moss and death. The air did not move, and for a moment, they stopped to listen, to acquaint themselves with their surroundings. Water dripped, vermin skittered, and wings fluttered above their heads.

They began to move further inside the black, murky chamber underneath the palace, side by side, picking their way as though they walked on unsteady ground.

"Why did you choose me?" Favián asked.

"Pardon?"

"You could have chosen Lochlan. Or Elin. Or both. Instead, you chose me to come with you to rescue Arwyn." Favián's voice was low and monotone, like an absentminded child hauntingly reciting a lesson, but there was something else about the way he spoke that drew Zeph's attention. Favián's voice was also the steady hand of a man who cared, and whatever airs he was putting on for Zeph's sake, he was not fooled.

Zeph waited a stretch of time before answering, and then finally, he said, "I know you love her." Favián's head snapped up and Zeph held up an open palm. "I don't blame you. She makes it easy to love her." Zeph looked straight ahead. "I chose you because I know how much you care. And…"

A scream rent the catacombs, causing both Zeph and Favián to jump.

"Arwyn!" Zeph yelled, taking off into a dead run, Favián doing his best to keep pace, but Zeph was faster and he reached what he hoped to be Arwyn's cell door long before Favián ever did.

Blind panic and rage lit through Zeph, and with a lift of his hand, he sent a wave of power through the door, crushing it like bone, then sending it sailing through the air behind him. He entered the room, lantern still in hand. Arwyn was on the ground. A hideous beast lay sprawled beside her.

Setting the lantern on the ground, he rushed toward her, afraid to move her. His hands fluttering over her, tears welling in his eyes. "Arwyn," he croaked. He touched her face; it was covered in blood. "Arwyn," he said, louder this time, his voice quivering. "Am I too late?" His ear fell to her chest. "Please, please, please," he chanted as he strained to hear her heart beating, his hands already heating with his healing powers.

Favián finally came rushing through the doorway, panting.

"Bring your light over here!" Zeph ordered, lifting his head. "See if that thing is dead."

"If it isn't, it will be," Favián said, his sword already in hand. As Zeph healed Arwyn, Favián approached the beast on the floor with caution. When he saw no signs of it breathing, he said, "I think it's dead, but to be certain…" Favián set down his light and wrapped both hands around the hilt of his sword and…a sickening sound of a head being severed echoed in the small space. "It is officially dead."

Zeph barely heard anything Favián was saying. He was much too concerned about Arwyn. "Heal, my sweets, heal. You can't leave me. I forbid it," he pleaded. Tears glittered like jewels on his lashes. "You can't leave." His hands grew hotter, brighter as he pushed his healing power into her. It was the oddest thing when it happened—her heartbeat, it was like a gust of wind, felt and heard, but unseen. His breath caught. *Thump—thump, thump.*

Glancing up at Favián with unsure eyes, he asked, "Do you hear that?" His ear wasn't to her chest, yet he could hear it plainly. *Thump—thump, thump.*

"Hear what?" Favián responded, his voice soft yet jagged.

Zeph looked back at Arwyn. "You don't hear it?

"I don't hear anything," Favián answered.

"Your heart is racing."

Zeph's hand covered the thumping organ. "You know my heartbeats?"

"Sometimes, I don't know if they are yours or mine."

Zeph smoothed his thumb over Arwyn's cheek, then he took his sleeve and began wiping away the blood on her face. It wasn't her blood. Her skin was smooth underneath. "Arwyn, open your eyes." He lowered his face to her ear. "I know your heartbeats, too, luv. I can hear them. And I promise you I can even feel them—in my own chest. *Please*, open your eyes."

Her eyelids fluttered, and Zeph pulled her into his arms and held her, clung to her. "I have you," he said. "You're safe now. I have you." He pulled back, needing to see her. The moment her eyes fully opened, and she realized Zeph had her, tears brightened her eyes, making them glitter in the dimness of the catacombs.

"You found me."

"I found you."

A tear slid from the corner of her eye. "I thought I would never see you again."

Zeph opened his mouth to speak but his tears clogged his throat. He had thought the same, he had just refused to entertain the thought aloud. He swallowed that down and asked, "Can you move? We need to get you out of here."

"We?"

"Favián is with…" Zeph's words trailed off, looking up to where Favián had been standing and finding him gone. "Favián?" he called.

A beat of silence, and then, "I'm here," he said. "I'm…outside the door."

"Can you stand?" Zeph asked Arwyn.

She nodded. "I think so."

With Zeph's help, Arwyn made it to her feet. Zeph picked up the lantern he'd placed on the ground. "Put your arms around me until you feel you have your strength."

"She killed the beast…killed the beast…killed the beast," whispered voices chanted.

Zeph waved the lantern around the cell. The walls began to swirl and move, and misshapen faces appeared with eyes and mouths that opened and closed.

Favián re-entered the cell, his eyes round as coins when he saw the moving, swirling faces. "Holy…"

"That was what was torturing me," Arwyn said, ire in her voice. She took the light from Zeph and marched over to the wall. The faces hissed as she brought the flame closer. "You are going to wish you had never met me," she said calmly, collected. She jammed the flame in the eye of one of the many faces, catching it on fire. It spread in a slow, creeping fashion until one entire wall was aglow in flames. "Let us go," she said as the whispers turned into shouts of agony. "I've had enough merriment down here." She stopped to kiss Favián on the cheek. "Thank you for my rescue. I suppose we are down to just your lantern now."

Favián's eyebrows shot up. "*Sí.*"

Zeph took Arwyn by the hand, pulling her firmly to his side. "I don't know if I should marry you or be completely terrified of you."

Arwyn smiled up at him, perhaps a bit smug, and it nearly knocked the breath out of him. "Just get me out of here, if you please. You can sort out your problems later."

Favián led them back out the way they'd came as Zeph kept one arm tucked around Arwyn, relieved to be holding her again. When they emerged from the mouth of the catacombs, Zeph loathed to let her go, although she did not appear to want him to. The snapping of a twig caused Zeph to push Arwyn behind him as he spun to meet the unknown.

He breathed a sigh of relief. "Tabris."

"I didn't mean to startle you."

Ignoring that, Zeph said, "Let's go. We need to get back to Lochlan and Elin."

They moved like ghosts, the four of them, silent and unseen, back through the city, the waxing moon looming above them like an ever-present guardian. Arwyn pulled at her sleeves, and Zeph wished he could find a bit of calm in all the quiet. But the lack of noise only served to scratch at his nerves. He couldn't help feeling it had been too easy—Arwyn's rescue. No guards within the catacombs, or even outside them. It all felt too...

"What's wrong?" Arwyn asked in a hushed tone.

Zeph glanced at her as they cut a path in the darkness, side by side, with Tabris and Favián in front of them. He wanted to be forthright with her, but he didn't have an answer. "I don't know," he said. "Something isn't right, though."

"I feel it," she said. "The wrongness. It's in the air."

Zeph could see Lochlan and Elin now, just up ahead. Things were about to happen. For better or worse, he didn't know, but it was time to confront the evil.

"Arwyn," Zeph started, "when we reach the palace, I want you to stay with Tabris. I don't want you near the king."

"Zeph—"

"I mean it," Zeph said, pulling Arwyn to a stop. "I intend to keep you safe. Please, do not make me beg, but beg I will if it means you are safe from Rolim, from his taint."

Arwyn stepped closer to him, placed her hand upon his chest. "I love you," she said. "I'll stay with Tabris because you asked me to. But I have a request as well." Her eyes glistened when she looked into his. "Don't do anything foolish."

Zeph shared a glint of a smile. "I'll try. But I'm afraid you know me rather too well."

"I do," she said. "That's what scares me." Tugging on her sleeve again, she looked ahead, toward Favián, and said, "He is here because of me. Promise me nothing will happen to him."

"We will do our best to protect him," Zeph answered, kissing her on the forehead. "We'll do our best."

But Zeph had a feeling—a very bad feeling.

As soon as Elin saw them, she ran to greet them, wasting not a moment to hug Arwyn. "Are you hurt?" she asked.

"Fortunately, I am not. Though I did think I would die down there."

"She killed a beast," Favián said. "And don't ask me about the faces in the wall." He shuddered. "She set them aflame."

"What?" Lochlan asked. "What faces?"

"I told you not to ask," Favián said.

"We'll explain later," Zeph said. "Are we ready?"

"Yes," Elin said. "More than ready."

Zeph looked over his shoulder—at the palace, a lofty bearing against the black night, perched on the mountain, mute and immobile, resigned as though it was a prisoner of war. He turned back to Arwyn, his heart twisting in his chest. He opened his mouth, fully intending to say those three little words, but like the palace, he felt mute and immobile. The words lay flat on his tongue, and though they tasted sweet, he couldn't bring himself to utter them aloud.

"Go," Arwyn said. "It's all right."

Zeph closed his eyes in frustration, rested his forehead against hers. "Arwyn," he said, his breath wisping across her brow.

"Be safe," she whispered.

"I'm not running," he said. "Remember that." He kissed the top of her head and turned to the group. "Let's go kill a king, shall we?"

Arwyn watched them go, and the further away they drew, a vapor of a chill spread down her arms. The feeling their entire world was about to change caused her to cover a sharp intake of breath.

21

They entered through a service door on silent feet. Voices carried from the kitchen along with the clanging of pots and pans. Zeph peeked around the corner, held up three fingers, and gestured for Lochlan and Favián to follow. Elin stayed where she was, peering around the corner just as Zeph faded into shadows, reappearing behind one of the servants, snapping his neck. Lochlan disappeared into shimmering orbs, and reappeared at the back of another servant, snapping his neck as well. Favián didn't have magical talents, but he didn't need them. He released his knife with a silent grunt, his right arm coming down hard and fast, the knife meeting its mark between the eyes. All three servants lay dead on the floor.

But a fourth one entered through the door at Elin's back. They saw each other at the same time. He lunged at her. She darted underneath him, her heart racing. He swiped at her just as she moved past him and managed to scratch the side of her left cheek. She shuffled backward, bumping into a shelf. He sneered, his lip curling as he prowled toward her. She had never killed anyone. She was an elemental and a healer. But the thing about healers was...if they could fix a heart, they could also break one.

Frightened or not, Elin would not cower. Not now. Not when she looked into the servant's eyes and imagined him hurting her brother, hurting all those she had helped on their journey. "That's right," Elin said with false calm. "Come get me." Her palms were hot behind her back. "I want you to."

The moment he was within arm's reach, she lurched forward, pressed her glowing palm on his chest, and commanded his heart to squeeze itself. His face turned red, then purple. His eyes wide as two full moons.

She made sure he was looking at her when she said, "Die."

Lochlan, Favián, and Zeph rounded the corner and stared at the dead servant at Elin's feet. She stepped over him, feeling half horrified and half satisfied. "Four down. Several more to go."

On their way out of the kitchen, Lochlan asked, "Are you all right?"

"Four down. Several more to go," she repeated.

"Elin."

"Yes, I'm all right. It was kill or be killed. And there are more I'd like to see dead."

King Rolim grew increasingly impatient, but he reined it in, knowing that in a short while everything he had planned would come to pass soon. He raked a long black nail across the pleat of the velvet curtains, gazing at the moon that glowed menacingly over the city. *His* city. Ever since he was a boy he had known he would rule Faery. Albeit, he had thought he would rule much later in life, not believing his mother would fall at the hands of a half-breed or his father at the hands of Zeph. Nothing could have prepared him for that.

But here he was, and here they were, and he would make them pay for what they had done. Not because he loved his parents. He didn't know love. He had never been shown any. He only knew hate and he had hated his parents.

If anyone killed them, it should have been him. However, that was only part of the reason he wanted them to suffer. Rolim just liked inflicting pain on others. He also liked destroying things. It was the very reason he took Arwyn—so he could destroy her. And in destroying her, it would destroy Zeph.

A loud crashing noise sounded from inside his throne room. He turned to his captain. "What do you suppose that was?" he asked with a gleam in his eye.

"I believe your guests have arrived, Your Highness."

Zeph waited for the king to enter the throne room, anticipating his arrival with an uncomfortable nervousness, though Zeph refused to show it to anyone. When the king's captain opened the wide double doors, he wished for the nervousness to fade and for steely resolve to take its place. Zeph fixed his countenance to appear bored when the king stepped through the doorway, his red-tinted hair falling to his waist, a contrast to his pallid gray skin and striking golden eyes. Rolim had a face that was wicked and beautiful. That was the thing about evil. It was often a wicked beauty.

A reckoning stretched out before Zeph, glimmering like sunlight on a spider's web as they met each other's eyes.

Zeph flashed a smile. "You kept us waiting. Not very polite of you."

"You kept me waiting first." Rolim's lips thinned as he surveyed the ruination of his throne room. "Did the statues upset you?"

"We're in a foul mood."

"I see. I also see you're in the mood to play games."

"Not particularly, no. We're simply letting you know that you are not to be king. This seat," Zeph said, reclining back, "does not belong to you."

Rolim tipped a red-tinted brow. "And it belongs to you?"

Zeph grinned. "No. I don't want to be king. I just want you dead."

"Pity that you won't get your wish," Rolim replied. "Now, remove yourself from my throne. You and your…" His eyes roamed to Elin. "—your sister."

"Have you the inclination to move, Elin?" Zeph asked.

"No, I don't believe I do," she answered.

Zeph shrugged. "Pity that you won't get your wish, Rolim."

"I could make you," Rolim said, his tone heated.

"You could certainly try," Zeph challenged, raising a finger in the air. "But I must tell you, everyone in this palace is dead. The guards. The cooks. The maids. We spared no one. All loyalists to you and all. So that just leaves you and your captain. I thought it only fair we mention it."

The king laughed. "You think you have me, is that it? Tell me, Zeph. Did you wonder why this all seemed a bit too easy? It was easy, wasn't it? No one guarding your precious little elf. Very little resistance as you made your way into the city. The palace. Perhaps it was cruel of me to give you and your sister false hope, but I am a cruel Fae and an even crueler king." Rolim clasped his hands and strolled back and forth. "What did you think? Truly?"

Of course, Zeph had known. He was still trying to figure out what Rolim was up to. It must have shown on his face.

"Ah," Rolim said. "You did think it." He smiled. "I'll help you, Zeph. I don't care that you killed my monsters and servants. I'll get more. You know why?" Zeph let his lids lower like he was bored. "Because I can. I think I'll use humans as my servants next." Rolim tapped his chin. "And I can use…say…Cait Sidhe to replace my monsters." He quirked a brow. "Incidentally, where is our dear Arwyn?"

Zeph rose violently to his feet. "What have you done?"

"I'm merely asking where my soon-to-be bride is? Oh, that's right," Rolim said, snapping his fingers. "She's right here. Tabris! Bring her in!"

Tabris stepped into the throne room with Arwyn in tow, holding her tightly to his chest, a paw covering her mouth. There was pain etching Tabris's face, a strain around his cat eyes.

"He's under my control," Rolim explained. "So, you see, it doesn't matter much to me that you killed some monsters. I can always gain new ones. You of all people, Zeph, should know how *Darkside View* works. My parents used it on you. Tapping into the dark side of someone's personality. We all have darkness within us. Don't we, Zeph? And I am a master at controlling the darkness in others. I had the best teachers, you see."

"Don't hurt her," Elin pleaded with Tabris. "Please."

"I don't want to," Tabris gritted out.

"But he will," Rolim interrupted. "If I tell him to. I can manipulate him however I want."

Zeph raised the captain's shadow, made it solid, a living being. He hadn't even realized he had done it, blinded by the rage that churned within his soul. Zeph blinked when Elin grabbed his arm.

"What is that?" she asked.

"Do not be afraid. I have brought a gift."

"You have?" said Eliniana. "Why?"

"Because," the woman said, a smile playing at her lips, "you are the Fae of Light, a very special young lady indeed. And you, Zuriel, are special as well."

He frowned, not feeling very special at all. "I'm just the Fae of Shadows," he said.

The woman's head tilted in concern. "You do not realize your powers?"

Zuriel shrugged. "I can make shadows dance. Is that what you mean?"

"You can do more than make shadows dance."

The captain stared stiffly as this newly formed being stalked around him and his king. The king only glared at Zeph.

Answering his sister, Zeph said, "*That* will do what *I* tell it to do." Zeph narrowed his eyes and ordered his shadow creature to kill the king.

But the king was prepared and struck the shadow creature with a powerful force of energy that incinerated it into a bright white orb of fire. His captain was incinerated as well, for whatever happened to the shadow reflected in the true body. Zeph had instinctually known that, somehow, which was why he had chosen his shadow creature to kill the king, certain the king would react just as he had.

"We're down to one," he said to his sister, noting that Favián had moved in behind Tabris while the king was otherwise distracted, and was currently holding a knife to Tabris's throat.

"You'll have to do better than that," Rolim said, feeling pleased with himself, not yet aware of Favián's presence.

"I have more tricks up my sleeve," Zeph said. "Would you like to see another?"

"I think I would like to see what your sister can do."

Rolim flung his hands in the air and released a wave of energy at Elin, but Elin threw her hands up and pushed back with all her might. Lochlan emerged, seemingly coming out of the wall with a roar, and launched an enormous fireball at the Unseelie King who thought he could attack his betrothed and live to tell the tale, his face a twist of rage. The fireball hit its mark and Rolim stumbled back on his heels. Lochlan continued to launch attack after attack while Elin continued to push back on the king's assault. She grew brighter and brighter until the room was lit like the sun. Zeph was nearly blinded by her light.

Bolts of light arced from her fingertips. Rolim screamed in agony. Her hair blew around her face, windows shattered, and the faces of the shattered statues began to melt.

"Elin, stop!" Lochlan yelled.

"You'll kill yourself!" Zeph shouted.

They screamed over each other.

Elin let go of her power and fell to her knees. Zeph and Lochlan were both there, holding her, smoothing back her hair. She lifted her eyes, saw the king crawling on the floor, charred, naked, clothes having been burned completely off, his long red hair singed off his head, but still, he was alive.

"I tried," she said, her voice faint as a wisp of smoke. "I tried."

"I know," Zeph said. "I know."

"I can't be k-killed," Rolim gasped. "I tr-traded in dark magic." He laughed, though it sounded like a high-pitched wheeze. "I am invincible."

"What did you sacrifice?" Zeph barked.

"What?"

"You said you traded in dark magic. Dark magic requires a personal sacrifice. What did you give it?" Zeph knew dark magic from having lived in Shadowland. He also knew to stay away from it.

Rolim looked up, grinned. "My soul."

Zeph closed his eyes, cursing under his breath

"What does that mean?" Favián asked.

"We can't kill him," he said softly. "Dark magic is…" Zeph shook his head. "It's not even magic. It's…not of this world."

"Zeph," Lochlan said.

"What?"

"Your chest, it's—glowing."

Zeph looked down, rubbed his hand over the pale purple light that glowed there.

"Come here, Zuriel, I want to give you something." He padded across the stone floor and climbed into bed beside his sister. The woman held out a purple rock, smooth on all sides. "This is a magic stone. I brought it straight from the Middle World. One day you will know how to use it and what to use it for. Until then, keep it, and when it is time to use it, the stone will let you know."

Zeph's eyes met his sister's. "Give me the stone, Elin."

Her eyes welled with tears. "No."

"Elin, give me the stone. I can end this." His eyes flitted over to the king, who was already beginning to heal. "Give it to me."

"Zeph—"

His eyes came back to hers. He smiled softly at her. "You know you have to." He touched her cheek with the pad of his thumb. "It makes sense that it was me, you know. You have too much good in you." He nodded, accepting his fate.

"It makes sense that it was me."

"Don't do this. We'll f-find another way."

"There isn't another way." He kissed the top of her head. "Give me the stone, Elin."

"Zeph!" Arwyn called out, her face a mass of confusion. "What are you doing?" She wrestled free from Tabris, who was no longer under Rolim's control in his weakened state, and she edged away from him.

"Arwyn," Zeph said, choking on her name. He felt the smooth stone in his hand as Elin handed it to him. "I'm righting wrongs, my sweets. The only way I can." He placed the stone on his chest and watched as it became a part of his skin, adhering to his flesh, purple light spreading throughout his body like an intricate web. "We can't kill him. But I can send this evil straight to Hell, away from here." He looked up at her then, those three words formed again on his tongue, and this time, he was able to say them. "Thank you, Arwyn. Because of you, I know what it meant to be loved, for I loved you."

With that, he looked away from her, knowing he couldn't watch her tears fall. He had made her cry too many times before. He looked evil in the face instead as Rolim stood to his full height. Zeph let out a roar, ran like a bull toward him, knowing exactly where he wanted to place his horns. And as he ran, Zeph scattered into tiny particles, as he had before, only this time the particles glowed a bright purple, then formed into a tight ball just before hitting the king square in the chest. The king exploded into the same bright particles of light and then—nothing.

Zeph and the king were gone.

The only thing that broke the silence were Elin and Arwyn's screams.

Greater love than this no man hath, that a man lay down his life for his friends.
~ John 15:13

22

rwyn fell to her knees, scanning the spot where Zeph had just been. "Where is he?" she cried. "Where did he go?"

Elin knelt beside her, though she didn't speak, didn't answer. She just stared at the same blank space that Zeph no longer occupied.

"Tell me what just happened," Arwyn croaked. "I don't understand."

Favián and Lochlan were silent. Arwyn looked up at them. Their expressions were grim, somber.

"Someone, answer me!" Arwyn demanded.

"He opened a portal. A space in between realms. Twilight." Elin spoke with care, with caution, as though her words were weapons and she was trying to not inflict injury. "He sent the king there…since he couldn't be killed…he sent him away. He can't come back."

"W-Who can't? The king?"

"Neither can come back," Elin said, her voice so small it was unrecognizable.

"How do you know this?" Lochlan asked.

Her eyes fluttered. "The stone's magic told me."

"What?" Lochlan was beside Elin then, cupping her face with both of his hands, forcing her to look at him. "What are you talking about, Elin?"

"We'd forgotten about the lady. She came to us when we were children. She brought us that stone. She said we would know what to do with it when the time came." Elin's face crumpled like paper. "She said the stone's magic would tell us."

"What lady?" Lochlan asked. "Elin, what lady?"

"I think she was an angel. She said she was from the Middle World."

Lochlan fell back on his haunches. He blinked several times while mouthing *Middle World* and *angel.*

Arwyn abruptly stood, her face pinched in pain. "No!" she said. "No! I don't accept this. Zeph can't be stuck in Twilight. I refuse to believe this."

"Arwyn," Favián said, his voice sounding lost, distant.

"Zeph!" Arwyn shouted. "ZEPH!" She circled the room, calling his name. "Zeph, come back! You can't leave! I-I forbid it." Her voice cracked, like thin ice breaking. Favián grabbed her from behind and held on. She bucked, trying to free herself. "Let go of me."

"Shh, just let me hold you."

"I don't want you to hold me! I want Zeph! I want him to c-come back! Where did he go?"

Favián didn't let go...would not let go. "I don't know, *mi corazoncito.* I don't know."

"I want him back, Favi," she whimpered, sinking to the floor, him sinking with her. "I want him back."

"I know," he said, his voice falling on her ears soft as snow. "I know."

23

Zeph felt himself falling, falling, falling, screams echoing all around him, hands reaching, tugging, snatching him from Rolim's body.

He was sucked through a veil, and it was like tearing off his skin.

Then it was over, gone, like a gust of black wind.

He shouldn't be surprised this was the way his life would end.

A door banging into an empty room.

And there was no one there to say...*Farewell.*

24

Two days passed and Arwyn refused to leave the throne room. She didn't eat. She didn't sleep. She refused to speak to anyone. She stared at the spot Zeph had been standing when he last spoke to her and did nothing else.

Favián stayed close by, never leaving her alone, knowing Zeph would not only expect Favián to watch over Arwyn, he would want him to.

Favián's mouth twitched. He thought about the time they'd first met, how unlikeable Zeph had been. They had come so far, he and Zeph. Somewhere along the way, he had grown to care for the prickly Fae, and now he was...

Favián shut his eyes and clenched his fists. *Damn you, Zeph.*

"How is she?" Lochlan asked, taking a seat next to Favián in an unlit corner of the room.

Favián shook out his hands and drew his knees up to rest his arms. "I'm worried about her."

Lochlan nodded in understanding. "Elin is having a difficult time as well. I don't know what to do for her."

"How are you holding up?" Favián asked.

Lochlan's head fell against the wall. He stared up—at nothing. "I hate him," he said quietly. "I hate him. I hate him. I hate him." A tear slipped down his cheek, a quiet descent. "For leaving. And I keep hoping that my heart would listen to what my head is telling it." His voice wobbled. "But the damned thing is broken."

Favián laid a hand on Lochlan's shoulder. "I feel the same."

"And then there's the angel story," Lochlan said. "Favián, I think the angel visited me too once. I didn't remember it either until Elin mentioned it. But it feels so familiar."

"Did the angel give you a stone as well?"

"No, I'm sure she didn't. It feels more…" Lochlan trailed off, his eyes darting left and right. "Like she wanted me to know she cared."

"Favián?" Arwyn said, standing before them, swaying on her feet.

He sprang up, ready to catch her if she fell. She was weak, and he was past concerned. "Do you need something?" he asked.

"I want to go home. Take me to Searly."

"All right." Favián nodded. "We'll go home."

Lochlan stood too. "I'll find Elin and then we'll all go."

Elin stood at the highest point in all of Faery, on the barren cliffs overlooking Death Sea, looking out from a safe distance, listening to the swell and sway of the waves below. The flint-gray sky was tinged in yellow around the edges, like pages in an ancient book that foretold a prophecy, hinting at doom.

Lochlan approached her slowly. "I've been searching all over for you."

"I'm sorry," she said. "I just…I needed to come here."

"Why?"

She glanced at him over her shoulder and then stared back to the cliffs.

The colors of the sky were changing, hidden fires burning low under the crumbling gray. "For eight days Zeph was on this mountain, alone, dying." Her chin quivered. "Have you ever been that alone? I haven't. Even after I lost my parents. I had you and Searly."

"What did Zeph tell you?"

"That when he thought he'd lost me, he wanted to die." She spoke to him while looking out into the sea. But she wasn't present. She wasn't with him. She was living somewhere else. "He came here and poisoned himself. You know the rest."

She took a step toward the edge of the cliff, then another. The wind picked up strength, blowing her hair around her face, whipping her skirts around her ankles. She closed her eyes and mumbled, "I'm sorry."

"Elin," Lochlan said, reaching for her hand. "What are you sorry for?"

"I should have tried harder. We could have found another way."

"He chose—"

"He didn't think he had a choice!" Thunder rumbled in the distance, lightning struck close by, and clouds rolled and tumbled overhead. The palpitating pulse of the ocean began to thrash against the shore. "He didn't think he was worthy to live. He accepted his fate in this—that dying this way was what he deserved." Her voice was caught in the wind and carted off, like that of her brother's soul. "He was mine," she whimpered. "My twin. My other half. He was p-part of me. I feel like I can't br-breathe without him. And I want him back!" she bellowed. "I want my brother back!"

Lochlan wrapped his body around hers, holding her tightly so she could break, and he would be there to keep her pieces together. "I know. I know."

"It's not fair," she cried. "It's not fair. He had no choices. He was just a child. They took him away from us. Made him do things he would have never done if they'd left him alone. They did this. They're the monsters. He didn't deserve to d-die. Not like this. N-Not like this."

"He had a choice," Lochlan said softly in her ear. "He sacrificed his life for you. For all of us. Don't you see? In the end, he chose love. He chose love, Elin. Don't take that away from him. Don't."

A sob of defeat broke from Elin's lips, the high-pitched whine of her pain reverberating off the mountain. Her heart was a steady, hard rhythm underneath his palm. Fat drops of rain fell around them as steady and hard as the rhythm of her heart.

Lochlan held her firmly in his arms.

"I needed more time with him." Her eyes slid closed. "I needed more time."

He rested his cheek on her head. He, too, had prayed for more time. "Let's go back to Mirova. Lick our wounds. Let Searly help put us back together."

"And then what?" Elin asked absently.

But Lochlan did not have an answer. And then what, indeed.

Searly knocked on Arwyn's door. There was no answer.

"Arwyn, may I enter?" he asked softly. He put his ear to the door, hoping he would hear sounds of her moving about. "I brought food."

"Leave it by the door, if you please," she said weakly. "I'm not hungry."

"No, no. I'm afraid I can't do that. I must insist you eat something this time."

"I said I'm not hungry, Searly. Please."

"You need to eat." Searly opened the door. "We are not negotiating." He set the tray of food beside the bed. She rolled over and refused to look at him. Searly sighed. "Arwyn, just a few bites."

"He left me," she whispered. "He said he wouldn't run. He said he wouldn't leave. But he did. He left me."

"He didn't want to," Searly said, sitting next to her. "They told me everything that happened." Searly reached out his hand and stroked her long lavender hair. "He loved you. Very much. He wasn't leaving you. He was saving you."

"Excuse me," a strong male voice said.

Arwyn and Searly both turned to see who their visitor was.

"I was walking past. Your door was open, and I couldn't help overhearing." Xavier took a tentative step forward. "May I say something?"

Arwyn sat up, dried her eyes as best as she could. "Speak freely, Xavier."

"I wanted to say that I'm sorry for your loss." Xavier let his eyes fall to the floor. "I wasn't kind to Zeph when he was here. I think everyone knows that."

"Xavier—"

"Please, allow me to finish," he said to Arwyn, his eyes lifting to hers. He had the look of a man in a spiritual crisis, pinched and pained.

Searly squeezed Arwyn's hand and nodded for Xavier to continue. Whatever he needed to say, Arwyn should hear it.

"I learned it's much easier to live a cloistered life, praying, getting lost in the repetitiveness of monastic living. I thought myself a holy man, doing God's work. And then…" Xavier walked to the window, stared out. "Everything changed. I became a man filled with hate. It consumed me. I can see now how hate can blind a person. Because I did not see the changes. Not in myself. And not in Zeph." He turned to face them both. "Three times Zeph saved you, Arwyn, by my count. Possibly other times we aren't aware of. And the first time, Zeph was under the influence of evil as I understand it." Xavier's expression was pensive. "I won't pretend to understand the magic he was under, but I think about that." He shook his head. "And somehow, he rose above it to save you." A tear slipped down Arwyn's cheek. "Zeph battled demons I couldn't possibly imagine, though I didn't know. None of us knew. But now that we do…" Xavier's eyes began to glisten. "Now that we do, I am saddened that he is gone. I wanted you to know that I think you saved him, too." He nodded to himself. "I think you saved each other." Xavier's eyes found hers again. "Saint Paul says… *And now abide faith, hope, love, these three; but the greatest of these is* love." He smiled at her, a genuine smile. "Love is powerful, Arwyn. Never doubt the power love has. I would do well to remember that. Thank you for teaching me that lesson."

Arwyn stood and reached for Xavier's hands. "Thank you. I appreciate your words."

"I'm sorry that's all I can offer you."

"You offered kindness. That is a lot."

"If there is anything else I can do, please ask."

"Thank you, Xavier. I will."

After Xavier left, Arwyn closed the door, pressed her head against it, and let her tears fall once more.

"He wasn't wrong, luv," Searly said.

Arwyn nodded. "I know."

Searly allowed silence to coil around them like a sleeping cat. She didn't move from the door and he didn't move from the place beside her bed. He had had his own moment of breaking down shortly after their arrival. Although Searly was good about keeping his wits about him, he was still only a man. His heart had cracked right down the middle when he'd learned Zeph's fate. He had wanted to blame Arwyn for his emotional state because she had projected her emotions on to him when Zeph was brought back into their lives. But he knew that wasn't fair, nor was it true. Searly cared for Zeph and losing him had been a fist to his gut.

He glanced around the room. The small space felt so much bigger than it was. Zeph's presence had been so large that the monastery would now seem extraordinarily empty without him there.

"You know you can stay here for as long as you need—for as long as you want," Searly said, dragging his words, tasting the tang of sadness on his tongue.

"I know," she said. "And Favi? What are his plans?"

"His plans are to be wherever you are."

Arwyn traced her finger over the scarred woodgrain on the door. "I am nowhere," Arwyn whispered. "I exist. But I do not live. I am nowhere."

25

"Everything will be all right," a soft, feminine voice said.

Zeph's mind was foggy and unclear. He thought he felt himself being lifted off the ground, but that couldn't be. His mind was playing tricks. He was locked behind a veil, trapped forevermore. "Leave me be," he murmured. "Leave me be."

"Shh," she cooed. "Look at me, Zeph."

Zeph cracked one eye open. A shimmering lady hovered above him, sparkling in gold and silver. His breath caught.

"Do you remember me?"

All Zeph could manage was a nod.

She smiled a beatific smile. "Your story is not over. I have a gift for you. Look."

A beautiful bright light floated toward him, then two. He blinked. The lights faded, and two shapes emerged. A silhouette of a man and a silhouette of a woman glided toward him, and with them they carried the scent of honeysuckle and bluebells and rich mosaic wildflowers. The scent of his childhood. The good ones. The happy ones.

Tears pricked Zeph's eyes. "It can't be," he whispered.

The angelic woman, still at his side, said, "You did well, Zeph. I never lost faith in you. And neither did your parents."

"But I—"

"Sacrificed yourself for the greater good."

"I killed them," he rasped.

"Zuriel," his mother said gently, her soft iridescent hair cascading all around her.

Then the man stepped forward. He wore a smile, just like Zeph's. "Son."

Their voices were soft music and it was almost too painful to hear.

Zeph's lip quivered. "What's happening?"

His mother walked toward him, her face a benediction, and embraced him.

The angelic woman spoke up. "They have obviously forgiven you."

"They have?" Zeph asked as he held on to his mother while staring at the face of his father.

"Shh," his mother said in his ear. "I have my boy in my arms. Let me hold you."

His father stepped forward and wrapped his arms around them both. Zeph pinched his eyes closed, not believing any of this was real.

After a time, the angelic woman said, "It's time for you to go home, Zeph."

Zeph pulled away from his parents, eyes wet, head confused. "Home?"

"Yes," she said. "That's your gift. For your unselfish sacrifice. For all the pain you've endured. For being asked to endure it at all."

"I don't understand."

"You're going home," she said.

"But..." Zeph blinked, looking at his parents...at the angel. "Where is home for me?"

His mother tilted her head, looked at him with understanding, and said, "Wherever your heart leads you."

26

rwyn waited for everyone to be abed and then she left her chamber, a coverlet wrapped securely around her, for she was chilled and too tired to properly dress. The door to Favián's room opened when she passed by. Arwyn froze, like someone caught doing something wrong.

"Arwyn, where are you going?"

She closed her eyes and breathed through her nose. "Just taking a walk, Favi. Go back to bed."

"Do you want company?"

"No."

"Arwyn—"

"Please, Favi, I wish to be alone."

"For how long?"

She opened her eyes and turned toward him, answering honestly. "I don't know."

Favián's mouth was tight around the edges. "I'm here, you know. Whenever you need me."

"I know," she said, knowing she wasn't giving him any ground. She had built a wall around herself and was letting no one in. No one at all. There was simply no room with all the grief that surrounded her.

He stared a moment longer, nodded once, then returned to his room. She breathed out a long exhalation and turned her back on the closed door. Once she made her way to the communal room, she sat on the chair facing the fire, craving its warmth, and curled her feet up underneath her, the coverlet snug around her. She let her head fall against the back of the chair as she listened to the crackle of the firewood in the hearth.

A kiss of a breeze across her face caused her to stir. Arwyn's eyes fluttered open. Realizing she must have fallen asleep, she sat up, blinking the blur away.

"You should eat something," a familiar voice said.

Later, Arwyn would remember that moment as the most exquisite and tortured moment of her life. It happened in such sweet slowness, as if he knew she would need every second to understand, every second to accept that he was real, for she had felt she was dreaming.

She turned her head toward his voice, and there he stood, shouldering the door, as though he'd been watching her sleeping. "They said I could go home."

"Zeph?" she squeaked. She leapt to her feet, her heart thundering against her breast. She squeezed her eyes shut. "Please be real."

Zeph ate up the distance between them and then she was in his arms. "I'm real," he said. "I'm very, very real."

"You left me."

"I'm so sorry."

Something broke in her. Something between a laugh and a sob, between heartache and relief, between sanity and insanity. Something broke.

"Shh," Zeph whispered. "I'm here now. I'm here, my sweets. Feel me. I'm here."

She clung to him like he would disappear, and a sharp pain pierced his chest, quick and unexpected, like a crack in a bone.

"I wouldn't have left you like this. Please know that."

"How are you b-back?"

"I don't know. They said I earned it. I don't know if that's true. But here I am. I'm with you, and I'm never leaving you again."

He pulled free his neckcloth, took one of her hands in his, and wrapped their joined hands together with it.

"Wh-what are you doing?" she asked.

"Binding us together—if you will have me. I said before I didn't know whether to marry you or be terrified of you." He tried to offer her a grin. It trembled because he was nervous. "I want to marry you, Arwyn. Nothing about you terrifies me. Only you saying no, perhaps." His lashes swept up to look her in the eye. "Will you marry me, my sweets?"

"Yes," she said.

"Right now? This minute?" Life, Zeph learned, was precious, and he would take better care with the time he had.

"Right now. This minute," she answered.

Zeph breathed a deep sigh of relief and jumped straight to his vow. "I take you to be my wife and I promise to love you all the days of my life."

Arwyn inhaled a deep breath, looked him in the eye and said, "I take you to be my husband and I promise to love you all the days of my life."

Zeph unwrapped their hands, brought hers to his lips, and kissed them. "Thank you," he said.

"For what?"

"For loving me when I was so unlovable."

She shrugged. "I like a challenge."

His lips found hers. He kissed her long and deep. "Lucky for me," he murmured as he trailed kisses down her neck.

"Thank you," she said breathlessly.

"For what?"

"For not giving up."

"You wouldn't let me."

"Because I love you."

He drew back so he could see her...all of her. She looked at him right back, her scrutiny like a well that pulled on you, drawing you in. He traced the lines of her face with the tips of his fingers. "When they said I could go home, I didn't know where home was. They told me to close my eyes and follow my heart. So I did. When I opened them again, I was looking at you, sleeping in that chair."

Arwyn hugged him then. "Heartbeats," she said. "You followed the heartbeats."

"Yes," he said. "I did."

"Who told you to follow your heart?"

Zeph pressed his forehead to hers. "My mother."

"Saints in Heaven!" Searly shouted. "You're alive!" He rushed toward them, pulling Zeph into a fatherly embrace. His eyes were shimmering. "Alive," he said again.

"Searly," Zeph said. "It's good to see you."

"Aye." Searly let him go, looked at Arwyn and hugged her as well. "He came back for you. Oh, the joy! I can see it in your face." He palmed her cheeks. Then his eyes went wide. "I have to tell everyone." Searly stepped out into the hallway, shouted their names. His voice echoed off the walls in the dead of night. "I'll be right back," he said as he hastily made his way down the corridors, calling out names. "Zeph is back! Come quickly!"

"I was hoping we could—"

Zeph's words were interrupted when Elin and Lochlan orbed into the communal room. Elin's face, oh her face, was a story unto itself. Arwyn could read it like text. For only a few moments ago that had been her standing there.

"Elin," Zeph said softly.

She shook her head, disbelieving. "Truly? You're here?"

"Truly," Zeph answered. "I'm here."

Elin launched herself into his arms. Zeph caught her, stumbling back a few paces. She sobbed, hard and fast. Arwyn noticed Lochlan drying his own eyes when he thought no one was looking.

Then Favián entered the room. His eyes found Arwyn's first. He smiled. She smiled back. He made his way toward her, watching her all the way.

"I'm happy he's back, Arwyn. For you. For Elin. For myself." His eyes roamed to where Zeph and Elin stood, embracing. "I don't understand this—magic—this life—but I won't question it if it gives you a happy ending."

"I don't understand it either, Favi." She took his hand and held it. He looked down at the way her fingers intertwined with his. "I won't question it either."

"I, Lochlan William Archer of Mirova, take you—"

"Prince," Searly said.

"Pardon?" asked Lochlan.

"There is no need to deny your heritage any longer. Your father was King of Mirova. Your mother was a Faery Princess. *You* are a prince. Thus, you are *Prince* Lochlan William Archer of Mirova."

"Searly," Lochlan hissed through clenched teeth. "*Not now.*"

"Very well. We have that on record." He waved his hand. "You may proceed."

Elin did her best not to laugh. "You were saying, my love?"

Lochlan closed his eyes. "I was saying that I..." His eyes darted to Searly, then back to Elin, softening instantly "—take you, Eliniana Lumis Vitae, to be my wife."

"And I, Eliniana Lumis Vitae, take you, *Prince* Lochlan William Archer of Mirova, to be my husband."

Zeph smirked at his sister. And then he smirked at Lochlan. The longer he stood witnessing his sister's wedding the gladder he was that he and Arwyn didn't go this route.

A few more words were spoken and Searly pronounced Lochlan and

Elin husband and wife. A celebration ensued, but Zeph was eager to get his wife alone. They'd not yet had the opportunity. The past few days had been a whirlwind.

While Zeph had been away, thought to never return, Elin had made some decisions. She wanted to go back to Faery. She wanted to help put Faery back together. They had no leadership, and she was afraid someone nefarious would try to fill the void. After Zeph returned, they all spoke into the wee hours of the morning for the past several mornings until they had all agreed they would go back and do what they could to help. They would be leaving first thing on the morrow.

As the celebration wore on, Zeph took Arwyn by the hand and whispered in her ear. "Come with me." He gave her a titling smile.

She arched a brow. "Come with you where?"

"Away from the noise," he said. "Just for a few minutes. I promise to bring you back."

Arwyn looked over Zeph's shoulder. He knew what she saw. Dancing, laughter. But he needed a bit of quiet. He needed a few minutes with just the two of them.

"All right. Lead the way," she said.

Zeph took her inside the monastery. It smelled of incense and hope. He'd grown to love that smell. It comforted him. And he was going to miss it. As they walked they held hands, something else he'd grown to love, holding his wife's hand. They had yet to mention to anyone they had married the night he'd returned. It was something they'd kept just between the two of them. Not that they were hiding it. They just weren't ready to share it. It was theirs alone for now. They would tell the others soon enough.

As they approached the library, they heard voices. Favián's and Searly's they recognized; however, there was a third they did not.

"I did not realize you were coming," Favián said. His voice sounded flat, unlike himself. Zeph pulled Arwyn to a halt, his Fae ears keen on listening.

"When Searly wrote to me, I felt I had to come."

"Why?" Favián asked.

"I was…" the man paused, took a breath and started again. "I was wrong. I see that now. I came to tell you that, Favián. You're my son. I miss you. I want you to come home. Your *mamá* and I miss you."

"You came to tell me you were wrong?"

"Yes."

"But you want to take me home."

"Not because I want you to fight in the king's army. And not because I expect you to stay. I want to mend our father-son bond. And so your *mamá* can see you. If you knew how she cries at night."

"She cries?" Favián asked.

"You are her only son. You've never been this far away from home. She'll get better with it over time. But she needs to see you, Favián. She hasn't heard from you since you arrived here."

Favián sighed. "I'm sorry, *Papá*. I should have taken better care."

"I understand you have made new friends. Searly told me. Good ones."

"I have."

"One in particular. A girl. Arwyn, is it?"

Zeph's eyes slid to Arwyn. She held his gaze. He tucked his arm around her and pulled her toward him. She rested her head on his chest, waiting for Favián to speak.

It seemed like a lifetime ticked by before Favián finally spoke. "I think going home is a good idea."

"You do?" Searly asked.

"I do," Favián said. "You heard *Papá*. *Mamá* misses me. And I miss her. I'll come back. I just—need to sort some things out—with my father," Favián added.

"Very good, very good," his father said. "We can leave tonight."

Zeph was happy for them. Truly. Favián deserved to have his father in his life. But why did it have to feel like Zeph was losing a piece of himself? It would be hard to say goodbye. But for Arwyn it would be so much harder. He looked down at his wife's face.

She was in tears.

Epilogue

"Come find me," a little boy said.

Zeph turned and couldn't keep the grin from sliding across his lips. "I wonder where he could be?" Zeph mused. "Is he under this rock?" He made a big show of looking underneath. "No, not there." Zeph heard giggles coming from the thick, tall wheatgrass that swayed in the sweet-tempered breeze. Zeph made his way toward it when a little boy jumped out, hair white as milk, arms flailing. "No fair. You knew I was there all along."

Zeph wanted to deny it. He tried to, but his tongue grew thick in his mouth. Curse the inability to lie. "All right, I knew. Your shadow was showing. A tiny bit. We'll work on it." Then Zeph pointed a finger at him. "And next time, don't laugh."

"I tried to hold it in."

"We'll work on that, too."

Together, they walked back to the monastery, side by side. They did this twice a year, every year for the past six years. It was tradition now.

"Uncle Searly will be upset if we're late." The boy looked up at Zeph with sharp blue eyes. "Mum especially."

Zeph's lips tilted into another grin as he looked at the setting sun, lowering like a rose on a stem. "We won't be late. We'll pick up our pace."

They entered the refectory just as everyone was sitting down to eat. Arwyn gave Zeph a reproving look, but Zeph appeased her by kissing her tenderly, once, twice, three times on the lips.

"You're forgiven," she said.

"We weren't late," Zeph said.

"That's debatable," she replied.

"You've already forgiven me," Zeph responded.

Arwyn pursed her lips. Zeph grinned again. It simply could not be helped. He took the seat beside his wife. His son took the seat on the other side of his mum.

Immediately thereafter, supper and chatter ensued.

Everyone looked forward to this gathering every year. Their lives in Faery were busy, though it was rewarding, too. Zeph shouldn't complain. He loved his life.

Looking around the table, he realized someone was missing. "Where's Favián?" Zeph asked.

"He couldn't make it this time," Searly answered.

"How disappointing," Elin said. "I was looking forward to his visit."

Searly looked up from his plate and offered everyone a reassuring smile. "He's assured me he will make it up to everyone soon."

Arwyn smiled, though it was a disappointed smile. She missed Favián. She had been looking forward to seeing him.

Zeph reached for Arwyn's hand underneath the table and gave her a gentle squeeze. She responded by gently squeezing back.

"Stop kicking me," Zuriel said to Alanis. She was Elin and Lochlan's daughter, and Zeph thought his niece was the most beautiful girl he'd ever seen, aside from his wife, of course. And holy hell did Zuriel give Alanis a difficult time of it.

"I wouldn't kick you if you wouldn't steal my fruit," Alanis said. "Eat your own fruit."

"Yours tastes better."

"That doesn't even make sense," Alanis said. "It's the *same* fruit."

Lochlan stared at Zeph across the table with narrowed eyes.

Zeph cleared his throat. "Zuriel, leave Alanis's fruit in peace, please."

"But—"

Zeph held up a hand. "No stealing fruit."

"Don't kick your cousin," Lochlan said to his daughter.

"But—"

Lochlan cut her off. "No kicking."

"Have I never taught you kids the insult game?" Searly chimed in.

"Don't, Searly!" the adults answered in unison.

"What's the insult game?" Zuriel and Alanis asked.

"It's a game where you insult one another. All in good fun, of course. Your fathers have played it before."

"They have?" Alanis asked, looking at her father with skepticism.

"He wasn't very good at it, I'm afraid," Searly said.

Lochlan's narrowed eyes turned to Searly then. "Thank you for that."

"I'm nothing if I'm not honest."

"Can I insult Alanis?" Zuriel asked excitedly.

"No!" the adults responded.

"Well, that's not fair. You got to do it," Zuriel pouted.

"See what you started?" Zeph said.

"If you teach them how to do it the right way—"

"No!" the adults answered.

"You all take the fun out of being a godparent," Searly mumbled.

After supper ended, Zeph took a walk by himself, wanting to visit his parents' graves, preferring to do it alone.

He sat on the ground like so many times before and put his back against a tree, crossing his feet. He didn't speak. He just sat with them, drawing little circles in the dirt with his finger. It was dark, and Zeph still liked the company of the dark. The moon was out, but it was wan, far away, like the hoot of an owl.

"You did it, you know," Searly said.

Zeph had heard the footsteps approaching, so it wasn't his voice that startled him. It was his words. "What did I do?" he asked.

Uninvited, Searly took a seat beside Zeph. "Arwyn sent me out here. She said you three will be leaving soon."

"We would stay, but Zuriel has a tough time sleeping in a bed not his own."

"I'm just happy you came."

Zeph nodded. "We'll always come, Searly."

They listened to the sounds of nature a few more minutes before Zeph couldn't resist asking once more, "What did I do?"

Searly pointed to the crosses on the graves. "You gave yourself the story worthy of your parents. A pretty remarkable story at that." Searly inclined his head and looked at Zeph the way a father would look at his son. Zeph would know because it was how he looked at his own son.

For a moment, Searly's face appeared to melt like hot wax, but Zeph realized it was the burn of hot tears. He turned away and made haste to wipe away any evidence and said, "Thank you."

Searly slipped an arm around Zeph's shoulder. "I'll walk you back."

"Will you tell me the story again? Please?" Zuriel begged. "I love the story how Father became king and you became queen."

Arwyn tapped him on the nose with the tip of her finger "All right. But you must close your eyes because it's late." She reached over and blew out the lamp.

"I promise," he said.

Zeph listened from just outside Zuriel's chamber door, a smile playing on his lips.

"Not so long ago," his wife said in a soft, lilting voice, "a cruel Unseelie King wanted to rule all of Faery."

"His name was Rolim," Zuriel said.

"That's right," said Arwyn.

"And Father killed him."

"He sent him away, rather," Arwyn replied. "To a faraway realm where he can never escape."

"That's even worse," said Zuriel.

Arwyn drew quiet, and then said, "Yes, I certainly hope so."

"And then Father became King of Faery."

"Well, not just so. That came a bit later. You see, your father was not supposed to come back either from the realm of Twilight."

"But the angel sent him back," Zuriel said.

"That's right," said Arwyn. "And when everyone in Faery saw your father and learned what happened, they saw it as a sign and declared your father king."

"He didn't want to be king, though," Zuriel announced. Zeph could picture him sitting up in bed, chest puffed, chin raised. "He told me."

Zeph could hear the smile in Arwyn's voice when she said, "No, he certainly did not. He had to be convinced. Your Aunt Elin and the rest of us helped set up a new Faery Court in the meantime. Faery needed leadership, rules, laws. Or else it would fall into disarray. It was important that everyone was represented. To this day, the Royal Court has a representative from every village, big or small. Once the court was assembled, they held a vote. Who would be king?"

"And they voted Father."

"That's right. They voted your father. After the second time of Faery saying with their voice they wanted him to be their king, he conceded. Your father has been their king ever since."

"He's been the best king ever!" his son said with a punch of enthusiasm.

Zeph bit his lip, biting back a laugh, and entered the room. "If I've been a good king, Son, it is only because your mum is the most excellent queen."

"Oh yes," his boy corrected. "I didn't mean to exclude you, Mum. Not at all."

Arwyn laughed and tousled her son's hair. "It's all right. Now, you promised you would close your eyes if I told you this story and you talked all the way through. It's bedtime for you, my luv." She kissed his cheek. "See you in the morning."

"See you in the morning," he repeated.

"Good night, Zur," Zeph said.

"Good night."

Zeph took Arwyn by the hand and led her out. "Ready for bed?"

"You go on. I'll be there in a few minutes."

"Everything all right?"

"Of course," she answered. "Searly gave me a letter from Favián before we left Mirova. I thought I'd read it before bed. I'll be along soon."

Zeph kissed her forehead, let his eyes fall shut as he smelled her hair—wild berries, the scent making his heart do wild things. Those three little words formed on his tongue. He had become so familiar with the taste of them now. He liked the texture, the form, the feel of them so much that he rolled the words around a bit before saying them. But then he did. And even though he'd been telling her these words for the past six years, they always felt monumental.

"I love you," he said. "So very much."

Arwyn breathed him in, inhaling, as though she was making him a part of her. "I know," she said. "And I love you."

He released her with reluctance. "Take your time, my sweets. Come to bed when you're ready."

Arwyn unfolded the letter from Favián and began to read.

Dearest Arwyn,

I met someone. She's kind, thoughtful, always thinking of others. She reminds me so much of you. We met on one of my journeys and we fell in instant like with one another. She makes me laugh. I've wanted to tell you about her for a while. Every time I sat down to write the letter, a part of me couldn't get the words to come.

I think a lot about the first time you and I met, about how easy it was to talk to you, and how easily you made me laugh. I was just a boy then. But you made me feel like a man sailing on top of the world. I'm still sailing whenever I think of you.

So, it's best if I think of you less and think of Miryam more. Miryam, that's her name. You would like her. She is so lovely. But you like everyone because that's the kind of person you are. Zeph is incredibly lucky to have you, and Faery is incredibly lucky to have a queen as wonderful as you.

And I, Arwyn, am incredibly lucky as well. You're my—sister, right? And I have the most amazing sister the world has ever known. Tell your son that I got a present for him. I will bring it with me on my next visit. I'm sorry I couldn't make the trip this time. I was busy getting married.

Surprise!

I hope you are happy for me. Of course you are. I can practically feel your excitement from here. Thank you. I wanted you to be the first to know. You may tell the others now. I can't wait for everyone to meet her.

All right, I must be going.

I'll see you soon, mi corazoncito.

With love,
Favi.

Arwyn traced the letter with the tips of her fingers, tears brimming in her eyes. "Yes, Favi," she whispered. "I'm happy for you." She kissed the letter and held it to her heart.

As Zeph waited for Arwyn to come to bed, he unfolded his own letter he'd received from Favián, only this one was years old and only consisted of a few lines. He'd found it in his room the night Favián left the monastery with his father.

He had kept it with him ever since, taking it out to read daily. It was a reminder for Zeph, and as he read, he silently thanked Favián for being one of the first to call him his friend.

Do not fear your darkness, Zeph.

You are the space between the stars, the weight under the sun, the canvas of the moon's glow, stitching the fabric of the sky in place.

You are neither man, nor monster, my friend. You are the magic that makes everything else shine.

Until we meet again,
Favián

The End

Note from the Author

Now that everyone has read Zeph's story I have another story to tell you. I told this to my beta readers/friends and debated whether to share this with everyone else. I decided I would, so here it goes...

This book almost did not end the way it did. Toward the end of my writing process, I realized that Zeph was going to have to sacrifice himself in that scene with Rolim. I saw the scene in my head exactly as you read it, and the scenes that followed it, all the way up until that scene with Arwyn and Searly after she went back to the monastery. But I could not figure out how to bring Zeph back. I spent an entire weekend in tears thinking Zeph would die at the end. I saw him with his parents and I thought... is this it? He gains their forgiveness...he sacrifices his life, and we're supposed to accept this as his 'happy ending'?

I messaged Christie, my good friend and beta reader, on a Sunday and said, "I have to talk to you. I think Zeph dies." I had to tell someone because I had cried the whole weekend, unable to figure out how the hell to get Zeph back to Arwyn and Elin and everyone else. To Christie's credit, she didn't book a flight to Alabama to kill me. Though, she was NOT happy with me at all. But I was not happy with me either. I had wracked my brain trying to figure out solutions. And it's not as easy as figuring out a different scenario. Zeph showed me everything that happened. He showed me his death... weeks in advance... before I had even made it that far into the book. I had always envisioned that final showdown to be different. I hadn't worked it all out yet, but I just assumed it would be a victorious battle. I was looking forward to writing it. And then... Zeph goes and thwarts my plans like he has at every turn of this book. I refused to write a single word that weekend, determined that I could come up with something else. But I hit a wall. Which was why I ended up reaching out to Christie, begging her not to throttle me and listen to what I had to say.

She said, "Ooookay...I'm listening. I'm freaking out but I'm listening."

After I told her the jest of what Zeph was making me do she went quiet for a while. I started to pack my bags thinking I had at least twelve hours to disappear if she was leaving by car to come take me out. To my surprise, she started to ask questions that led to more questions and by her doing that... my mind opened up again and I figured out a way to BRING ZEPH HOME.

But for two days, I sat in my room, much like Arwyn sat in that throne room, and I refused to do anything because I thought I had lost Zeph. So, when I wrote those scenes...I relived those moments They were real for me. As an author, I'm not just telling stories. I'm living them. These characters are in my heart, buried in my soul. I never write a book for the money. There are easier ways to make money. But there's not too many ways you can touch a person's heart whom you've never met than by sharing your heart and your soul with them. And I've certainly shared mine when I wrote this book.

Favián's note at the end was a quote Christie wrote about Zeph that she pinned on our Pinterest board we started over a year ago. I wanted to honor her for saving me and Zeph (lol) by talking me off the ledge and put it in the book. It seemed right that I attribute it to Favián. Who else would have said those words to Zeph, but him? And it seemed right that that's how the book should end, since it almost ended so differently.

I debated whether to tell you guys my writing struggles. There have been many. I've never written a villain turned hero before, so it was a huge challenge for me. I've always written sweet heroes. Zeph was not sweet. He was the most complex character I have ever written. And there were many times I didn't know if I could finish it. But I was drawn to him, nonetheless, and kept pushing forward. This book is my biggest accomplishment to date because I wrote something I was scared to write and wasn't sure if I could write, but I did it. If I never write another book, I will look back on my writing career and be pleased with what I have accomplished. It's not about fame or fortune. It's about connecting, and I hope I connected with you on some level through Zeph's story.

Acknowledgements

I would like to thank an incredible group of ladies who are there, always there, when I need an ear to listen, a keen eye, and honest feedback. They are my beta readers, friends, and confidantes. And I couldn't imagine going through my writing process without them. They are: Anne Woodall, Trisha Rai, Melyssa Winchester, Sharon Hanson, Astrid Heinisch, and Christie Parker. Thank you all SO MUCH for getting me through this journey. Again, I feel that words are inadequate to fully express my love and appreciation for you, but I hope you know me well enough by now that you do know how much I love and appreciate you. Please never doubt that. You all have helped me, mostly by just a shout from the sideline, "You can climb over that hurdle!" or "You can do it!" but it was those words of encouragement or that kick in the butt that I needed that got me through days when finding the right words seemed too difficult of a task. Thank you for believing in me—even when you didn't know how I was going to turn Zeph's story around. You believed in me and that's how I pushed through. Thank you!

To Claudette Cruz, thank you for editing for me.

To Emily and her staff at E.M. Tippetts Book Design, thank you for the amazing job you do and your professionalism. It's always a joy to work with you all.

Thank you to RBA Designs for the beautiful cover art.

And a special thank you to cover model Valery Kovtun and photographer Anna Pototskaya for allowing me to use your amazing photo/art. Thank you!

And to my family, we made it through another book. You all deserve a medal.

About the Author

Pamela Sparkman grew up in Alabama. She became an avid reader at a young age. The written word has always fascinated her, and she wrote her first short story while still in elementary school. Inspiration for her stories always begins with a song. She believes music is the pulse of life and books are the heart of it.

When she isn't writing, however, she's spending time with her family and taking one day at a time.

Email:

Sparkman.pam@gmail.com

Facebook:

https://www.facebook.com/pamelasparkmanauthor

Goodreads:

https://www.goodreads.com/author/show/7761886.Pamela_Sparkman

Instagram:

https://www.instagram.com/pamelasparkman/

Website:

http://www.authorpamelasparkman.com/

Newsletter:

http://www.authorpamelasparkman.com/contact

OTHER TITLES

Contemporary Romance

Stolen Breaths (Stolen Breaths, #1)

Shattered (Stolen Breaths, #2)

Skin Deep (Stolen Breaths, #3)

Each book in Stolen Breaths series is a STANDALONE novel.

Historical Romance

Back to Yesterday

Fantasy Romance

The Moon Shines Red

Made in the USA
Lexington, KY
19 August 2018